POST HUMOUSLY YOURS

POST HUMOUSLY YOURS

CHARLES D. BRAUN

Library of Congress Cataloging-in-Publication Data

Names: Braun, Charles D., 1969–xxx, author.
Title: Posthumously Yours / Charles D. Braun.
Description: 240 pages. – First edition. | Laguna Hills, California: Type Eighteen Books, 2026.
Summary: "Charlie Braun has been trying to make his exit from the world since the day he was born with the umbilical cord wrapped around his neck. After his mother passes on to the next life, he feels completely free for the first time in his life and prepares for his final exit. A darkly humorous look at a life less lived, and a provocative exploration about living (and ending) life on one's own terms."—Provided by publisher.
Identifiers: LCCN 2025941952 | ISBN: 9798998947766 (paperback) | ISBN: 9798998947773 (ebook)
LC record available at https://lccn.loc.gov/2025941952

Published by Type Eighteen Books
www.typeeighteenbooks.com

Printed in the United States

CONTENTS

FROM THE PUBLISHER

Authors of fiction are often asked about possible autobiographical connections. Readers want to know if the main character is actually a cloaked version of the writer, or if any of the supporting characters are based on family members, coworkers, friends, or even enemies. These connections, for the writer of fictional stories, can be direct, indirect, or subconscious. And they can be nonexistent—a fact readers sometimes have a difficult time accepting.

We'll never know how much of *Posthumously Yours* is related to the life and times of its author. Charles D. Braun is a pseudonym, and the writer is no longer with us to field questions about his life or inspirations. What we do know is that he worked as a copywriter and was a lover of pop culture and especially, music, and we know that before he ended his life, he sent a box to a colleague—someone he knew only peripherally. In the box was a letter with a final request, and this manuscript.

We've taken care to honor the author's intentions and tone, and the structure of this remarkable story. Because of copyright protections, we couldn't print the song lyrics he referenced by artists such as Kate Bush, Suzzy and Terre Roche, Jackson

Browne, Suzanne Vega, Roseanne Cash, Roland Orzabal, Phoebe Snow, and more. Suffice it to say, the author was greatly influenced by wonderful lyrics, the kind that reach your soul and help you find your way when feeling lost.

Charles D. Braun, the character in this story, is a creation of fiction, and his perspective and struggles are his alone. The wit, talent, and intellect of his creator shine brightly in these pages. The novel raises multi-faceted questions involving ethics and existentialism, family connection and mental health, and readers should be aware that the story deals heavily with suicidal ideation and suicide. As its publisher, we believe this to be an important book that will engender much discussion about difficult topics, and a wide appreciation for one man's unique view of the world.

—Mary Vensel White, Type Eighteen Books, 2025

A portion of the proceeds for this novel will be donated to the American Foundation of Suicide Prevention (afsp.org). Are you in a crisis? Call or text 988 or text TALK to 741741

CHAPTER ONE

FAMOUS LAST WORDS

FIRST, the good news:

If you look in the upper right-hand drawer beneath the Altoids and the Gideon Bible, you will discover a five-hundred-dollar bill acquired on July 14, 1969, the day I was born (and the denomination was discontinued by the Federal Reserve). As you might imagine, it is worth considerably more today—up to eight hundred and fifty as of last week. Consider it your finder's fee.

Obviously, you have figured out the bad news. This was not a burden I wanted to place on anyone, never mind a stranger. While I've tried to downplay the drama—no blood, no bloated and bluish effigy to cut down from a doorway, and a climate-controlled, Swiss-made, HyperHEPA-filtered air purifier to neutralize any lingering scent—your discovery is not something I would wish on anyone, much less a complete stranger. So, while it might not mitigate the initial trauma, the least I can do is introduce myself:

According to my mother, I've been trying to make my exit from the world since the day I arrived with the umbilical cord wrapped around my neck (intentionally, she claimed). Whenever anyone learns my story, I don't know whether to read their look of astonishment as admiration or contempt. They want to know how anyone could have made it well into their colonoscopy years without having had such universal experiences as skinny dipping, receiving a speeding ticket, travelling beyond North America, texting, reading Shakespeare, experiencing a hangover, watching *Gone with the Wind*, *Casablanca*, *Star Wars,* or porn, opening a social media account, texting, sexting, possessing a cellphone, owning a pet or a plant, buying a lottery ticket, pulling an all-nighter, writing a love letter, sharing a room, house, bank account or vacation with a significant or insignificant other, engaging in PDA (the "P" being public or private), or understanding how football is played. (This is the highly abbreviated list.)

Even those who might get past the football thing could not imagine living this long without ever having been married, in a long-term relationship, or in love. For myself at least, I always had an answer—until now.

CHAPTER TWO

IF IT'S THE LAST THING I DO

10.13.83 Wilbraham, Massachusetts

PLAYING SCRABBLE WITH MEL, as we did since she bought the game for my seventh birthday, was like trying to beat the house in Vegas. In my entire life, I might have won a dozen times, yet she played each game like it was a national tournament. Watching this woman—who supposedly bought the game, hoping to develop the vocabulary of her only child—morph into this take-no-prisoners competitor was simultaneously fascinating and disturbing.

She insisted that I displayed a certain precociousness and mastered the rules, if not the game, a full year before reaching the suggested "8 to Adult" age specified on the box. What she observed wasn't as much talent as aptitude by attrition—what's left over when you don't have math, science, or other academic skills. "Charles has an impressive grasp on his native language," Mrs. Volk wrote in a third-grade report card, "and he spells like an eight-year-old." I was a real prodigy, all right.

Assessing the board one evening, I found myself suppressing a smile.

"You're thinking of a dirty word, aren't you?" Mel inquired hopefully.

"That's right," I replied, "and I'm not going to tell you which one."

She looked at me with wide eyes. "You really think there's a dirty word I haven't heard in eighty-three years?"

Truth be told, there probably wasn't a dirty word she hadn't said in eighty-three years. Yet, although I was approaching my sixtieth birthday, I couldn't acknowledge to my mother that the word "clit" was in my consciousness. "Clitoris" had been included in conversation—along with every other female body part—stemming from another birthday gift: the Our Bodies, Ourselves book, wrapped in Peanuts-themed paper, for my thirteenth birthday. Nevertheless, "clit" reminded me too much of the other C word, so I told her I was thinking of a word that wasn't allowed.

As she scanned the board silently, a gleeful smile emerged.

"Fuck!" She pointed to the F in the word "roof." She thought I planned to add a U, a C and a K—twenty-three points for the K on a red square.

I reminded her I didn't have a U or a K, and obscenities weren't in the Scrabble Dictionary, a source Mel always dismissed as having been written by the Daughters of the American Revolution.

I told her the word I was thinking of was sexually explicit.

"You don't think fuck is sexually explicit?" She took the tile from my hand and returned it to the rack. "That explains why you're not in a serious relationship. For your information, that thing you aren't doing is called fucking."

Mel had always meticulously avoided specifying pronouns or even species when inquiring about my hypothetical sex life, amending the stock line "I just want you to be happy" with some comment about my loneliness in aging. At my age, I knew she'd gladly settle for "unhappily committed" to any mammal—living or otherwise—who didn't have an R after their name on the voting rolls.

She said this half sardonically but never with a sense of irony warranted by her own history. Here was a woman whose only child was conceived through her only known liaison—with a sperm bank—extolling the virtues of a committed relationship. Even as a devout agnostic, I'd always considered my birth a modern-day version of Immaculate Conception.

In an era when kids with divorced parents were from "broken homes," my situation always seemed perfectly normal to me. So did our unspoken agreement that each of us was allowed to keep one subject off-limits. *Mine* was that she could never dispute the immortality I had attributed to her. All my life, she'd quote *her* mother, who matter-of-factly announced she would like to die at eighty-one. Why eighty-one? Because, well, "enough already!"

My mom always considered her signature achievement as having any lack of similarity with her mother. "The greatest gift she ever gave me was ignoring me," she used to say. So, I was surprised the day she succumbed to a bout of her mother's morbid practicality and reminded me she had reached the age where even the life insurance company which claimed "you cannot be denied for any reason" would reject her.

Once during our weekly drive to the Big Y in Springfield for groceries, she pointed to the cemetery and asked, "Where will I be spending eternity, there, or on your bookshelf?"

The question was so straightforward—"Sugar or Splenda?" —that I responded in kind, telling her I assumed she'd already made her own arrangements. It wasn't like the question hadn't occurred to me, but it was a clear violation of our unspoken pact.

"Never mind," she said. "Surprise me."

To me, burial seemed simultaneously solitary and claustrophobic, a situation that let the whole eternity thing drag on far too long. Cremation was more of a clean break, but I could never get past the name, deceptively reminiscent of soft serve ice cream, her favorite food. Cryonics struck me as wasteful, dated, and perhaps a bit exclusive—a Republican's way out. Natural Organic Reduction, or human composting, was environmentally sound, but, at the end of the day, it didn't seem all that different from roadkill albeit six feet under. Each of the standard options for eternity seemed less appealing than the last.

I was never smart enough for science fiction, but I wondered if something could be arranged along the lines of the transporter in *Star Trek*. A person could be converted into an energy pattern through "dematerialization." Or there was the episode in which two crew members were transformed into small, chalk-like cuboctahedrons, before one is crushed like sand. Simple, clean, environmentally sound—but unfortunately, still science fiction. Ashes now, dust a couple of hundred years later: the difference was not the mode of disposal but only the timeframe. Despite Mel's advancing age, I managed to defer my decision until the end and made the unsurprising choice.

I kept my eyes on my tiles. She insisted that "fuck" was obviously the root of "fucking," which remained the act of having (or, in my case, not having) sex.

"Look it up," she said, sliding the dictionary across the table. I told her I didn't care what it said and that, in any case, it wasn't the word I was thinking of.

She returned to studying the board but after several minutes her unnerving smile reappeared. "You don't have a U, you don't have a K, but you didn't say anything about a C," she said.

I begged her to drop it.

"It's four letters, right?" She tapped her fingers on the table. "A four-letter C word."

No, I insisted, definitely not *that* one.

She thought it sweet that I felt the need to protect her from the word. Yes, she acknowledged, the sexual aspect of the word had lost its meaning, and the F word was simply the go-to swear.

"You're right," she proclaimed flatly, "Fuck is the new shit."

Although discussion of her death was off limits, Mel had a favorite related topic: what I would do alone in the world when she was gone. All my life, I had her life to justify my own. Imagining her gone, all I could come up with was the hope that everything would magically get better—eventually. But it only got worse.

The laboratory results from my annual physical were as I had always feared: cholesterol 150, glucose 90, blood pressure 90. Even my normally dour doctor added a smiley emoticon to the report. With my luck, I would live forever. First, the loss of my only family member, now the specter of immortality hovering over me like an act of retaliation from a deity I never believed in. Nature, it appeared, was not going to make it easy. If I wanted out, I'd have to do the dirty work myself.

I had read that every year nine million Americans contemplate suicide. Surely, most had experienced the milestones that had eluded me. How could someone who had been nothing, done nothing, and expressed no desire to become anything, make it to the ironically named status of sexagenarian when younger people with far more experience and potential were gone? I was thinking not just of the Woolfs, Plaths, and Hemingways, but all the anonymous people for whom the fear of ending their life was eclipsed by the fear of carrying on.

For more than an hour, I tried to produce someone who knew me well enough to convince me of a reason for my existence. But I had no such person in my life. With Mel finally gone, there was nobody relying on me, literally nobody on the planet would ask me to reconsider. I could finally slip out the back door, and nobody would even notice. For the first time in my life, I felt completely free, untethered by responsibilities and guilt, relieved, exhilarated, and terrified.

The only thing keeping me alive was the angst about everything that might or might not come after. Planning an exit was more difficult than I had imagined, compounded, perhaps, by a genetic disposition toward hypochondria. Mel presented her paralyzing fear of illness and pain in practical ways: "What would happen to you if anything happened to me?" she would ask before deploying me as a human shield against a line of would-be hand shakers at a wake. Although I kept my eye on the ultimate finish line, I never developed a healthy adolescent appetite for self-destruction. Even during the last twenty years, when our caretaking roles had reversed, I still watched my cholesterol levels, wore my seatbelt, and yielded on yellow—when I probably should have been taking up cigarettes, heroin, and risky sex.

When I finally decided to pursue professional help for my feelings, I'm sure a part of me was seeking permission not to do something I was apprehensive about. Instead, the voice on the other end of the phone dampened my hope with an initial disclaimer that she was a volunteer, not a therapist—and an ally, not an advocate.

"We don't give advice," Maeve explained with a lilting brogue. "We're here to listen and support you."

It had been a few weeks since I buried Mel. I sat at my desk with the phone pressed against my ear.

"Really?" I said. "So, if I decided to polish off a fifth of Jameson with a Drano chaser, you'd say 'Cheers'?"

"You have a plan?"

"If I did, that would not be it. I assumed someone working a suicide prevention hotline would try and talk me out of killing myself."

"Is that why you called?"

"Maybe I was looking for some reason to live, something I'm missing."

Maeve thought about this for a moment. "Are there others who'd be unable to go on without you?"

"Not anymore."

"No friends, family, loved ones?"

"You are the only person on the planet who would know I was gone."

Her voice lowered an octave. "That sounds very lonely."

"Actually," I said before ending the call, "I've never felt so free."

CHAPTER THREE

TODAY IS THE WORST DAY IN THE REST OF YOUR LIFE

IT SEEMED SO sensible at the time. I had time on my hands and money in the bank. I probably should have looked for a facility with a religious affiliation like Hospice of the Good Shephard or Holy Trinity House, instead of one whose parent company had its own symbol on the New York Stock Exchange (LSS). But I had never been hospice shopping before and didn't want to displace someone with a real spiritual connection or physical need. The parent corporation of Haven House (the name referred to its location in Connecticut's second-biggest city and not its purpose) was Life Support Systems, LLC, the only organization I could find that would waive the usual terminal illness requirement and accept an "unspecified chronic malady" for admission.

The next time I phoned the helpline, I made a point to call during the same night shift so I could tell Maeve how she inspired me to move to hospice. Although she refused to accept credit, it didn't stop her from visiting me there. I assumed she must be violating some policy, but Maeve said that she was the executive director—shorthand, I figured, for "I make the rules."

It was Maeve who tried to plead my case so I wouldn't be

the first resident to be expelled from the hospice. Who knew it violated resident etiquette to order a white clam pie from the original Frank Pepe's in New Haven, where I had moved for its pizza scene in preparation for my last meal?

Did the admissions counselor really expect someone who had nothing physically wrong to survive for nearly a year on a menu consisting entirely of Ensure and IV chasers?

"This is not Residence Inn by Marriott, and I am not a concierge." My case manager Gini scolded me as she helped herself to a slice. "Your neighbors are concerned with nutrition, not umami."

"Maybe the aroma will jolt their senses back to life."

Gini was in her thirties, with the disappointment of an older person. "Many experience nausea from medications," she told me. "Also, the smell of garlic and seafood is disruptive. And the noise."

I grabbed the remote and muted the "Mister Sparkle" ad from the eighth season of *The Simpsons*.

"Not that noise," she said gesturing to the television, "*that* one."

As she pointed to me, I silenced my snorting laughter.

She nodded, her severely cut hair unmoving. "The other residents are here to make a peaceful exit surrounded by their loved ones."

"Same here," I said, hoisting a slice with one hand and the remote with the other.

For nearly six decades, Mel had been the only person I lived with—in the first half, she was my caretaker. In the second, our roles reversed. When I arrived with my vague prognosis, Gini suggested palliative care, but as soon as my ability to pay out-of-pocket indefinitely was established—courtesy of the estate Mel had inherited from her parents and bequeathed to me—she found me a private room. For a while, we had conspired to not ask or tell anyone about my actual health, but as the gap between the "real" patients and me became more apparent, I could feel my tenuous welcome waning.

I decided to spend each day at Haven House like it was my last, choreographing every detail from the menu to the entertainment. I planned to watch every episode of *The Simpsons* (except season one, before Dan Castellanetta changed the voice of Homer and the show became funny). I had a rotation of pizzerias on speed dial, from Modern on Mondays to Sally's on Sundays; ice cream from Ashley's to Milkcraft (with occasional diversions to Dip-Top for soft serve in Mel's honor); and a treadmill to maintain my exceptional numbers in case I decided to opt-in to life when the year was up.

Already, I had surpassed the average hospice stay of seventy-eight days more than threefold and was fast-tracked for a Guinness World Record. Like *The Simpsons*, there was no end of my run in sight— a prospect that seemed to unnerve the staff.

"They want you feckin' gone," Maeve confirmed after a meeting with Gini. We sat in the dining room over tepid paper cups of tea.

"This place is half-empty," I said. "It's not like anyone is waiting for the room."

"It's not about that."

"My comatose neighbors are actually complaining about the smell of garlic?"

She shook her head. "The staff don't think you belong here."

"Am I dying too slowly?"

"Trouble is, you're not dying at all."

"I might be. I haven't decided yet."

"They don't know that. Maybe you need to tell them, so they have something to look forward to. Otherwise, they think you're just letting on."

"Letting on?"

"Pretending."

"I came here because hospice staff are supposed to be angels."

"You told me you came here because no proper place would admit someone who is perfectly healthy."

"You think I'm perfectly healthy?"

"Physically. They see you on a treadmill, watching cartoons and ordering pizza. They don't understand what you're doing here."

"What did you tell them?"

"I said you needed some time to figure things out but honestly I'm not sure."

Maeve was always careful to begin any comment resembling a personal opinion with those helpline disclaimers about being there to listen, and not judge or to provide support, not offer advice. She didn't need to. I told her that, once, I had written one of the largest checks of my life after watching a commercial for an organization providing free surgery to children with facial tumors. Yeah, she said, it's impossible to turn away from those faces. I told her that was exactly what I had done. At first, I recoiled and changed the channel. My complete lack of empathy was so startling, I pulled out my checkbook.

It was similar with relationships. Paralyzed by performance anxiety driven by interconnected bouts of coitophobia and cardiophobia and undermined by an underlying case of pantophobia, I was quite certain I wasn't the only one who felt nothing following their anticlimactic climaxes. After winning a free session at a high school fundraiser, a psychic put it best: I was an acquired taste few women would ever acquire.

My 'relationship' history was atypical. In my fortieth year, I was headed for a Charles Schulz exhibition at the Norman Rockwell Museum when I came across a macrobiotic restaurant called "Eat Me Raw." It turned out to be a series of classes in orgasmic meditation (aka "OMing"). Held at a monastery-turned-yoga-and-wellness-retreat in Stockbridge, OMing was a daily morning ritual in which a dozen women, naked or nearly so from the waist down, achieved orgasm manually assisted by a male "research partner." Although I knew the other participants would be more experienced, the rules seemed reassuring. Both partners kept their eyes closed, while the males remained fully clothed and let their fingers do the talking, no strings attached. As one participant later told a reporter in a titillating story in the *Times'* "Style" section: "When you go to a massage therapist, you don't take the masseuse to dinner afterward." The whole performance aspect seemed more cognitive than strictly physical, a playing field in which I felt marginally better equipped to compete, especially after reading everything about g-spots in the self-help section at the library.

What I did not anticipate was the unmistakable look of having drawn the short straw on my partner's face the moment she saw me. Suddenly, any confidence from my prep work was replaced by the memory of stepping up to bat in sixth grade gym while the entire outfield advanced towards home plate. The dour, elfin blonde I was paired with proceeded to our mat silently. As the other male partners put on their plastic gloves, my partner's eyes were shut tightly, and her mouth scrunched as if she was anticipating a hysterectomy paired with a colonoscopy. I slid my index finger inside her and began to get the lay of the land.

Stark silence pierced the blissful moans from around the room. I continued my efforts until a hand suddenly emerged like Thing on *The Addams Family*. The hand grabbed my wrist and began guiding me, taking the responsibility of locating the target literally out of my hand. By this point, I had forgotten the prep work and was glad to let her drive.

An ecstatic soundtrack of little fireworks exploded all around us. Seconds that felt like minutes went by before she finally pulled my hand out and replaced it with her own, a third-string relief pitcher replaced by the coach after a single inning. I peered through one eye to confirm the others around me were not looking and crept quietly out of the room.

"Were you attracted to her?" Maeve asked.

"Our eyes were closed."

"When you met her."

"I barely saw her. It's not supposed to be sexual for the guy. It's all about the woman's climax."

"So, these men who showed up at seven a.m. had no motivation but satisfying a stranger?"

I considered this. "I guess it's supposed to be like reparations."

"You felt nothing yourself?"

"Embarrassed, mostly."

Her analysis was simple: from the loss of my only family member to the inability to feel real empathy for others, to the lack of even the most basic attraction, I was hollowed out and unable to experience real emotion. It sounded perilously close to the way psychologists describe mass shooters and other psychopaths, but Maeve assured me there was a difference. Psychopaths feel something through cruelty. They get satisfaction from having power over others or an ability to make people suffer. I didn't have any of those feelings, she explained. On the contrary, I had no feelings at all.

"It almost doesn't matter what you do or don't do," she explained. "Either way, you're already emotionally dead."

This, of course, was a complete turnaround from the script she used at the helpline. Ever since she had proposed that we meet in person—a clear violation of the code of ethics—Maeve had dispensed with the script about being there to listen and not give advice. She had become my de facto therapist and maybe a step beyond, volunteering sometimes surprising opinions about the existential question I was facing.

She'd often camp out in the only chair in my room. "I'm going to ask you a question," she said, "and I want you to tell me the first thing that comes to mind. Is there anything or anyone you would miss?"

My answer was immediate. "The white clam pizza at Frank Pepe."

For as long as I could recall, the one part of my body capable of experiencing sensation was my taste buds. As a child, I wrote elaborate menus detailing the items for my last meal, forever daydreaming about my next one. When you are searching for a compelling reason to continue, and the best part of waking up really is Folger's in your cup—it's probably time to consider the alternative.

When I confessed to Maeve that contemplating the logistics of suicide, I wasn't sure I could go through with it. She had a ready answer: Fugu Sashimi, a Japanese fish that, depending upon the skill of the chef, is either a delicacy or deadly.

"If I could just get past the fear thing."

"'The only thing you have to fear...'"

"...are guns, blood, sharp objects, botching the job, and spending the rest of my life breathing through a tube and crapping through a bag."

She blinked. "There are less violent alternatives."

"Yes, being discovered five days later, Blue Oyster Cult playing on a loop like Pachelbel's Canon..."

"There are ways to get over your fears."

"How many of them?"

"As many fears as you have."

"Are you familiar with Phobophobia?"

"If fear was the only thing keeping me around, I think I'd be more scared of living."

"Oh, I'm scared of that, too."

"Give me one non-edible reason why life is worth living," I insisted.

"I don't know, maybe hope."

"Hope for what?"

"That I'll finally get over my fear."

"Maybe I can help."

Until that point, all I knew about Maeve was that her family was back in Ireland. Since we'd met, she had befriended me, sharing a little more of her own story. Her parents had passed away—her mom from cancer when she was a kid and her dad while she was here in the U.S. of a cause she did not disclose. Her only sibling, a brother, and her adult son remained in Ireland. Maeve had moved to the states to attend the Divinity School at Yale which offered a joint degree with the School of Social Work at UConn. Her initial placement was at the Hartford Multi-Service Center, where she made a troubling discovery: though her clients sought therapy for a range of problems, all had seriously contemplated or attempted suicide.

Her plan had been to return to Ireland after graduation. But as part of her master's project she applied for a grant to launch a suicide prevention hotline—except they wouldn't call it that.

"All roads can lead to that outcome," she explained, "but I didn't want people to think they had to be contemplating killing themselves to call. I thought a helpline would cover more ground with less stigma, you know? I mean, some people hear 'suicide,' they think 'crazy'".

"Do you?"

"I think someone can be suicidal without being crazy."

"They can be perfectly rational—"

"If you're asking if I think you're crazy," she said. "I'd say no."

"Based on what?"

"Based on the fact that I'm not qualified to offer a diagnosis, since I'm not your therapist."

"But you are a therapist. You've seen crazy. Do I fit in?"

"Coming from a family of crazy people, you seem pretty level-headed to me."

"That's quite a ringing endorsement."

"I think it's crazy for someone to consider suicide before they've tried everything else first. But I'm guessing you didn't get to be your age without exhausting your other options. I assume you've tried therapy."

"Nearly every day of my life."

"Meds?"

"None that altered reality."

"I used to tell the kids at the Multi that everything can change overnight."

"How about when you're about to turn sixty?"

Maeve proposed the idea of spending the days leading up to my milestone birthday by sampling some of the experiences that had eluded me. At the end of the year, if I decided I'd had enough, she would take me out for Fugu.

The standard line that therapists give hopeless clients—that everything can change overnight—seemed apropos for those with a whole life before them. As closing time approached, it seemed unlikely, if not impossible, that my entire life would take a 180-degree turn. Having made it this far, I figured there was little at stake in Maeve's proposal. I agreed with a caveat.

"If things don't work out let's rent Harold and Maude and send out for pizza, instead of ordering toxic blowfish."

"Watching that movie always makes me feel good about what I do."

"You do remember she killed herself?" I asked.

"And he went off singing into the sunset."

"And you see that as a happy ending?"

"Remember what she said at her surprise eightieth birthday party: She couldn't imagine a lovelier farewell. She was able to choose her own ending."

Here was something different: an acknowledgment there might be valid reasons beyond terminal illnesses and infirmities to discontinue life and even choreograph one's own ending—all from a social worker who ran a suicide prevention hotline. I wondered what Mel would have thought. As a therapist, she, too, was a rebel, someone who molded the training she received to fit the reality she found in the field. I knew that Mel was dedicated to preventing suicide among teenagers, but I could not imagine how she would have responded to the idea of a healthy adult planning an exit strategy. Yet Maeve's proposal had no downside.

"Make me a list of all the classic movies you've never seen, the books you've never read, a language you'd like to learn," she said.

"Maybe I need to think bigger: you know, drugs, alcohol, marriage, kids."

"It's hard to make up for fifty-nine years in a few months. Maybe you should think about starting a little smaller."

"I could call an escort service and see if they deliver."

"You're getting pushback for ordering pizza, and you want to invite brassers to visit you in a hospice?"

"Brassers?"

"Call girls."

"I'm not a prisoner here, Maeve. I can walk out anytime."

"Fair enough. Just make sure that's what you want, because once you close the door, I get the sense your friend Gini out there is changing the locks."

"Do you think I belong in hospice?"

"I wouldn't have chosen it, but you seem to be less isolated here than you would be rambling around that empty house alone. At least it's a safe place until you figure out what's next."

"I guess."

"You've had one home all your life. We need to build up your confidence. You seem to have a support system here."

"The chaplain and I have had some decent conversations."

"Trying to make a deathbed conversion, is she?"

"We talk about everything but religion. She thinks my soul is beyond saving. There's a nurse here who comes by every day to play Battleship. His mother is the dietician here. I guess you could call them friends."

"Don't confuse friendly and friends. In social work, we call it transference, where the client develops feelings for the therapist. Happens a lot with bartenders, too."

"I don't have feelings for anyone. That's why I'm here."

"After all those years taking care of your mom, you said you finally felt free. If you form personal attachments, you lose that freedom."

"Maybe."

"The staff here are professionals doing their jobs. Once you leave this place, you will never see them again. For you, that's a good thing. If you really want to keep your options so you can decide what to do at the end of the year, you can't afford to make friends."

"What about you?"

"I'm your advocate."

For someone I had recently met, Maeve seemed to know me well. At a time when the home I had grown up in suddenly felt completely unfamiliar, a short-term rental would have amplified the solitude and anything long-term would represent far too much commitment. For the mercenary failings of its parent company, Haven House felt strangely homey. So, I couldn't afford to get too comfortable.

My primary nurse, a stout version of James Carville, named Vic, would set up Battleship, which had become my substitute for Scrabble, in my room, then come in between his other patients to make one move at a time.

Much to my surprise another favorite turned out to be the chaplain who made a grand entrance into my room dressed as the grim reaper. Upon learning of my agnosticism, Candace shrugged, plopped herself down at the foot of my bed, kicked off her shoes and began massaging her soles.

"If I asphyxiate you, we can list bromodosis as the cause of death."

"Kill a lot of your patients with foot odor?" I asked.

"You must have been an etymologist in a previous life."

"Please tell me you don't believe in reincarnation."

"Most patients want to hear that I do."

"One life is more than enough, thank you."

"Oh, right. Gini told me about your death wish. I guess I'm here just in time."

"Gini has an even bigger death wish for me than I do."

"Ah, Gini. Haven's real angel of death. She doesn't like it when anyone overstays their welcome. Too much paperwork. Is there a particular reason you want to give her a win?"

"I've stuck it out for fifty-nine years because I felt guilty abandoning my mom. Now that she's gone, I feel like my work here is done."

"I'm sorry for your loss, but what about the rest of your family?"

"That's the lucky thing. It was only the two of us. There are no ties keeping me here any longer."

"Friends?"

"Gini would probably be the closest."

"That's rough."

"Or Sally. Her Original New Haven Clam Pie is one of the main the reasons I moved here."

"In Rhode Island, we keep our clams where they belong: in the shell. I was raised on my mom's Stuffies."

"Stuffies?"

"You chop the clams, mix them with breading and spices and bake them in the shell. *That's* a reason to keep on living."

"It's nice you have that memory of your mom."

Candace scratched her neck under the black robe. "I have more than a memory. She moved in with me last year."

"Do you have siblings?"

"I didn't think so until I discovered my dad was quite the player. I was visiting him at Christmas a couple of years ago and started noticing most of his guests had a family resemblance. Two brothers, three sisters, at least. Apparently, he dated half the women in Praia."

"You're Cape Verdean?"

"Impressive. Most Americans have never heard of the country never mind the capitol."

"I only know because it was an answer on Jeopardy."

"I've got to stop wasting my time with Wheel of Fortune. It was a ritual with my mom. She said I was her black Vanna White."

"Our ritual was The Mary Tyler Moore Show every Saturday night."

"My mom used to say I could turn the world on with my smile. And that I had dimples to die for."

"When my mom said I looked like JFK, Junior, I thought she had Glaucoma. And dementia. So, what was it like discovering your long-lost family?"

"It was a relief. Here I was, thinking that when my mom was gone, I'd be alone in the world."

What was a source of comfort for Candace seemed like a burden to me. The older we got, the more I felt the obligation to be there for Mel, but she had given me a reason to live beyond the weight of responsibility to care for her. All my life, I had to pretend I was feeling the same emotions everyone else did, when what I was really feeling was nothing. I could watch tragic news stories on television or tearjerker movies without any feeling of genuine emotion. I never recalled crying or the sense of elation I heard others describe. When I tried to explain my mindset to Candace, she mentioned Sarek, Spock's father and the Vulcan side of his parents' mixed marriage.

I suspect detachment protected me from being bullied for being different as a kid. If others thought I was weird, as I assumed they did, they mostly kept it to themselves. Maybe they didn't know how to react or how I would. My superpower was the ability to slip between the cracks and disappear. My grades were neither good nor bad enough to attract the attention of teachers. I avoided the gaze of classmates and their cliques, and I escaped with a blank space in the yearbook from the high school where my mom would become a virtual celebrity as a counselor—all exactly the way I wanted it.

Mel was the exception, the one person for whom I felt an unambiguous, genuine sense of attachment—proof I was not totally detached from humanity. For years, I told myself I needed to be there for her. Once she was gone, I felt truly untethered and responsible to no one. If I were to continue, I'd need a reason. The idea of helping strangers seemed like a good one, even if there was no genuine feeling behind it. With my estate, my value to others was higher dead than alive; apparently, even my soul was not worth saving. In her near-daily visits, Candace rarely mentioned religion. For a chaplain not to proselytize felt near sacrilegious. I asked if she thought I was beyond redemption.

"You said you were raised to believe that religion was 'magical thinking,'" she said by way of an answer.

"I have nothing against magic."

"I can't turn non-believers who want to hedge their bets at the end of their life into believers."

"So, basically, it's too late for me?"

"As long as someone is still breathing, it's never too late. But that's not what I do here."

"I thought you were a chaplain."

"I'm not an evangelist. Did you ever consider a therapist?"

"I have an advocate who makes house calls."

"The Irish chick who comes in every day with the attitude? How do you know her?"

"She runs the Hampden County Helpline. I called one night, and we had a rapport."

"So much for anonymous suicide prevention hotlines."

"They don't use the word 'prevention.' They believe callers need to reach their own conclusions."

"Press one for yes, two for no?"

"Don't you think we have the right to decide for ourselves?"

"The last thing a desperate person needs is encouragement to take the easy way out."

"If it were easy, I wouldn't have waited fifty-nine years. All Maeve ever encouraged me to do was think of a better reason to live than fear of dying.

"How many times have you tried?"

"None. That's the problem. Fifteen-year-olds are decisive enough to decide and brave enough to act."

"They aren't decisive or brave. They're impulsive. They don't realize that everything can change tomorrow."

"When you're fifteen."

"Where is it written?"

"I'm supposed to go back and relive a life I never started?"

"Or you could start now. All you need is a reason."

"I used to stick around for my mother. Now, the only reason is fear. And maybe Modern Pizza on Mondays."

"As I sci-fi nerd, I used to read this fantasy writer, Richard Riordan, who taught a class he called Magic Problem-Solving 101. He said his students called it Whatever Works."

I thought about this. "Then I guess I'm here to figure out if anything works."

CHAPTER FOUR

ODD MAN OUT

"YOU STILL HERE?"

Vic greeted me every day this way with a mischievous, conspiratorial grin. I often countered with a reminder that he would miss the free pizza when I was gone, but I think he liked hanging out in my room because he had a willing audience. Nursing was Vic's vocation and wordsmithing his avocation; he readily acknowledged suffering from a debilitating lifelong affliction of logorrhea. I won't pretend my mind didn't often drift off, but his daily visits took the pressure off holding up my end of the conversation. While he occasionally threw a question my way, he'd seamlessly steer my response back to something about himself. When I disclosed that even as I approached sixty my mother continued to ask if I needed a bathroom break, he countered with an anecdote about his mother, who left instructions for houseguests looking for ice to check the freezer.

I felt like I knew the entire Tomassini family: his wife, Arlene, who juggled part-time shifts at a florist and a candlepin bowling alley; their son, Carter, a DJ and musician;' and a French bulldog, Fitz, who confirmed the adage about people resembling their pets. "It was like looking in the mirror," he quipped about their first meeting. "I knew I was in love." I knew his mother, Erma, the dietician at Haven, whom he credited for saving him from an abbreviated, inebriated, saturated lifestyle. "After all these years," he said, "I'm still trying to figure out if she is Ann Richards or Mary Richards." Also, I had briefly met his brother Ryan, a commercial fisherman from Stonington, who met him for their weekly "salon" at Contois Tavern. While Vic had the strongest resemblance to his late brother Eamon, it was Ryan who reminded me of their dad's blue-collar roots. Literary references naturally worked their way into Vic's conversations, but he was the only member of his family to attend college or possess a retirement account.

The whole notion of nursing school was originally a practical way for Vic to use the veteran's benefits he earned as a member of the Coast Guard. Stationed aboard the cutter Albacore, he was responsible for enforcing two permanent security zones along the Thames River (the Connecticut one, all fifteen miles of it). To hear Vic tell it, his military service was basically spring break. "I built up an immunity to the fine aroma of puke that prepared me well for nursing," he quipped.

Although I had few first-hand impressions of Vic from a patient's perspective—there were no IVs to attach, no pills to dispense or bedpans to empty—I could see why nursing was a good fit. Like Candace, his jovial presence was a welcome respite from the hushed voices and sterile surroundings in the corridors and common rooms. Between the irreverent humor and the endless stories in his un-hushed delivery—Vic was a refreshing reminder of life outside those hermetically-sealed windows.

Perhaps we were so well suited because I was looking for someone to fill the empty space—not just here, as Haven's longest-surviving guest, but throughout my life. Even as a child, I had always been something of a cipher by design. I had no desire to tell my story—what story? —so I learned to become an interviewer. It rarely took much coaxing. The most frequent compliment I received was that I was a good listener, which meant, I assumed, that I rarely interrupted.

So, I was unprepared one day when Vic of all people tried to turn the tables, peppering me with a list of random questions. Did I have any family? Was I ever married? Did I have children? Pets? Did I go to college? What did I do for a living before retiring?

"That's a lot of questions."

"Sorry. They're your secrets to keep. It hit me that I may have been talking to a G-man or something."

"My life is an open book but not one anyone would want to read."

"That's okay. You don't owe me any explanation."

"What made you ask?"

"The other night I mentioned something we were talking about to Arlene, and I realized that after all these months the most personal thing I know about you is which topping you like on your pizza."

"What were we talking about?"

"I told her a patient at work must have been dying from boredom because there was nothing else wrong with him." He raised his eyebrows. "She asked me all these questions about you, and I didn't have any answers."

I had assumed that Vic knew why I was there, but this was the first time he'd acknowledged it. And this time my foolproof strategy to deflect the conversation back to the speaker had failed me. The only seat in the room was a lounger that looked like a ragged cousin of Chairy from Pee-Wee's Playhouse. Vic dragged it over to my bedside, pulled out his cell, and placed a call to Modern. It was Monday: his shift was ending, and he had plenty of time.

CHAPTER FIVE

BEGINNING OF THE END

AS A WRITER, I have one good sentence in me, maybe two. After that, it's all downhill. I'm probably the last person in the world who should be telling you this story. The job fell into my lap because I'm in the center of it all. Which, I suppose, is ironic because for the past fifty-nine years I've made it a point to keep out of everybody's business, including my own.

When the experts insist the answer is to "Write about what you know," all I think is, "Sage advice—unless you don't know shit." I mean—what if, at the stage when your peers are wearing second wedding rings, you're still wearing braces? Suppose the sexual anxieties you share are similar to those of their teenage children? What if you never had to face going home again because you've never left in the first place?

Nothing is more humbling than trying to write from experience and realizing you haven't had any. The truth is it never completely hit me that lacking a life might adversely affect my professional ambitions, until I started writing about other people's lives at The Palmer Pilot where my career in journalism began and ended.

Palmer, Massachusetts, is one of those small, blue-collar

towns where the profusion of lawn ornaments makes the whole place look like a giant miniature golf course. Shrunken jockeys leer at Blessed Mothers and naughty cherubs tinkling into plaster fountains. Silver globes rest atop chalky, white pillars next to red-flagged barns, half-crushed from the minor leagues of mailbox baseball. Set back from sprawling yards and winding driveways, a pastel ranch might just be another prop—an aluminum-coated windmill at the eighteenth hole. Billboards nearing the border to Wilbraham line US 20 anchored by a Friendly's sundae shop exhibited football players, ski bums, beach volleyball players and other preppy athletes Alive with Pleasure for Newport Menthols and a spartan, image-free query ("Lonely? Depressed? Desperate?") with a phone number for the Hampden County Helpline.

Until recently, Palmer was a company town and on the map because of one factory synonymous with a single product. The connection may not have been as famous as Detroit with automobiles or Pittsburgh with steel, but it was every bit as strong. For more than half a century, Palmer, Massachusetts, was the tampon capital of the world.

The year was 1936. Tambrands, Inc. had just introduced Tampax, the first sanitary protection worn internally. Ads in national magazines enticed women with "an assurance of daintiness you have never known before." Business took off and by 1942, the company, then based in New Brunswick, New Jersey, prepared to build a new plant to meet the booming demand. Who knew that building materials would become scarce following the Japanese bombing of Pearl Harbor? Searching for a new home, a company executive from Massachusetts visited an abandoned textile mill in Palmer. The community had such confidence in the company's future that the chamber of commerce offered to put up the twelve-thousand-dollar mortgage and invested their own money in Tambrands stock. The company returned the town's faith by hiring local residents at an unheard-of salary of twenty-five cents an hour, a wage so high that some feared it would up the ante for less prosperous employers and drive everyone out of business.

Palmer was still a company town when I got there. It was working class but prosperous; the kind of place where good wages and security made it unthinkable for all but the most ambitious to escape. Tambrands was not Ben & Jerry's with its factory tours and free samples, but people were proud of where they worked. Those old mill buildings might as well have been churning out new Jaguars as the most famous feminine hygiene product in the world. There were no smirks or giggles, no bike shop named Cycles or diner called Flo's.

But in neighboring towns across the border, smart-ass college kids derisively referred to Palmer as Tampon Town. Wilbraham, Massachusetts had a corporate face of its own as the birthplace of Friendly's Ice Cream, the company logo rendered in topiary off the Mass Turnpike. But where Palmer was primarily rural by attrition and dilapidated, Wilbraham was purposefully preservationist, filled with horses, tire swings and lawns that all seemed to be part of a real golf course. Yet, for all its bucolic affluence, the mark of success was to get as far away from home from this one zip code town as possible. After senior year in high school everyone made a mad dash for the border, and anyone lacking the brains or balls to get out in time was sentenced to life in Palmer, like some mutant who refused to evacuate Cherynobl. That would be me.

In Wilbraham, even the public schools were seen as feeders to Smith, Amherst, Williams, and Mount Holyoke. As the town's only representative at Holyoke Community College, I had made it a whopping twenty-three miles from home, not far enough, it seemed, to satisfy the editor, Derek Thompson, that I might be qualified to be a reporter. Instead, he offered me the job of announcements editor, a role which allowed me to track the progress of my peers and put my own life in context. The news came in waves. First, academic honors: dean's list, Phi Beta Kappa Society, Magna cum laude. Within a year, I began to get press releases from as far off as Silicon Valley and Jakarta trumpeting new management trainees and corporate V.P.s. Then, marriage engagements, a final checkpoint into the real world.

Through it all, I steadfastly clung to the same address, the same car—a 1983 Mazda GLC that had yet to hit twenty thousand miles, the same rubber-toed high tops and painters pants I wore in high school, and until then, the same job. My journalism career at *The Pilot* ended before it began, with the inspirational words of Derek's father, the publisher, and his grandfather, the founder. Lark Thompson was a salesman who used to brag that he had never read a newspaper before starting one—a claim not difficult to believe once you'd seen the first issue which was proudly displayed in his grandson's office. "Through the generosity of the merchants of Palmer," the masthead fawned.

From the start it was clear *The Pilot* would build its reputation on police blotters, health code violations, and the business smarts of its proprietors. Lark Thompson knew that for all its connections to the town's economy, Tambrands liked to keep a low profile. No company that contributed so much to its hometown and stayed largely invisible was about to advertise in the local newspaper. But that didn't stop Thompson from treating Tambrands like its most coveted customer. Thompson said the company anchored the whole local economy including the advertisers who supported his business, and he decreed that every mention of Tambrands would read like a press release. Lark Thompson knew he could never battle the competition for the story, not when the Wilbraham *Hampden Times* had a small but seasoned team of real journalists. Instead, he would beat them at something more important to the average Palmer reader. Unlike the *Times* which derived its revenue from subscriptions and the quarter cover price, *The Pilot* would be delivered to every resident free of charge and make all its profit from advertising.

"Everyone thought he was nuts," Derek explained, trading a conspiratorial smile with his grandfather's portrait across the room. For the first time during my job interview, he took his feet off the desk and sat upright.

"The bankers asked how he planned to stay in business when his competition was selling newspapers and he was giving them away," Derek continued. "He told them they were in the business of selling newspapers, and we were in the business of selling ads."

Bankers weren't Lark Thompson's only critics. The editor of the *Times* took one look at the wedding announcements and store coupons on the cover of his new rival and said that any reader with half a brain could see you get what you pay for, forgetting that no such readers lived in Palmer. *The Pilot* may have been litterbox lining where I was from but here, it was exactly the newspaper the town deserved.

"People in Palmer don't care about this," Derek said, imitating his grandfather waving a copy of the *Times*. "They care about *this*." He slapped a quarter down on the table and paused for the usual affirmation. The first time he told me the story I didn't know what he was waiting for, so I sat there staring blankly, praying he would continue. Instead, he looked back at me and was puzzled at first then genuinely disappointed. Clearly, I had missed the cue to leap to my feet and yell, "I believe!" In retrospect, it was all downhill from there.

I thought of Derek's expression over the years I worked at *The Pilot*, usually when he'd question my dedication to the profession, which was often. I always wanted to ask him whether we were talking about his profession or mine. The only problem, of course, was that he turned out to be right: advertising was the profession, as the folks at the *Times* would discover upon their demise. Derek not only knew the business, but he knew me, too, better than I would have admitted when he terminated me.

Back then it all seemed like a total whitewash, an excuse to appease the dickheads at the chamber of commerce, the suck-ups at town hall, the morons who worked at the plant, and any other loser townies who were offended by my unforgivable mistake. How was I to know that the information from the high school about the plans for the prom were all a hoax, that there was no Alice Cooper tribute band called "Toxic Shock" covering "Only Women Bleed"? Fact-checking was the job of a reporter and as Derek had reminded me for the past twenty-six years, I was anything but that. As the announcements editor, my role was not to write but to condense, which is exactly what I had done. Nowhere in my listing was the information I had received about the crowning of the Applicator Queen, or the place settings at the function hall decorated with feminine napkins, or any of the other hints that this was all a prank by the seniors from my hometown high school.

Yet even when I showed him the press release I had received, Derek could see only what I left in, not what I had taken out. The relationship between Tambrands and Palmer was still strong. For him, the only thing worse than the possibility of pissing off the biggest employer in town was the prospect of being blamed for driving them out. Only three years later, the company was celebrating its fiftieth anniversary with a market share of sixty percent. Yet for the first time, more than half of the company's sales were outside the U.S., and a new factory in China sparked rumors that Tambrands might close the local plant or sell to another company that would. The last thing Derek wanted to do was to give them an excuse to leave.

"Forty-seven years," he sighed. "That plant has kept this town in business for forty-seven years."

"And now, I've single-handedly ruined the local economy?"

"I'm not saying that," Derek insisted. "But we can't afford to take any chances."

"And one joke in the local newspaper might push them over the edge?"

"That's the part I don't understand." He shook his head. "If you knew it was a joke..."

I had already explained it a dozen times to Derek and his father, not to mention to the Chamber of Commerce members who had filed into our newsroom. Their visits were supposedly unplanned, but I knew they were coming by the way work suddenly piled up around me, which would keep me here in case I was planning an escape.

Who else would drive past the smooth blacktop out front, heading down the narrow alley with its two unavoidable craters and onto the small gravel patch out back? How else could anyone get inside without being announced by the creaking of the floorboards on the wraparound porch and the screen door?

It took about a half-hour before I would be called in to perform my act of contrition, enough time, I assumed, for Derek to give me a proper introduction. *Charlie isn't like this. He may get a date wrong or misspell a name every now and then, but there's no way he would deliberately jeopardize this newspaper and this town to perpetuate a juvenile prank.*

I would then make an entrance with my head bowed and offer an explanation: It was late, and I was coming straight out of prom season into graduation and June weddings without a break. I was exhausted and somehow allowed myself to slip into autopilot, entering information quickly to keep up. Was it smart? No. Was it careless? Absolutely. Was it intentional? Of course not. At this point, I would look up remorsefully, stifling the impulse to add, "*Was it satisfying? You'd better fucking believe it.*"

Maybe I didn't do as good a job concealing this part of myself as I'd assumed. These businesspeople seemed to buy it, if only because Derek had reminded them that I'd been with the paper for years without a major incident. Yet, no matter how many times I repeated my explanation it was clear Derek remained suspicious.

"Between us, it was time to part company, don't you think?" he asked.

I kept my eyes on the severance agreement he had given me to review, squinting at the page.

"I mean, you would admit—"

"Derek," I interrupted.

"Right," he said. "Sorry."

I had once told Derek he reminded me of Mark Rossmore, his son's orthodontist and my own. Mark suffered from the occupational hazard of initiating a conversation after stuffing a symphony's worth instruments into a patient's mouth. The fact that I had no problem telling Derek this surprised and heartened me. I was a grown-up who couldn't walk down a corridor without hearing "Tuck in your shirt" from complete strangers, who could not put on a tie without assistance or wear one without looking like a ten-year-old playing dress-up, who constantly was asked to slow down or speak up as if the words were being smothered by a wad of grape Bubble Yum—yes, I was used to looking authority straight in the eye. Somehow, neither Derek's status as my boss nor his stature as a strapping six-and-a-half footer had prevented me from looking down on him. The tasseled Gucci loafers and not-quite-Rolex watch, the polyblend suits, the manicured fingernails and neatly trimmed moustache all screamed poser. At times, I'd notice him eyeing me suspiciously. Maybe this explained why I had been stuck in a pre-entry-level office job for years, passed over for the reporter's position in favor of one new college grad after the next.

"Can you honestly say there was a time when you were dedicated to this job?" Derek asked.

"The day you offered it to me," I replied.

"My point exactly." He bolted upright. "You haven't put anything into it since then, and you know why?"

"Because I was bored? Because I was overqualified?"

"There is no such thing," he snapped. "I don't care if you're sweeping the floors or selling ads, you prove yourself by doing it well, not by acting like you're too good for it. You had your shot."

We had been down this road before. I resented his suggestion that ghostwriting copy for the classified advertising manager—his literally illiterate adolescent son—constituted a shot as a journalist. Before I could stop, I heard myself taunting Derek about some people getting clearer shots than others. "We're not all on the family plan" is the way I phrased it.

"Did I ever tell you why I hired you?" A smile broke out across his face. "It was that Salvation Army Thrift Store suit you wore on your interview. You walked through the door, and I thought, 'It's the same suit this guy wore to his first boy-girl party in eighth grade."

"And you thought you'd help me out so I could afford new clothes?"

"Just the opposite—I knew you were from Wilbraham," he said rubbing his thumb against his fingers. "I thought I'd help you out because obviously, it didn't make any difference."

I looked over at Lark Thompson glaring disapprovingly from the wall and told his grandson how much I appreciated the sacrifice, particularly considering that the nation's leading journalists must have been fighting for my spot.

It was one thing to hear this from some Ivy League prick slumming on his front porch for a semester, but how could the graduate of some community college—someone who, by all rights, ought to have been thrilled for steady employment —be so ungrateful? Derek thanked me for making the meeting even more fun than he'd anticipated and slid an envelope across his desk. "It expires in twenty-four hours," he warned as I tucked the letter into my shirt pocket. "And don't let pride get in the way because things are only going to get worse."

The intern phone rang off the hook regularly. It had been two years since Derek had managed to lure an unsuspecting journalism student from Mt. Holyoke. There was no reason her old desk was still filled with remnants from her semester at *The Pilot*: a cutout headline, a cocktail menu from Massholes where Derek courted new clients from his private two-top by the bar; a line of paper drink umbrellas strung together from the Scorpion Bowls she would share with Derek and his account executives after work. I pictured their offices upstairs stocked with family photos and children's drawings, awards and clacking metal balls--all the artifacts of real jobs and real lives.

I reached into my top drawer and pulled out a folder containing announcements and photographs from former classmates, including the frayed, yellowing card that made my stay at *The Pilot* seem almost worthwhile. I could pack six years into a single folder and disappear without a trace.

The idea of "Indian summer" was usually a white lie but this time it was true. I rolled down the windows and rolled up my sleeves. I heard gravel spitting from my wheels and "Low Rider" seeping through the hole in the dash where the radio used to be.

I took a couple of potholes in stride, absorbing their impact with my eyes wide open. Main Street was still as a Sunday, but I felt like I was on the final float in a parade. I passed the gothic town hall with its twin stone gryphons standing guard at the entrance, the Christian Science Reading Room in its tidy, perpetually empty storefront, the Merit Self-Serve with its triple lure of lottery tickets, bait, and Camels by the carton at the lowest price allowed by law, and St. Anne's, which showed signs of life only when a hearse was parked out front. Most of these landmarks were familiar from the police blotter, the community calendar, and the obits.

Driving past Massholes, I recognized Barbara Milgroom's cherry Caravan from its smoldering ashtrays, Tim Reidel's Cutlass with its stickers for D.A.R.E., M.A.D.D. and the N.R.A., Len Gore's limited-edition Caprice Classic—the one that climbed Mt. Monadnock. I knew the cars better than the owners, yet I could imagine the conversation.

"You hear about Charles Braun?"

"Everybody in Palmer heard about Charles. It was in our newspaper. It was in the goddamn Times, *for fuck's sake."*

"How the hell was it in the Times *when he just got canned this morning?"*

"He got canned?"

Finding a space in front of Palmiere Patisserie was no surprise, but the parking meter threw me off. For all the town's efforts to go upmarket, its so-called business district still had no attractions that could justify more than a nickel an hour for parking. I couldn't remember seeing the word "expired" on a Palmer parking meter in years.

As Derek escorted me from his office that afternoon, all I could think about was a sandwich that had intrigued and eluded me for the six years I'd been tethered to my desk. Was the simple, hand-lettered sign in the window promising nothing more than "Tuna Melts Today," a holdover from the previous business, a Wonder Bread Thrift Store? Surely, the description was an understatement for *Tuna Fromage et Tomate.*

Palmiere was supposed to represent a renaissance for the downtown business district. Nobody explained the new Palmer to its older residents; most probably assumed the name was a misspelling of the town. Occasionally, the scent of croissants and baguettes would lure some curious townie but most grumbled about the prices and kept their distance. An all-American redundancy like "Tuna Fish" may have been a noble attempt to lure back the natives with comfort food, but management wasn't fooling me. This was a prize worth waiting for: the lunch on the Left Bank I never experienced.

Inside, a hefty woman behind the counter with a tightly wrapped blonde-grey bun delivered the unwelcome news: the sandwich press had been shut down for the day. I was about to leave but realized I had no place I had to be. A small courtyard looked bright and invitingly empty, and the server's accent sounded authentically scolding, which I liked. The idea of sunlight and solitude was so appealing, I ordered a café au lait and took a seat at one of the empty tables with Orangina umbrellas and black plastic Gauloises ashtrays.

The moment I opened the folder I recalled the anonymity I'd achieved in Wilbraham. I made my way through the public school system without making friends or enemies, chess club president or varsity football, National Honor Society or the detention list. In twelve years, I rarely said much more than "Here." Had I been singled out with an honorific in our yearbook, it undoubtedly would have been for most non-descript. It always amazed me that these strangers with their glamorous postmarks and grown-up lives would scribble a personal note on the back of their photograph or in the margins of their announcement.

"Hey Charles," a note on state department letterhead began. Another, written on a business card from Sharon Fielding at Columbia Law School where she was a professor, wondered if we might have been in the same Principles of American Law section there. In her publicity shot, Terry Donahue, whom I'd known slightly as a neighbor, remarked that my name sounded "vaguely familiar" and insisted we get together the next time I was on the Dutch side of Saint Maarten.

A handwritten note was clipped to the back of one of the photographs.

"Hey Charlie," it began. "You probably don't remember me."

I knew it was probably another case of mistaken identity, but the opening was so unusual that I skipped right to the photo. The fact that Karen Nyman even remembered my name was astonishing. Even in third grade, she was as unattainable as Laurie Partridge. Later, the toughest jocks' conversations, which usually involved "nailing," "banging," and "porking" were somehow reduced to innocent, half-stuttered fantasies about getting up the nerve to ask Karen to the school dance. And, with so many other girls preening for attention, she seemed genuinely oblivious to her own allure.

"We were in the same Spanish class with Mister Paul at MRHS," she wrote.

Originally, I sat far behind her in my usual place of choice, right corner, back row. But then Mister Paul, aka Señor Paulo, Don Francisco, and Señor Manos, began to notice what was going on every time he turned his back on us to write on the blackboard and sat us in a giant half-circle. For every guy in the room, the upside of the new seating plan was the prospect of closer proximity to the source of Karen's Love's Baby Soft perfume.

Mister Paul began his opening routine by standing before the class and reciting the Spanish alphabet phonetically as if it were an Army chant. Our job was to repeat it without losing our shit at the sight of this lumbering cartoon figure with a push broom mustache.

"Ah, bay, say, chay," he'd begin, arms waving wildly like a conductor.

"Ah, bay, say, chay" his unwitting recruits called back.

Adding to the challenge during the recitation, an attendance sheet circulated the room, collecting signatures in the left column and comments on the right. Mostly, the subject involved one of two timeless themes: Mister Paul's lineage as the love child of Ned Flanders and Roseanne or his personal hygiene. The assumption was that the turtleneck, blazer, thick corduroy pants, and tassel loafers he seemed to wear each day were, in fact, a single uniform. Occasionally, there were holiday-themed contests (guess the number of flakes on Senor Paulo's shoulders) or artwork (various illustrations of Mister Paul's dick including one with an uncanny resemblance to a Keith Haring Wang). The job of detaching the right column before Mister Paul connected the names always fell to Ray Giacopelli, who sat on the far right. Ray had developed a way of signing and tearing the attendance sheet in a single motion to avoid suspicion. When that didn't work, he'd throw in some remark about Menudo or Pele or Black Gucci loafers and look longingly into our teacher's eyes. Mister Paul would appear mesmerized. For that split second, Mister Paul seemed to have blocked out everything and everyone else in the room.

The rest of us looked like we were watching the most intoxicatingly gory horror film ever made. Ray was like a hypnotist testing his powers before he'd snap his fingers and break the spell. With the slightest change in Ray's expression, Mister Paul would leave his trance and demand that Ray repeat himself—this time, en español, por favor.

Most people in the room concealed snickers, but I found the expression on Mister Paul's face too disturbing to laugh. Karen looked more confused than amused, as though she was trying to follow a conversation not in English or Spanish but in some unintelligible third language. The only other person not laughing was Michelle Ellis. When I glanced over, she was smiling, not at him but at me. It was a look I'd gotten to know well over the years. Michelle was one of seven minority students who made the daily five-mile trek to Wilbraham from Springfield, a gritty city with rundown overcrowded schools best known as the birthplace of Dr. Seuss. "Voluntary desegregation," they called it, a chance for inner city kids to trade one kind of poverty for another. Back in kindergarten, school bus A-14 was greeted with innocent curiosity. Why is her hair all knotted up? Why can't I ever go to her house to play? In junior high, their numbers grew, and our questions changed. What kind of name is Shamika? Why do they always sit together at lunch? John Reidel, Tim's son, thought he had an answer.

"They're in a huddle," he explained to the natives at a nearby table. "They're like, football, football, football. Why else do you think they make up half the varsity team?"

John's theory didn't account for the fact that seven of Wilbraham's twelve minority students were female, and the name he gave them, "The Dirty Dozen," sounded strange coming from a guy with perennial pit stains. John had his reasons. Tim Reidel wasn't pleased when he learned his son had been relegated to the JV squad, not after all the years he spent coaching him in Pop Warner. According to a story in the *Times*, Tim, a former sales rep at The Plant, was talking about running for school committee on a platform for cutting the town's bussing arrangement with Springfield. The campaign apparently never got off the ground, but, when word got out, a few of the Springfield parents pulled out of the program.

By my freshman year, the Springfield students were suddenly all the rage. Want to know what to wear to school? Check out the kids at A-14. Want to seem *really* cool? Hang out at their table at lunch. Having a party? Better make sure at least one of them is on your list. Looking for a way to become the envy of every teenager in Wilbraham while astonishing your ex and your parents in one fell swoop? Become one of the fortunate few to date one of the school's newest celebrities. Almost overnight, we had a Black student council president, a Black football captain, and a Black cultural club—never mind the fact that the school was 95% white. Boomboxes replaced Walkmans, Run D.M.C. and N.W.A coexisted with Metallica and AC/DC, and several locals sported high-top fades and dreads. Kids we had ignored for years were suddenly resolutely hip—with one exception. The aura had completely eluded Michelle. She was unclaimed by the white kids, who found her inauthentically black, and by the black kids, who thought she was suspiciously white. With her granny glasses, knitting bag, and oral presentations on Barbara Streisand, Michelle was not so much black or white as she was grey. More than once I had heard kids from Springfield wonder hopefully if her light bronze skin meant she was Hispanic.

The day she slipped me a note with the heart over the 'I' in her name, inviting me to an Air Supply concert, I couldn't come up with an excuse fast enough to get out of it. Besides, Michelle and Karen were the only people in class who, besides me, chose to leave the comments section on the attendance sheets blank. We probably each had completely distinct reasons, but it felt like a common bond.

"I can't remember a word of Spanish, but I still hear the alphabet in my sleep," Karen wrote.

. . .

For some reason, my mind kept flashing back to that tuna sandwich sign on the window. For six years, I had flown past it every morning as Derek or Barbara or Len waited inside for their cappuccinos and croissants. At noontime, I would watch them file out of the office, knowing I could make it into town and be back at my desk before they had paid their lunch tab at Massholes. Every year, my craving grew, yet it felt as if each step at work was being monitored by hidden security cameras. How could I get back the six years of lunch breaks I was entitled to?

I returned to Karen's note. Obviously, she was being polite, but later, my therapist had a different take.

Mel: Of course she's flirting. You don't recognize it because you've never tried it.

Me: It was on the back of an engagement notice.

Mel: I'm not saying she's offering to run off and have an affair. She's just fantasizing.

Me: Why would she be fantasizing now about someone she was never interested in then?

Mel: Maybe she was, and you just didn't notice.

Me: Karen Nyman is the kind of girl guys fantasize about, not the one doing the fantasizing.

Mel: Do I really need to remind you she is no longer a girl? Or that women aren't only the object of men's fantasies—we are entitled to have them, too?

My instinct for self-preservation kicked in. I knew the language and tone well enough to recognize our session had concluded. I also realized we were treading outside of professional territory here. Most of the time we were successful at drawing boundaries, but every so often, I was reminded of the problem with therapist and client sleeping under the same roof. I dismissed her advice for what it was—good intentions.

Six months later, I felt confident I had made the right decision. The proof was in the picture: Karen, cheek to cheek with Borden Hammond, a Yale Law School alum who appeared to be straight out of The Preppie Handbook. The copy described the ceremony and the reception in mind-numbing detail. Wedding announcements had always struck me as second only to birth announcements as the ultimate symbol of narcissism. Please, tell us, a mass of complete strangers, where you had your honeymoon. Bermuda, you say? And now a baby? Wherever did you get such an original idea? If newsworthiness were any criteria, why not "Charles Braun, a graduate of Minnechaug Regional High School in Wilbraham and Holyoke Community College, announces thirty-nine years of near total abstinence?" Or how about "Charles Braun, son of Lucille Braun and Anonymous Donor, proudly announces the longest tenure in any entry level position?"

I'd figured that Karen, who once seemed barely aware of her celebrity, might have been above it all. Apparently, she was nothing more than a fresh, powdery smelling hologram with an easy smile and a soft, unassuming voice. It would have made it so much easier to ignore her note if only she hadn't added that question just below her photograph.

"So, Charlie, what were you thinking about all that time, anyway?"

Those bold, black letters called out like a ransom note with the words cut out from different magazines and nothing like the smooth, flowing script that came before. Somehow, without a word, I had become more than a random name in class. In one way, my therapist had nailed it: as I had been studying Karen, she had been studying me, too. Even after all these years, the realization was stunning.

The other 'personal' notes from classmates reminisced about the 'good old days' as if we ever shared them. Eliza

Cummings, now an editor at Harper's, apparently confused me with a teacher she never had but recalled hearing wonderful things about.

"I'm really sorry to hear you had to leave teaching for this," she wrote. "The profession needs people like you." To reward my dedication, Eliza passed my name along to her mother. As the proprietor of Five Spice Catering, named for the five colleges in the area, Iris Cummings helped plenty of teachers 'just like me' paying for the basics the rest of us take for granted.

Then there was Ray. Just seeing his name on that creamy, textured envelope with its Park Avenue address drained the blood from my face. A press kit included an artsy black and white photograph of Ray behind a baby grand piano on a grand concert stage. He was wearing a tux with a top hat and tails and the same goofy, gap-toothed grin I remembered from school.

"What do the New York Philharmonic, Carnegie Hall, Carole King, and Stevie Wonder all have in common?" the copy read. "The magician who keeps their instruments in tune: T. Raymond Giacopelli." A grown-up roadie. I could feel my circulation returning. Wherever he went, whatever he was doing, Ray would always be the same delinquent who carved his own "Reserved" sign in wood shop for the detention bench in the principal's office. Even now, Ray was probably walking to work every morning wearing his letter jacket, returning home each night to a living room crammed with trophies going back to his junior varsity glory days.

"Como estás, Carlos?" he'd written on the flipside of his business card. Just seeing my name in Spanish again was enough to bring on post-traumatic stress. I thought of the time Ray had witnessed my escape from a private tutoring session with Mister Paul. "You give Señor Manos a bona?" he whispered as I tried to slip out of the room unnoticed. I smiled like I thought it was funny, too, although I had spent the last hour haunted by the same question. The whole time I could smell Mister Paul's cologne, strong yet sickly sweet like an industrial bathroom air freshener. Whenever I'd forget a word or couldn't answer a question en español, Mister Paul would sigh and shake his head then lean in toward me and repeat exactly what he'd said more softly than before. As long as I could hear the coins jingling in his pockets, I figured it was okay. I had looked beneath the table to see Lunes y Martes, Mister Paul's corduroy hand puppets, slowly making their way toward Senor Pinga in the middle.

"They don't call 'em hand puppets for nuthin'," Ray snorted as I brushed by. His theory, widely accepted if the attendance sheet was any proof, was the reason Mister Paul called students up to write on the board and was to be able to keep his hands in his pockets. That was where he kept them during our private session, yet, somehow, when Ray cornered me outside the room, it felt as if he'd caught us doing something besides studying.

If I made any lasting impression on Ray, I was sure it would be like that kid who put on a puppet show with the master. Instead, he simply wrote that the folks back home might get a kick out of his photo. "It must have been rough to have to move back," he wrote. "But hey, you gotta do what you gotta do to feed the family." Somewhere between the principal's office at Minnechaug Regional High School and the stage at Carnegie Hall, even T. Raymond Giacopelli had found himself a life.

Derek may have known nothing about running a newspaper, but he was right about one thing: I never cared about that job. In fact, I dreaded every moment at work, not just because of the people and the boredom and the bitterness of being cheated out of the job I had trained for, but because I couldn't open the mail without my hands trembling. Every postmark, every word, every photograph took its toll. A bride's fourth marriage, a baby photo, even the death of a former classmate in a skiing accident was hard to digest without feeling envious. If there was any comfort in their self-inflicted diseases and divorces, it was blunted by the lives they had to show for their mistakes.

Hickeys, scars, tattoos, wrinkles, drugs, alcohol, broken homes, dysfunctional families, alimony payments, genital herpes—in a way, each was a badge of honor. When I met a person with AIDS, I didn't see images of death; I saw signs of life. Whether they measured their success in achievements or afflictions, my old classmates had war stories, turning points, places they could pinpoint when some decision they made had defined their future.

I could remember those events just as clearly—the places, the dates, the times. But for me, everything was defined by a decision I didn't make: a hangover averted, a relationship deferred, a move postponed and ultimately avoided. Each time, I saw the opportunity dissipate, yet it felt like watching someone else's life unfolding instead of my own.

I thought of this when I sat down to write from experience at Palmiere that afternoon and realized I didn't have any. In exchange for all those years of stories I might have accumulated living in a real city, working as a real reporter for a real newspaper, I was walking away with a folder of other people's accomplishments. Four years studying journalism for the opportunity to spend my career promoting the achievements of peers who had surpassed me. As someone who could not muster up passion, compassion, or other human emotions, it came almost as a sense of relief to discover I had one after all: envy. For all this, I had my boss emeritus to thank. It did not take me long to reciprocate.

In this neighborhood of ornate country estates, our modern and modest Lincoln Deck House stood out for its relatively diminutive size and psychedelic decorations—the mailbox with the Grateful Dead ice cream cone kid, the abstract sculpture that proved a Rorschach Test of neighborhood fantasies, and the more explicit condom windsock promoting Mel's futile campaign to provide free prophylactics in the high school's health center. Like her home, she was a polarizing figure in town, beloved by students and some of the parents whose kids she advocated for but reviled by other parents who resented her for empowering them. When she transferred from the middle school to MRHS after I graduated and students called her Ms. Braun, she told them to call her Lucy until the assistant principal pointed out the passage in the handbook prohibiting students from addressing staff by their first name. Her way of circumventing school policy was to suggest "Miss Lucy," which I shortened to M-L and pronounced "Mel," and I would address her as such for the rest of her life. "Mom" had always seemed far too generic for such a singular personality, nor did it capture the unconventional dynamics between us. Her more cynical explanation was that I wanted the hand-thrown monogrammed Simon Pearce coffee mugs I bought for her birthday to stand out from the "World's Best Mom" variety.

When I walked in, she was seated in her therapist's chair, a Victorian wingback she had reupholstered, reading a copy of a women's magazine with Susan Sarandon on the cover.

"I can't believe you fell asleep in that movie," she said. "That final shot with her and Geena Davis driving off into the abyss still haunts me."

I pulled up the ottoman and slid an envelope with my severance agreement over her magazine. She skimmed it and removed her readers.

"Any place that would let their most loyal employee go over one little mistake after all these years..."

"Are you kidding? I'm sending Derek a thank you note."

"Take a deep breath and think it through."

"You're always encouraging me to be more assertive."

"Assertive, not impulsive. He holds all the cards."

"Not anymore. I'm free."

"You don't want him to rescind the severance package."

"You didn't read it carefully. There are strings attached."

She looked at the agreement again. "Just one. You agree not to sue or defame him."

"Why would I sign away my rights?"

"He knows you don't have the money to sue him after what he paid you all these years."

"And he knows you do."

"How would he know that?"

"He knows the net worth of everyone in town. The Larkins are very well connected."

"Exactly. I don't want him to blacklist you from another job."

"That's why I'll keep the threat of a lawsuit hanging over his head. Besides, the chance to tell him what I thought after all these years is a lot more valuable to me."

"How about if you take his money first and then tell him to go fuck himself privately?"

"You always told me the greatest reward of the family estate is the freedom to speak our mind."

"Responsibly."

"When was the last time you ever held back from saying what you thought?" I asked her.

"As a matter of fact, two hours ago. This kid was sent home for wearing a tee shirt that said, 'Eat my shorts.'"

"Aye caramba! That place never changes. I don't know why you stay there."

"For my kids. Every day I walk by the bench outside the principal's office and the same girl is there for skipping class."

"Nothing like pulling a kid out of class to encourage them not to skip it."

"I told her I was going to get a plaque for the bench in her honor. But it's not like I can go to the mat with Ted Weeks every time. I constantly must choose my battles."

"Yeah, well luckily for me I don't."

"I'm not sure it's a good thing you feel so unaccountable."

"You want me to feel accountable to Derek Thompson?"

"I don't care about Derek. I worry about you leaving one job before you have another."

"I didn't leave. I was fired. He said firing me was even more fun than he'd anticipated. You think I should have held out for my gold watch?"

"I'm sorry, Charlie. Derek sounds like a bigger prick than Ted if that's possible. It wasn't your fault. Fortunately, you have no financial pressure so you can take your time to figure out your future."

I thought about my limited experience, my lack of presentation skills, my advancing age, and my waning ability to project even a false front of confidence. Even with all the time in the world, the future seemed far out of reach.

CHAPTER SIX

WHAT ARE YOU WAITING FOR?

NOTHING IS HAPPENING and I don't like it. I don't like the stillness. I don't like the silence and, most of all, I don't like the suddenness.

Only a month ago, I was sitting here, watching surveyors with DayGlo vests fan out across Sugarbox Farm across the road. Just last week hard hats were marking off sections and moving in backhoes, from Ashton House all the way to Sand Mountain. Yesterday, when I looked outside, it had all disappeared: the workmen, the machinery, even the little red flags dotting the fields. Still, I had refused to return the Standard chair with the insignia from Smith College, Mel's alma mater, which I had positioned in front of the window to monitor the activity. When I suggested to Mel this might be the calm before the storm, her professional diagnosis was acute paranoia, and her fear was she would come home one day and find me in survivalist gear with our pantry stocked with kits filled with freeze dried foods and poison pills.

At town hall they claimed nothing was going on, but I never could understand why the surveyors and construction workers would just pick up and leave.

"You've got to be able to tell the difference between good news and bad," Mel said. "That's one thing you've never been able to do."

"If no news is good news is the best you can offer, I think I want my nickel back."

Before our daily therapy session, I'd drop a nickel into a Chock Full O'Nuts can on the kitchen table. It was a practice I'd adopted from her kids at school who would deposit five cents into one jar after an office visit and recoup it from another filled with Nik-L-Nips. Sometimes, I would add a card with a five-star rating and a note. This time, however, my fears were grounded in reality.

Two years ago, I had spotted the sale of Sugarbox, our next-door neighbor and one of Wilbraham's only remaining farms, in the Pilot. The buyer was Hampden Real Estate Holdings, but there was no listing in the phone book, and, needless to say, no story in *The Pilot*. There had never been a story in the *Times*, either, which made me even more suspicious. We always assumed the company was a front for some sprawling housing development that would turn Wilbraham into an upscale Palmer.

One of the only consolations of going without steady work for so long was the chance to keep tabs on the situation. The day after the announcement in *The Pilot*, I had letters out to every house on our street, trying to mobilize against the mysterious invaders. For the next two years, I trailed every town official and real estate agent in Wilbraham, until I had become that crazy person everyone whispers about: the kind who has no life and insists on making everyone else's miserable. For the most part they were right: I enjoyed being noticed for the first time in my life, even if it was for all the wrong reasons. I experienced a perverse pleasure walking into the clerk's office on Christmas

Eve fifteen minutes before closing time to request some obscure document or ominously photographing from our porch the goings-on across the road with a Polaroid. I was on my way from anonymous to notorious.

The only thing holding me back from delving more deeply into full, tin-foil-hat territory was Mel's reputation. For better or worse, she was universally known, and I didn't want to make her work even more difficult living under the same roof as Wilbraham's version of Norman Bates.

All of which was not to say this wasn't the beginning of the end. Real estate holding firms weren't buying up the few remaining farms in Hampden County to grow heirloom squash. Workmen wouldn't greet twenty-dollar bills with blank stares unless they had some greater incentive to hide the identity of their employers. At some point, my neighbors would be grateful for my efforts, if not for me; eventually, maybe I'd even consider a career, relationship, or place of my own. Until then my job was to protect the only home I had ever known.

Over a few months, as the battle seemed imminent, my vigils at the window grew longer until my one-man campaign became a full-time gig. From the time Mel left for work first thing in the morning until just before she pulled up in the driveway for our daily four o'clock session, I remained planted in that chair for hours at a stretch. Maybe I had built up an immunity from my days at *The Pilot,* but I was rarely bored. Usually, I alternated between binoculars and the blank book I'd learned to store beneath the chair for Mr. Hollis's mail deliveries or Mel's occasional, surprise early-release days.

The prospect of her coming home and finding me "obsessing" over my "crusade" again instead of conducting a job search kept me on my toes. But it wasn't merely my obsession keeping me occupied. Back in my "journalism" days, Derrick said the reason I'd make such a crappy reporter was that my mind was never in the real world. On his more charitable days, he suggested that, technically, I showed some promise but maybe fiction would be my strong suit. As it turned out, he was half-right. Journals aren't usually considered fiction; however, the one I started after I left *The Pilot* was filled with speculation about real people. In television they might have called it a docu-drama or some other oxymoronic hybrid. On paper it was exhaustive theorizing about the lives of all the people I had almost known.

Although it may have been difficult for my former class-mates who worked eighty hours a week to imagine, being unem-ployed could be quite time-consuming. Sure, there were the trips to the unemployment office and a round-the-clock job search, but what really filled my days were the previous one-hour tasks that had mysteriously morphed into a day's work. Choosing shampoo (once a reflexive grab) now meant a thorough comparative study of ingredients, price per ounce, and manage-ability. I used to skim through *The Pilot* at stoplights. Now I found myself reading it cover to cover—even, I'm ashamed to admit, the ads. A visit to the grocery store became the focal point of a day.

That all changed with the siege. Between my work as a private investigator and one-man campaign to save Sugarbox, I was busier than when I had a real job. Nobody would wait two years, invest millions for land, hire a surveyor and construction workers, then pull up stakes and leave. Whoever was behind Hampden Real Estate Holdings had plans, real plans. Even if they decided not to develop the land, they were going to sell it to someone who would. Rumors ran the gamut, which speculated about everything from luxury housing to a golf course to a retire-ment village. Whatever the truth was, I was certain we'd only seen a hint of what was to come.

On the morning, the crew had disappeared it was pouring so hard I could barely see across the street. I kept my place at the window anyway.

"I want to ask you one thing," Mel said, scooping fruit salad into a Tupperware container. "How will you know when it's over? I mean, how will you know when you've won?"

From the moment she drove off until it was time to leave for my check-up with Mark Rossmore, I sat in that chair like a blind man, listening for trucks or equipment. All I could hear was the wind, rain, and an occasional passing car or school bus. As Mel pulled out of the driveway, I thought about her question. There were probably a thousand companies in line behind Hampden Real Estate Holdings, each counting on some opposition but knowing that, eventually, people would return to their everyday lives. What would they do when they finally encountered the ones without lives to get on with? Maybe I'd never know when I'd won but I could tell when I hadn't.

By the time the downpour let up, it was nearing eleven. Starting up my car on a rainy day could occupy a morning. After a half-dozen attempts, I slammed my fist so hard against the steering wheel that I flew back against the seat as if recoiling from an airbag. Leaning back, I closed my eyes and counted. The starter clicked. I could hear Marlon from the service department warn "Easy, don't flood it." There was nothing wrong with the ignition, the wiring, the battery. Everything was in miraculous shape, especially for a car that had been through all those Wilbraham winters. Even the body showed amazingly little wear. He said it reminded him of a '67 Mustang convertible he keeps garaged except for two days a year—the Fourth of July parade and the annual gathering of Mustang collectors.

I had only returned to Palmer a few times since my last day at *The Pilot,* but things always appeared exactly the same. Even the smallest addition of a Procter & Gamble flag flapping by the main entrance of the factory stood out like a Nixon silhouette on Mt. Rushmore. It was eleven-thirty and the parking lot at Massholes was already jammed. I recognized the red RX-7 out front. The first time Derek drove it to work, I noted we both had Mazdas. "We have so much in common," he snickered.

As I walked out of his office on my final day at *The Pilot*, I said, "We really do have so much in common. Our Mazdas have the same rotary engine." It was a lie I knew would land. Now, I hadn't seen him in three years, yet I thought about our last conversation often.

Slowly, I began to see all the little things I'd missed. Of course I wasn't qualified to be a reporter. I couldn't be, not as long as the person I worked for wasn't qualified to be an editor. I toiled for my paycheck, while his was handed to him. Yet for all his money, he was still from Palmer, and I was from Wilbraham. How had I missed it all these years? He had hired me to strike back at all the people of Wilbraham who would glance at the sign, "Entering Palmer, Massachusetts, Incorporated 1775," on their way to Smith or Mount Holyoke and only picture a Tampax box. The whole story about the damage I had done was just an excuse. The factory hadn't closed. The paper hadn't folded. The town hadn't disappeared. Derek had kept me in the same degrading, entry-level job to give the townspeople of Wilbraham the finger.

As time went by, these revelations became an increasingly larger part of my daily four o'clock sessions with Mel.

"Let it go."

"You were the one..."

"It's true, but if you let that ass-wipe deprive you of any more time, he really will have won. The best way to get even is to move on."

At Massholes, I pulled up alongside Derek's car in the distant corner of the lot and saw the stacks of newspapers piled halfway to the ceiling. Peering into the window, I counted at least a half dozen familiar artifacts: from a radar wire dangling beneath the sun visor to a pair of cigar butts protruding from the ashtray. The car had to be at least as old as mine but looked every bit as youthful. I stood the tip of my car key against the door and began slowly twisting like a corkscrew on a wine bottle. Vandalism felt surprisingly unrewarding, and all the effort had barely left a scratch.

I returned to my car and stared at the hole in the dashboard where the radio had been. I reached for the 8-track under my seat and plugged it into the cigarette lighter. The only three working tapes had belonged to the previous owner, and the tapes had become so stretched that the distinction between Karen Carpenter and The Boomtown Rats had begun to blur. "I Don't Like Mondays" was playing as I pulled into a space in front of the medical arts building.

What George Roundy, the Warren Beatty character in "Shampoo," was to the hair salon, Mark Rossmore was to the orthodontist's office. The resemblance wasn't physical. I could never understand how women could possibly be drawn to a doughy little elf with a Muppet coif. I wouldn't have believed it if I hadn't seen Jeanie, Mark's assistant, flipping through the *Sports Illustrated* swimsuit issue from the waiting room, comparing the models to past women in his life.

"Confidence is sexy," Mel said when I asked if she understood the attraction. "He oozes confidence."

"He definitely oozes."

"You say that because you are the opposite."

"I'll take that as a compliment."

"It wasn't meant that way. There are guys who aren't half as good-looking as you..."

Here was another recurring conversation that confirmed the adage, "The man whose mother is his therapist is a fool as a client."

The most objective description of my appearance I ever received was in second grade when our student teacher Miss Ballantine gushed over my desk-mate Tug's sparkling blue eyes and Ricky Schroder mop. When she noticed I was listening, her face reddened, and she made a point of complimenting the handsome painter's cap I wore every day. Later, I overheard her say to Miss Volk, "When I went home that night, I looked up 'non-descript.'"

The hat had become an extension of my head ever since the carpenter who was building our house left it behind. As soon as he arrived each morning, Carmen set down his plaid dome top lunch pail and engaged me in a thumb war. For months after he left, I wore it everywhere but the shower.

Mel believed that the attachment to the cap stemmed from a missing male figure in my life. Truthfully, I probably wore it for the same reason he did—as cover; in his case, for a balding head, in mine, for a thick mane I always feared made me look like a girl. Yet Mel insisted I bore a striking resemblance to the actor Robby Benson in his "Ice Castle" days, then Dustin Hoffman, and finally, in that infamous comparison that made me concerned about her lucidity and her sight, JFK, Jr.

"I'd take what Mark has over what you have any day."

"Bad breath?"

"It doesn't even phase him."

"It should, Mel. And it should phase you. He's a dentist. *My* dentist."

"That's how comfortable he is in his own skin. You should take notes. It's not often you meet someone that secure."

"Especially with no reason to be."

I suddenly had a suspicion she had pulled Mark aside and pleaded with him to share any trade secrets with her poor, fatherless son. So Mark took me under his wing and made every dental appointment feel like a visit to the Playboy Mansion.

"Notice anything different?" Mark asked as he pushed a button, and the chair reclined. Suddenly my feet were high above my head, and he was staring down at me like a bushy white cloud.

"Mmm-hmm."

"I spent twenty grand on this chair, and it was worth every penny. And you know why?"

"Mmm?"

"For the view. I'm telling you, Charlie, there's nothing like it. The day it was delivered, my first patient was Amber Crosby. You've seen Amber, right?"

"Mmm mmm."

"You must have gone to high school together, no?"

I shook my head.

"What year were you?"

I held up eight fingers, than three.

"She was a little before your time. You'd have remembered her." Mark cupped his hands beneath his chest as though he were holding a pair of beachballs. "Always wears low-cut blouses with no support. Anyhow, Amber takes a seat, and I push this button and she's going back and boom! The right one falls right out—and I mean all the way out."

"Mmm."

"Bite down hard. Tap, tap, tap."

I ground my teeth back and forth against the dental paper.

"So, I'm standing there thinking, Do I excuse myself? Do I ignore it and go back to work? Do I put it back? I mean, what would you have done?"

I squint as if the light is in my eyes, but Mark removes the instruments from my mouth and hits the button on the chair.

"Wasn't there a bib?" I ask.

"Maybe you didn't get the full picture. We're talking

bowling balls, and I don't mean candlepin. You think a paper napkin is going to make a difference?"

"They used to put those lane bumpers up for me. I'm better at mini golf."

"You don't need to be a pro bowler, my friend. This is simply a guy question."

"I guess I'm just not a breast guy."

"Every guy is a breast guy."

"What about leg men?"

"They mean legs plus breasts. The rest is extra-curricular. You're not fifteen anymore. We can talk like this now, right?"

"Um, I guess."

"I'm sure it wasn't easy growing up without a father to tell you these things—not that you need a dad to draw you a diagram. It should be instinctual."

"Okay if I rinse?"

"Of course. So, anything happening on the job front?"

This was Mark's way of asking when I'd make my next payment, but I took pleasure in being obtuse. As a victim of his side-hustle in orthodontics, I'd been wearing a retainer for fifteen years, probably making me a candidate for the Guinness Book. At the front desk, Jeanie inquired about payment. When I reminded her I was on the payment plan—a veiled reference to the unspoken bartering arrangement Mark had with Mel for therapy—her voice dropped to a whisper. She explained he needed to lean on all of us because half of Mark's patients were working at the factory. Jeanie must have read the confusion on my face. She slid a copy of the *Times* across her desk. "Proctor & Gamble to Acquire Tambrands," the headline roared. "Fate of Palmer Plant Undetermined." The handwriting had been on the wall for years. Two hundred jobs were eliminated when the facility shifted from manufacturing to research and development. Rumors about a complete shutdown began even before I'd left *The Pilot*. If Tambrands and Palmer were still synonymous, it was only because no other company had stepped in to replace them.

I wish I knew who or what possessed me to stop in at Saint Anne's that morning—God knows it was nothing remotely spiritual—but I found myself inexplicably drawn there. The church was empty and there was a green light above the reconciliation room. The name of the priest on the door, Father Sean, brought to mind Ol' Lonely, the Maytag repairman from the old commercial, and his basset hound Newton. I kneeled behind the screen, took a deep breath, and improvised the Sign of the Cross. Following a moment of awkward silence, Father Sean asked how long it had been since my last confession, prompting the line I had memorized so carefully.

"Forgive me, Father," I began in a hushed tone, "this is my first confession."

"That's not a sin in and of itself. But you may want to work on that sign of the Cross. What would you like to confess, my son?"

"My first sin is nothing."

"You'll have to speak up a little. I thought you said nothing."

"That's right," I said. "I haven't done anything."

"We're all sinners, my son."

"Really. What have you done?"

"I beg your pardon?"

"Sorry, Father. Like I said, I'm new to this."

"Better late. Did you just convert to Catholicism?"

"I'm afraid I'm not actually Catholic, father. That was going to be my second confession."

"We need to pause here. Confession is reserved for practicing Catholics."

"Yeah, I figured that one might be a deal breaker." I rose to my feet. "I'm sorry for wasting your time."

"Hold on," he said. "Are there any penitents waiting out there?"

"Um, I don't think so."

"May I ask why you chose to come here today instead of your own house of worship?"

"I don't really have one. I figured confession would be kind of like therapy."

"But if I understood you correctly, you have nothing to confess."

"I'm not sure. Is wasting a life considered a sin? What about ending it?"

No reply. At first, I wondered if he had heard me. Jesus glanced down at me from the wall disapprovingly. I had violated protocol and invaded a sacred space. As I got up to leave, a business card emerged through the lattice passage with the number for the Hampden County Helpline. I started to take another stab at the Sign of the Cross, then turned it into a thumbs-up sign and muttered thanks.

Driving by the empty parking spaces outside Palmiere on the way home, I realized that by my next appointment with Mark the place would probably have reverted to a Wonder Bread Thrift Store. I stopped inside and picked up a copy of *The Pilot* from the ubiquitous pile in the entrance of seemingly every business downtown. True to form, the headline read like a press release: "New Factory Owner Proctor & Gamble to Bring New Life to Palmer." Nowhere was there any mention of cutbacks or closings.

I skipped to the "help wanted" section, a prerequisite not so much for the jobs as for the entertainment value. As far away as Amherst, I had seen the listings pinned on bulletin boards in bookstores and posted above urinals in men's rooms. Most were simply examples of mangled grammar or creative spelling. A few were suitable for framing like a job under the category of journalism for an "Oyster Shucker/Seafood Processor."

I was about to order when I felt a pair of hands slide across my temples and over my eyes. Each finger was so thin and delicate that light started to shine through the cracks.

"Guess who?"

"Hey, Michelle."

"That's the greeting I get after all these years?" She pursed her lips and crossed her arms over her apron.

"I can't believe you recognized me," I said.

"Especially with all this stuff," she said, running her fingers through my hair. "Salt and pepper."

"You haven't changed," I lied.

I was thinking mostly of the wispy line of fuzz above her lip I had first noticed in seventh grade. Her cheeks had become slightly bloated and her hair, once wrapped atop her head, now dangled by her ears. I thought of a fortune teller.

"You still work at *The Pilot*?"

"That was three years ago. How did you know I was there?"

"I used to see your name in the paper."

"You read *The Pilot*? Did your family move to Palmer?"

"No silly," she said. "I did. I went to the culinary arts program at Holyoke Community College."

The owner, Angelie, eyed us from the counter and cleared her throat. I was about to order when it occurred to me how little was left in my wallet and what a walloping tip I would need to leave for Michelle. I asked for a petit Café Au Lait with skim milk to go.

"No wonder you're so skinny," Michelle said, pinching my ribcage. She disappeared into the kitchen.

I smiled at Angelie, who closed her eyes and shook her head.

When Michelle returned, she carried a coffee in one hand

and an almond croissant in the other. She broke off a piece and held it in front of my mouth.

"Did you make this yourself?"

"With these two little hands."

"You want to be a pastry chef? Sorry, I mean you are. Maybe you'll open your own bakery someday."

"We'll see."

I tried handing her a five-dollar bill.

She waved it off. "You'll just have to think of a treat for me the next time you visit."

A thick, patchy vapor rose from the fields of Sugarbox. The rainstorm had left debris strewn across the farm, branches and tree limbs were scattered on the ground and small piles of dirt strewn about the walking trail.

Back home, I discovered a phone number written on the back of a cheque slipped between two mini croissants. The "i" in Michelle was capped with a heart. I heard Mel's Valiant pull into the driveway and reached for my laptop.

"You work too hard," she said kicking her boots off. "You can't write well sitting in one place without a break. You need to refresh your mind."

I nodded and continued tapping away at the keyboard.

"Really," she continued. "All the guests on Charlie Rose say for a writer to be authentic, they need to be out in the world, experiencing life."

"Does Palmer count?"

"I hope that's wrapping up soon," she said, filling the kettle. "It's getting a little embarrassing."

"You're the one who said lots of adults wear braces."

"They do, but—"

"You're the one who said nobody would even notice. Now you're telling me people have been making fun of me all these years?"

"The braces look fine. It's the way it looks to ask for free orthodontia."

"Since when did the queen of who-cares-what-people-think worry about appearances?"

"I'll admit that I'm embarrassed to have Mark Rossmore carrying you like some indigent when he knows I can afford it."

"*You* can afford it. I'm supposed to be an independent adult."

"There are better ways to exercise your independence."

"I thought we were swapping his services for yours."

"That was a joke. I'm a high school counselor."

"He probably tells you his sexual fantasies about your students."

"Mark is a lot different than he presents."

"Sounds like therapy to me. Do you have a crush on him or something?"

"What am I supposed to do, block my ears?"

"Send him an invoice."

"All I do is listen and nod."

"I thought that's what therapists do."

She shrugged. "Dentistry is a stressful occupation. Only doctors have a higher suicide rate."

"He would have made a great OB/GYN."

"You're lucky depression doesn't run in our family, at least on my side."

"I'm elated."

"How about if I loan you the money to settle up with him, and you can pay me back when you get a job?"

"I'd rather pay Mark back then."

"You feel better asking for charity from a stranger than from your own family?"

"Much."

"What message am I supposed to take away from that?"

"That I'm a grown-up—even if I am living in your house."

"Our house."

"Your house."

"This is really something we should save for your session."

"We talk about my problems in my sessions. This is your problem."

CHAPTER SEVEN

OUT WITH A BANG

ALL THE THIRTY-FOUR U.S. states with a city or town named Springfield would like to claim theirs is the hometown of *The Simpsons*. Living eight miles from the one in Massachusetts, I was fairly confident we could make a good claim. Any city that could be the birthplace of Dr. Seuss and the home of the gun manufacturer Smith & Wesson was eclectic enough to qualify; each figured into my life in a unique way.

Growing up, the only place I found scarier than the cemetery was the doctor's office. I would sooner have faced the dentist's drill of Mark Rossmore than a request to take off my clothes. Before my first appointment Mel tried to prepare me with books about happy visits to the doctor, but my reaction was similar to a dog when it hears the word "vet." My fear wasn't of pain from shots and throat cultures. It was the humiliation of everything below the waist. To coax me, Mel said we'd visit Dr. Suess at his home office in Springfield and persuaded my pediatrician to assume the alias, speak in verse, and wear the Cat in the Hat's chapeau. His referral to a child psychiatrist was less colorful. I was told I'd have testing, but all we did was play Candyland and other games I'd never seen before. Before I left, the psychiatrist asked me to describe my nightmares and to point to the part of my head that hurt. Then, he took me to a room with a wooden chest and instructed me to close my eyes and grab one piece of treasure. I got a squirt gun which, at Mel's request, I traded for a Magic 8 Ball. The real gift was the relief of a doctor's visit that didn't involve removing my pants.

Had I continued seeing the psychiatrist, I wondered whether he would have flagged some of the signs that continued into my adolescence, like that strange night in late May when I awoke to find myself in our backyard, firing a pellet pistol into the air. For years, I would sleepwalk, often making it as far as the kitchen. Most of the episodes ended with waking up at the tail end of a nightmare. In a therapy session following a night when I had woken up screaming, Mel asked me to describe the dream. Although I rarely recalled details, I was able to remember enough for her to recognize a pattern with my past descriptions.

"Have you ever noticed the one thing missing in all of your dreams is you?" she asked.

It was true. Even when they were populated with familiar faces—Ray, Karen, Michelle, Derek, Mel—I was never a participant. Instead, each felt like an episode of someone else's story. Night terrors were a part of the cycle. The term "a good night's sleep" was as foreign to me as "Feliz para siempre." The only time in my life I could recall feeling truly rested was after general anesthesia for hernia surgery. A few stretches of organic sleep were as close as I ever got to euphoria. I mention this in an effort to explain why those last days in May, when the birds began their symphony well before sunrise, were so stressful. Any other time, their back-and-forth warbling might have seemed charming. That May, it was a provocation, a full-on assault that left me enraged.

When I found the Model 78G pellet pistol in The Want Advertiser, my intention was to use it to ward off intruders like a scarecrow. The fact that it was made by Smith & Wesson, a name as synonymous with Springfield as Friendly's in Wilbraham or Tampax in Palmer, made the alien object more familiar. This was the company that sponsored 4-H, not the one whose products were popular with local gangs.

Yet I was completely rattled to awaken in our backyard, firing off shots directly into the pitch-black sky. I was relieved not to find any casualties on the lawn and grateful that the only human in earshot apparently remained fast asleep. It would have hardly mattered that the air gun was closer to a signal flare or starter's pistol than a weapon, any more than it did that a squirt gun was a toy. Bringing even a faux firearm into the house would have been a betrayal, calling into question Mel's entire value system.

I opened the trunk of my car and tucked the pellet pistol into the space beneath the spare. As a young child I spent every sleepless night certain I was the last person on the planet still awake. When I got older my thoughts were an endless loop of morose scenarios. I lived in such a state of perpetual exhaustion that I would find comfort in the words "final resting place." Lying in bed that night, I pictured the pistol pulsing in my trunk like "The Telltale Heart." I decided to dispose of it in the morning but feared I'd be stopped along the way or caught at the town transfer station. Just before dawn, the birds had been replaced by the hum of cicadas. I hurried out to the garage, recovered the pistol, and grabbed a spade. Just before sunrise, I finished digging, topped off the hole with dirt and grass, and marked off the spot with the largest rock I could find. I started up the stairs in my bare feet when the light snapped on.

"You're up early even for you."

"Those fucking birds wake me every morning."

"Or birds fucking. It must be their mating season."

"They crap all over our cars, too. We should park them in the garage even in the summer."

"Or get a scarecrow."

"They'd crap on that, too."

"Voulez vou un café?"

"Oui."

The first time Mel served me Café Au Lait on my sixth birthday it was mostly foam. Every year, she seemed to fortify the mix with more and stronger coffee. By eleven, I was up to half and half with medium roast. I suspect she thought the caffeine jolt might counteract my inherent lethargy, but she also was a connoisseur herself.

Mel adopted coffee culture while travelling in Europe as a student. Our countertops were filled with so much coffee paraphernalia--a Chemex, a French press, an Italian espresso maker, and what she described as the "house brand" of grinder and electric drip machine for a plain American brew—there was no room for a toaster oven, a microwave, or a blender. We had few visitors, so I was the guinea pig for concoctions like a homemade version of a new frozen cappuccino drink that reminded me of our favorite dessert, a coffee frappe from Herrell's in Northampton. Yet while the coffee snob in Mel dismissed the local favorite as "supermarket swill," she so earnestly wanted to establish my local bona fides and chose the New England spelling—Dunkin'—as my middle name.

I looked up at her on the stairs. "So, you're open to drastic measures for birdie birth control?"

"What did you have in mind?"

"Let me work on it and get back to you."

CHAPTER EIGHT

DON'T MENTION IT

IN A TOWN like Wilbraham the whole concept of "neighbor" was relative. The locals certainly bought into the Robert Frost definition of good ones, and living "next door" could mean an acre or more away. So, although Ashton House was technically closest to us, I only formally met its owners several years after they moved in, while I was soliciting support door to door for the Sugarbox project.

Having moved to Wilbraham from Los Angeles just ten years ago, Mitchell and Grace were practically newcomers, but they had learned the etiquette for speaking with natives. Inquiring if someone went to Minnechaug, the regional public school, or Wilbraham & Monson, the elite private school, was like asking if they went to state school or Harvard. Referring to one as a native was preferable to the condescending "lifer" or downright derogatory "townie." When Grace opted for the neutral question, "How long have you lived here?" she looked surprised to hear me describe myself as a "townie."

"Which means, what, you were conceived at the drive-up window at Friendly's?"

"I hate that place."

"And you call yourself a townie."

"Any place that calls their frappes 'milkshakes' is faux local. Or, in the Sniglet dictionary, focal."

"Actually, they call them Fribbles. Cece would mainline them if she had her way."

Cece was their daughter, three years old.

"And that's who Friendly's ice cream is for," I said. "Kids. No offense."

"You don't like kids?"

"I don't like rainbow sprinkles on my ice cream. And if I did, I would call them jimmies."

"Because that would make them taste more grown up?"

"Because that's what they're called."

"So where do you go for grown-up ice cream?"

"Herrell's if you're in Northampton, Hojos anyplace else."

"That's Howard Johnson's, right?"

"Don't they have them back home in California?"

"I think they might have had a few. They never caught on there."

"You had a deprived childhood."

"Well, I'll have to convert Cece. You seem to have captured her curiosity. She asked if you babysit."

"I think I did once when I was fourteen."

"It made a strong impression, huh?"

"I feel the same way about kids as I do about adults."

"Hmm..."

"Cece reminds me of one."

"Yes, we hear that a lot."

"Don't you warn her not to talk to strangers?"

"That's one of the reasons we moved here—so we wouldn't have to."

I caught myself before blurting out that I had seen lots of small towns on the new milk cartons with pictures of missing children. According to my career counselor at Holyoke Community College, my profile—over forty, never married, lives at home—raised a red flag with parents many of whom were also potential employers. My responses, he advised, should be concise and carefully scripted. When asked why I left *The Pilot*, I'd respond that it was to pursue freelance opportunities. I wondered how long this would remain a sustainable strategy, and at what point "unemployed" would become synonymous with "unemployable." It was more than just the vocational question. In a world where you are what you do, there was the practical matter of how to introduce oneself socially.

Fortunately, it was the rare stranger or casual acquaintance who could not be easily distracted by a simple sleight of hand. When all else fails, Mel counseled, change the conversation to everybody's favorite topic. Mitchell seemed more than satisfied with my vague response to his perfunctory question about my occupation.

"What do *you* do?"

"You're sitting on it."

"You built this bench?"

"Along with every piece of furniture in Ashton House."

"It looks like it came with the house."

"That was the idea. It's all based on eighteenth and nineteenth century designs."

"Our furniture is more mid-century modern."

"The prefab, right."

"It's a deck house."

"No need to explain. I'm a big believer in making homes that everyone can afford. Grace was stuck on something unique. She didn't realize this town is so filled with historic houses. It's the cookie cutter homes that stand out."

"My mom chose it for the setting as much as for the house.

She liked the open space. Which is why we're concerned about the project at Sugarbox."

"What are they planning?"

"Nobody knows."

"The developers must have filed permits. Have you checked with town hall?"

"They claim the trust that purchased the land hasn't decided what they want to do."

Mitchell's brows met over expensive glasses. "There should be full transparency. I'll sign that petition."

"Thanks."

"We only have so much land."

"Exactly."

"Wilbraham needs to generate some serious revenue. The nearest mall is forty-five minutes away. Maybe an office park would bring in the Raytheons, the Drapers."

"An organic farm would preserve it as open space."

"This town needs to expand the tax base. Part of the reason we moved here was for the public schools."

"I'm living proof they are overrated."

Mitchell said he and Grace were big believers in public schools. They didn't want to send their kid to an elitist prep school like Wilbraham & Monson to get a good education. His explanation sounded egalitarian enough, and his occupation was suitably bohemian.

Still, Mel seemed wary of him. For someone who was so non-judgmental with teenagers, she was surprisingly quick to form first impressions, often critical, of adults based on the most superficial evidence—or, in Mitchell's case, none at all. "There's something about him," she said the first time they met at Rice Fruit Farm. What this usually meant was that she suspected someone of being among the Wilbraham residents who voted two-to-one for Ronald Reagan here in the state once known for its singular support of George McGovern against Richard Nixon. "Massachusetts. The one and only," read a bumper sticker on her '64 Plymouth Valiant convertible, right next to her personal "Question Authority" mantra, which was an extended middle finger to those who called it Taxachusetts "like it's a bad thing" and, by extension, to her late capitalist father. The problem with dismissing Mel's snap judgments about people was that, as with Scrabble, it was inevitably like betting against the house. I don't know what the telltale signs were with Mitchell, but when I told her Grace had asked if I babysat, she seemed to take it as a personal affront.

"Why would he ask a man older than him if he babysits?"

"I don't know, maybe he thought I needed the money."

"Why would he assume you don't have a job?"

"I don't."

"You're a journalist."

"I'm an unemployed mail opener. And by the way, it was Grace who asked me to babysit, not Mitchell."

"I'm sure it was his idea."

"Some might call your opinion of him based on one encounter over organic raspberries a snap judgment."

"It was bread and butter corn. And yes, I am intuitive. It's a requirement for my job."

"So what do you intuit about their relationship that lets her off the hook?"

"They're clearly a mixed marriage."

This was usually her shorthand for a couple with opposite political leanings, but Mel claimed to be describing something more. Grace seemed like a free spirit; Mitchell was uptight and controlling. She was responsible and industrious, while he led the life of dilletante artisan. She supported the family as corporate counsel for Tambrands, working twelve-hour days during the Toxic Shock Syndrome crisis.

"I thought your problem was with housewives, not house husbands."

"I don't have a problem with either. But I believe women and men should have the choice to work outside of the house or at home."

"So then if Mitchell wants to be a house husband, what's wrong with that?"

"Housewives do housework. They take care of the kids. They don't indulge their hobbies."

"Mitchell builds furniture. Isn't that a real job?"

"Not if you build it to fill your own home."

"He told me everything is for sale."

"Ask him the last time he sold anything."

"If it doesn't bother Grace, why does it bother you?"

"Everyone who lives under the same roof should contribute in some way."

"That would include me, wouldn't it?"

"Tell me you're not thinking of becoming their live-in nanny."

"I meant your roof. I'm not working."

"When you were, you contributed to the household expenses."

"I bought a few groceries."

"You do the cooking and the dishes."

"I make grilled cheese sandwiches and unload the dishwasher."

"The truth is we don't need the money. We are both fortunate that your grandfather, who paid for a new science center for his alma mater but didn't see a reason to invest in college for his daughter, had no other heirs. If he'd had a son, you wouldn't be alive."

"Remind me to thank him the next time we visit the mausoleum."

"Of course, I probably wouldn't be alive, either. Thankfully, he never had to regret having a daughter who used his money to become a single mother."

"Did I mention how much I appreciate the reminder that I was the wedge between you and your father?"

"You weren't the wedge. You were the last straw. I wish I were a believer, so I could imagine him going crazy over his irresponsible daughter and illegitimate grandson living under the roof he paid for."

"You, Ms. Braun, are a disgrace to your father's legacy."

"I wouldn't have it any other way."

"Just wondering if you'd dislike Mitchell less if he was the breadwinner and Grace stayed home to build furniture."

"Very clever."

"Well, it does sound like a double standard, especially coming from a charter subscriber to *Ms.*"

"The double-standard is that women rarely have the luxury of dabbling in a crafts project and calling it a career."

"His furniture may not be your style, but it's hardly a crafts project."

"I'm sure it's lovely. As long as he's working at home, I don't see why he couldn't indulge himself in a little childcare and housework instead of hiring a nanny."

"If they have the money, what's it to you?"

"I couldn't care less as long as it's not you."

"Because working as a nanny seems undignified?"

"First, I was a sexist, now I'm a classist. It's a noble vocation. It's just not what you do for a living."

"Remind me, what is it that I do?"

Vanity surfaced late in the game for Mel, creeping up so innocently it might easily have been mistaken for some quirky side-effect of menopause. This was a woman who spent three bucks a year on cosmetics—only a single tube of lipstick that would outlast most car batteries—and she'd make a semi-annual pilgrimage to Filene's Basement for discounted clothes. But just after her sixtieth birthday, I noticed her black and silver strands had been replaced by a muddy hue the shade of rotting plums. Finally, I was able to turn the tables and diagnose the professional. After preaching against the superficial for so many years, Mel was a prisoner of her own rhetoric.

Around this time, she also doubled down on her only attempt at conventional parenthood, an overprotectiveness that manifested in earnest along with a package from Sears on my eleventh birthday.

"A motorcycle helmet?"

"You wear this one when you ride your bike."

"And you wonder why I don't have friends at school."

"In a few years, everyone is going to be wearing these."

"Let everyone go first."

Mel was one of the parents who called the General Foods hotline to confirm that Pop Rocks don't make kids explode. Wine coolers, combustible hoverboards, extreme diving off Becket Quarry—none of these risky teen behaviors on her radar were on mine.

Yet her worries about the physical safety of her "largest investment" trailed me well into adulthood.

My next opportunity to be an early adopter was the cost of doing business with my banker. I was considering the $800 option to add airbags to my new, $5,500 Mazda. Mel insisted it was a much better investment than the $400 premium speaker system which would only exacerbate hearing loss. What was wrong with the seatbelts she had always insisted I wear? Like bike helmets, airbags would become standard, she claimed.

So, I could feel our role reversal begin when I found myself gazing at the icy roads, wondering why she was driving a car that had only lap belts and contemplating how her six-minute drive from the high school could take three quarters of an hour.

"I've never been so glad to get home," she announced.

"Rough driving?"

"It's rough working with morons who are more concerned about a tee shirt than the kid wearing it."

"Flashdance collar? Crop tops?"

Mel tossed me the contraband, with the Drug Abuse Resistance Education program logo swapped out for one that read "Donut Abuse Resistance Education" and, beneath it, the line "Dare to keep cops off donuts." The principal, Ted Weeks, confiscated the shirt and when the student refused the replacement, a Minnechaug Falcons football jersey, he was sent home shirtless on a thirty-three-degree morning. Mel followed him with a tarp from her trunk and delivered him to a parent raging at her son's clothing choices. When Mel returned to school, she was greeted by a message from the town's D.A.R.E. officer, who accused her of encouraging the student. Only the week before she had tried to come to the rescue of a student who'd been asked to remove a Bart Simpson t-shirt because it read "Underachiever and proud of it, man." His transgression: glorifying ignorance.

"I have a black student who was called the "n" word by a custodian and a girl who was molested by her uncle. The school has a raging cocaine epidemic, and they're worried about students' sartorial selections. I feel like giving Ted the finger myself and letting him fire me."

"Sartorial—now there's a good Scrabble word."

"All the letters are one-pointers."

"I'll remind you what my therapist told me: you don't have to do this."

"And then these kids will go to—"

"That's the remarkable thing about getting fired. It won't be your problem anymore."

"Not bad advice for an amateur. I'm just venting. And how was *your* day?"

I reached into my pocket and pulled out a crumpled corner of the *Times*. Mel sat there twirling a pair of readers in one hand and holding the newspaper about three inches in front of her with the other. When I tried to suggest the glasses might be more effective on her eyes, she said the problem wasn't reading the notice, it was trying to figure it out.

"It says there will be an announcement about the farm. Isn't that what you wanted?"

"An announcement is a done deal."

"I don't think I've ever seen you so invested in anything."

"One day we're going to look out the window at Love Canal or something."

"We get a vote at the town meeting."

"You put a lot more trust in our neighbors than I do."

"I never said that, but I don't think they'd want a toxic waste site in their backyard."

"Mitchell would welcome a slaughterhouse if it contributed to the tax base, so he doesn't have to pay for Monson Academy."

"What's wrong with public school?"

"Didn't you just finish telling me?"

"That's the high school."

"No coke epidemic at Mile Tree Elementary?"

"People move to Wilbraham for the schools."

"Little do they know."

"It sounds like you and Mitchell have become pals."

"Far from it. He wanted to know if I could housesit while he and Grace are in Toronto for the long weekend."

"What house needs a sitter for three days? Does it get lonely?"

"They probably want me to water the plants."

"First, they ask you to babysit—now they want you to housesit. I hope you said no."

"What's wrong with being neighborly?"

"I can't believe you would agree to be their houseboy."

"I couldn't think of an excuse."

"That's why you always need to have one in reserve."

"You've always wanted to see what Ashton House looks like. Why don't you come with me?"

"I see it every day."

"I mean inside. You should see the furniture he makes."

"You said it's all knockoffs from dead designers."

"So is our furniture. They only died more recently."

"Eames is not dead."

"He died a few years ago."

"Charles died. Ray is still alive."

"He designed that famous chair."

Her eyes widened. "I rocked you to sleep in that famous chair. It's original. And they designed it together."

"I sit corrected."

"If I was into that Victorian crap, I'd go to some fusty old museum and see the real thing."

"Fusty. That's eleven points."

"Thirty-three on triple word."

"Okay, so forget the house tour. We can snoop in their medicine cabinet."

"Now you're talking."

CHAPTER NINE

FEAR ITSELF

EVEN IF THE Blue Jays hadn't been in first place in the American League East, most of the 41,500 seats in Toronto's Skydome probably would have been filled with fans who wanted to see their new stadium. The most coveted weren't the premium dugout section, the VIP seats in the second deck behind home plate, or even in private Sky boxes. In fact, they weren't seats at all. Of the 348 rooms in the new Sky Dome Hotel, only seventy had a view of the field. Since the grand opening a month earlier, suites with a view which had topped out around $600 were going for well over a thousand.

Mitchell had sold a highboy at a Filene's-Basement-level markdown to finance the trip out of his own account as an anniversary gift, without knowing whether he could get a reservation at any price. Yet, somehow, he secured the most coveted view for a Boston vs. Toronto game with Sox star pitcher Roger Clemens facing Toronto's Mike Flanagan, a New Hampshire native and graduate of UMass Amherst. Mitchell had secured tickets only a month after the Skydome opened, and it was even more impressive with the addition of Canada's musical royalty slated for "surprise" guest appearances to sing the national anthem. Everyone, from Gordon Lightfoot and Anne Murray to Bryan Adams and Sarah McLachlan were rumored to attend. There were even whispers of legends like Leonard Cohen and Joni Mitchell, which generated even more frenzy. Oh, and it was July 4th weekend, not that it meant much in Canada—but Grace knew of the fireworks to come.

She told me later about how the evening started.

"What were the odds?" she asked him.

"About the same as winning Mass. Scratch."

"And yet you did it all for me."

"I like to think I'm going to get something out of my investment."

The bellman followed Mitchell and Grace pushing a caravan of brightly colored cushions in geometric shapes straight out of Colorforms. A bottle of Veuve Clicquot chilled in an ice bucket with a card from Mitchell's mom who was sitting for Cece. When they asked to have the furniture in the living room of their one-bedroom, double field view suite removed so they could fit their exercise pads, he reminded them of the 24/7 fitness center. It took ten dollars to convince him that their equipment, medically approved for her post-partum restrictions and his sciatica, was irreplaceable. They ended up paying another ten dollars for housekeeping to remove the couch, coffee table, chair and ottoman.

As the stadium filled, Mitchell arranged the cushions, and Grace dimmed the lights. Both donned the hotel's plush cotton robes. The room was illuminated by a bank of television lights in the Dome. They planted themselves on cushions for the best seats in the house.

"Ladies and gentlemen, from Charlemagne, Quebec, please welcome CBS recording artist Celine Dion to sing your national anthem."

A chorus of cheers mixed with some jeers greeted "O Canada."

De son patron, précurseur du vrai Dieu,Il porte au front l'auréole de feu.

Ennemi de la tyrannie
Mais plein de loyauté.
Il veut garder dans l'harmonie,
Sa fière liberté;
Et par l'effort de son génie,
Sur notre sol asseoir la vérité,
Sur notre sol asseoir la vérité.

"She's no Sarah McLachlan but she's not *that* bad."

"They're booing the language, not her. We're on the English-speaking side of a turf battle."

Grace pulled two satchels of red tissue from her robe and handed one to Mitchell.

"Red socks—I guess we're choosing sides."

"Put 'em on."

"That might be seen as a provocation."

"Let's be provocative."

Mitchell popped the champagne. They lifted plastic tumblers from the honor bar.

"Joyeux anniversaire.

"Tres bien. Happy anniversary."

CHAPTER TEN

EXIT STRATEGY

THE WRAPAROUND PORCH of Ashton House had offered commanding views beyond Saltbox Farm and our house as far as the Boston & Albany Railroad on the industrial north side of town. The scenery from the only furniture, a couple of hammocks, was an ornate gazebo birdfeeder hanging from the canopied tongue and groove ceilings. Mel arrived after I had finished my housesitting duties and insisted on a solo walk-through. She emerged from her tour, waving a pile of Polaroids. My heart skipped a beat, but then I saw that the photos depicted details of the architecture and the furniture.

"I see you helped yourself to their camera."

"You think I should leave them money for the film?"

"I don't even want them to know you were here."

"I left it exactly as I found it—like a museum. The place reeks of "Sterile Chic."

She was not wrong. There were no plants to water—each one was dried, as though a botanical taxidermist had decorated the rooms. If there were toys or games anywhere, they were well hidden. The only sign of a child's room was a twin bed and night light. The wine refrigerator was full, the Sub Zero nearly empty, and the mysterious medicine cabinet stocked with nothing more interesting than free samples from Tambrands. Even the carriage house which Mitchell had turned into his workshop was so fastidiously kept that it crossed my mind he might buy reproductions and claim them as his own.

"What a waste of this spectacular setting," Mel proclaimed as she fell into the hammock next to mine. "What's the opposite of lived in?"

I handed her a Dixie cup of iceless iced tea and a paper plate with a slice of her favorite dessert—an apple, rhubarb, raspberry, strawberry and blackberry pie inexplicably called Fruit of the Forest. It was usually gone well before noon but not today. With the mass exodus from Wilbraham for the long weekend, we had the town to ourselves. I had tried to persuade Mel to spend the day with me in Northampton, with the lure of a walk on the campus of her alma mater and lunch at Paul and Elizabeth's where she could satisfy her interest in the beans and greens cuisine that first inspired her harrowing dalliance with macrobiotic recipes put us on opposite ends of the eat-to-live/live-to-eat spectrum. Yet the thought of the town emptying out around us seemed even sadder than a visit to The Enchanted Broccoli Forest. It hadn't occurred to me that the drive would have taken us through Chicopee, Holyoke, and Northampton, all of which had fireworks, crowds and traffic—three of her dealbreakers.

The aversion to crowds and traffic made sense, but I used to be puzzled by why a person with such strong visual sense would be opposed to fireworks. As it turned out, it was the noise. The moment I turned on the radio in the car, no matter how quietly, she would cover her ears as if experiencing a bomb blast. As a therapist, Mel might have diagnosed someone with her symptoms as phonophobic. In the client's chair, she preferred to describe her discomfort with loud noises not as a fear but a rational strategy. I assumed it stemmed from watching her grandmother lose her hearing and her teaching career with it, but that didn't stop me from reminding her there is no point in having hearing if you are too afraid to use it.

"Listen," she said squirting Ban de Soleil on her arms.

"I don't hear anything."

"Isn't it beautiful?"

"You know they have fireworks here in Wilbraham, too."

"I'll be safely home with cotton in my ears. Put some of this on your face. It's starting to burn."

"SPF 4. That means I'll have to lie out in the sun four times longer to get a tan."

"I should have gotten eight." She looked at her plate. "This even beats the fruit pie at Paul and Elizabeth's."

We dozed off, lulled by the warmth of the sun, the rocking of our hammocks, and the distant rhythmic pulse of sprinklers. I was awoken by the thump of a stack of Yellow Pages landing on the driveway. The sky had started to cloud over, and I went to retrieve them in case of rain. The Sunday paper lay a few feet away.

The turf battles between *The Pilot* and the *Times* made for light entertainment. But *The Springfield Republican* was the paper of record: a daily with a storied history stretching back to 1844 and a famous reader named Emily Dickinson. Her family not only subscribed to *The Republican*, but they were also friendly with two of its editors. Despite the name in recent history, they endorsed the Democrat in every presidential election. The word "Wilbraham" in a headline was so rare that I nearly missed the photos atop the fold—mug shots of Mitchell and Grace and an aerial view of the SkyDome.

It was, according to Grainger Fehrnstrom, their Boston defense attorney who was quoted in the article. His clients had no idea that every set of binoculars in the stadium was fixed on

Mitchell's butt pressed up against the glass and the back of his head thrusting between Grace's legs like a woodpecker. That was just the pre-game show, a three minute and thirty-nine second extravaganza culminating in two security officers bursting into the room and wrapping the couple in matching Blue Jays blankets.

It was a misunderstanding. Who would have imagined that the window in their room was not one-way glass? Why would they have assumed the cheers and whistles during their version of the wave, or the scattered boos while they were being led away, were for them? By the time it was all over, the clips of Prime Time Sports, the call-in show on Toronto's sports radio station, Fan 590, were in heavy rotation on WBZ Boston's Calling All Sports.

Bob: Please folks, I understand it was, yes, titillating, but we have been talking about this scandal for three hours now. Frederick in Cabbagetown, how about them Jays?

Frederick: Bob, I figured out the secret word.

Bob: Why do I get the feeling we're not talking baseball?

Frederick: I was there at the SexDome.

Bob: You and another 41,499 fans, Fred.

Frederick: Yeah, but I brought a digital video camera from Japan, and my wife reads lips. In slo-mo, she could tell which word the woman was moaning. It was "Merci."

Bob: Apparently, she was confusing Toronto for Quebec. Unless she meant "Mercy."

Frederick: Either way, right? I can't remember the last time my wife ever expressed that level of gratitude, can you?

Bob: I don't know your wife, but I'll take your word for it. Marty in Liberty Village, can we talk about—I don't know—Celine Dion's national anthem, McGriff's walk-off homer in the eleventh inning, or Brian Mulroney's tax reform bill?

Marty: How about politics?

Bob: At this point, anything but sports.

Marty: Does anyone think this couple would have walked if they weren't American?

Bob: Way to change the subject, Marty. In order for them to be convicted, the prosecutor would have to prove they were "intending to offend those they knew were watching." How do you prove intent?

Marty: Go to the videotape. There's no way they thought it was one-way glass. These people wanted to be seen. Americans are exhibitionists.

Bob: A lot of people who were there say they didn't see much.

Marty: That's because the back of his freaking head blocked her—

Bob: We're on a seven-second delay, folks. This is a family program, not a sports-sex show.

Marty: Right, like SkyDome is supposed to be a family place. It's right here in the *Star*: the maximum penalty for performing an indecent act is six months in jail or a $2,000 fine. The only reason they aren't paying is so Mulroney can avoid pissing off the U.S.

Bob: I don't know. A lot of people *there* seem pretty pissed off at them.

After 30 years as host of Sportsnet, McCown announced he was leaving Fan590, not because of "the incident," but perhaps not entirely in spite of it. The reaction was mixed back home. Some wanted the town to buy Ashton House and send the Cullens to Springfield, where they would feel at home among the adult bookstores. Families with children in Cece's preschool fretted about her future. Occasionally, random residents would flash a thumbs-up sign as at Grace, try to high-five Mitchell, or mime one of their moves from the video.

Then there was Mel, who was a support group of one.

Despite her antipathy for Mitchell, she balked at the "puritanical and judgmental" response of neighbors. She even sent me over to deliver a Fruit of the Forest Pie with a Post-it note encouraging our neighbors to hang in there. I decided not to tell her that Grace had asked to meet at Massholes.

Mel and I were the only adults in Wilbraham or Palmer who didn't frequent the local landmark, a low-slung, windowless concrete bunker crowned with a tangle of satellite dishes. Christened as Sterling Taproom in 1934, it was re-branded as Massholes decades later by Christos King, the porta-john magnate whose Throne King empire was locked in a perpetual battle with Springfield-based interlopers Pee Palace and A Royal Flush.

Massholes opened at 8AM but didn't serve breakfast, and they usually closed whatever time the last patron would stagger out with no regard to the one a.m. curfew on its liquor license. And somehow the establishment always managed to have a smoldering trough of cigarette butts at the entrance even when it was closed. Describing it as a dive bar would not have been fair for someone who had never set foot inside. I suspected "watering hole" would have been a safe bet given the surprising cross-section of patrons, (or, as Mel assumed, "the full range of brows: high, middle, low, and no"). The acoustics scared her off. Neither of us were drinkers nor second-hand smokers. We rarely socialized, and any lingering possibility ended when she heard from King's son--one of her crackheads at school—that his dad hosted a Reagan-Bush fundraiser.

So, I felt a sense of betrayal merely walking in through the nicotine haze to a corner table with a Joe Camel ashtray and a vase with a single, red plastic rose. I hurried hoping not to draw attention to my long list of dress code moving violations: shorts, flip flops, backward baseball caps (or, in this case, a front-facing painter's cap). Several sets of initials were carved into the Spuds MacKenzie stained glass "window" behind my table. My waitress was a dead-ringer for Sudie Bond, the actress who played Juanita in Mel's favorite movie, "Come Back to the Five and Dime, Jimmy Dean, Jimmy Dean." She dropped a beer menu on the table without glancing my way or breaking her stride. A couple of shitfaced frat brothers wearing Theta Chi sweatshirts were entertaining themselves with a karaoke rendition of "She Drives Me Crazy." The monitors above the bar were split between a rain-delay of a Sox vs. Orioles game and an episode of St. Elsewhere.

I heard "Charles," stretched as though it had multiple syllables. "You know hats are against the dress code here. But I guess this one isn't removable." Clean-shaven and casually clad in Top Siders, khakis, and a polo straight from "The Preppy Handbook," Derek Larkin towered over my table. His skin was bronzed, his eyes red and glassy. We had travelled in such different circles that, even in a tight radius, I had remarkably managed to evade him from my last day at *The Pilot* years before. He parked his beer mug on the table and thrust out his hand. I latched my foot on the chair across from me and pulled it toward the table.

"I saw you here with your entourage and thought you might want to catch up," I said.

"You're a mind reader. Can you guess what I'm thinking now?"

"I'm surprised to see you in a place like this. What would you call it, a dive?"

"I would now."

"Did you ever know your little joke almost cost us *The Pilot*?"

"What a loss for journalism."

"And that kind of talk nearly lost you a couple teeth."

"Be my guest. I'd be glad to own whatever's left of *The Pilot*. Maybe I could turn it into a newspaper."

"We're doing fine now, but Tambrands could have levelled us. They own this town in case you haven't figured it out."

"They own you, Derek. Every business does, even the ones that don't advertise."

His eyes blazed. "Listen to this—a journalism lesson from the only employee we've ever axed. The highlight of my career."

"No doubt. Getting fired by you is like making Nixon's enemies list."

"Where are you working today, Charles, *The Republican*, *The Globe*, The *Times*?"

"Those are steppingstones to *The Pilot*."

"That's what I thought. Still living with your batshit mom?"

"She sends her best to your boss."

Our "pleasant" banter was interrupted by Grace, with her long blond hair wrapped in an upsweep. I admired her bronzed skin set off against a modest white sundress and open-toed sandals. A crystal dangled from the chain around her neck. Absent of make-up, Grace was a ray of natural light in the dank, dark room. She apologized for interrupting. I told her Derek was leaving, but she held out her hand.

He clasped it like a Venus fly trap around its prey. "No introduction necessary."

"Do we know each other?" she asked, clearly confused.

"Everybody knows you," he replied suppressing a smile. "You're quite the local celebrity."

"I'm surprised, Charlie," she said with her gaze fixed on Derek. "You don't seem like the kind of guy who would hang out with someone who would attack a complete stranger."

"No judgement intended," he said. "I'm grateful. You helped me sell a lot of newspapers."

"Derek's daddy owns *The Pilot*," I explained. "They couldn't sell newspapers. They can barely give them away."

"It was good enough to keep you working there all those years until we fired your ass."

"You don't have to worry about us being friends, Grace," I told her.

"I have a new respect for you, Charles," Derek said. "I could never picture you with any woman, never mind a porn star."

"She's also a lawyer."

"Here's to the First Amendment," he said, raising his glass.

"Grace works for Tambrands. Derek is a big fan of your company," I said rising and extending a hand. "This has been a nice reunion. Let's plan for another ten years from now."

Derek shook his head, turned away, then swung back, trying to land a sucker punch as I took my seat. His fist landed on Spud MacKenzie's black eye, shattering the glass. The room grew quiet. Derek smiled and was either anesthetized or in shock. I grabbed all the napkins from the dispenser and tried to mold them around his bloody hand which was still balled up in a fist. Grace yanked the back of my shirt and headed for the exit.

"What the fuck did you do to him?" our waitress asked as we hurried by.

"What the fuck did you do to our stained-glass window?" the bartender added, slipping beneath the bar flap and following us to the exit. He was pale, gray at the temples, and built like a bouncer. The chorus of "If I Could Turn Back Time" trailed us out the door.

"Like Budweiser doesn't have plenty more where that came from," Grace said.

"They didn't make it," he said peeling off his apron and tartan cap. "Some stained-glass artist made it from a picture of Yamas, Christo's pit bull. Probably cost him a fortune."

"Derek Thompson can write him a check," I said.

"You think he's responsible, but he'll probably blame you. I'd better get your number and his."

"You think Charlie put Derek's fist through the glass?"

"I only saw his hand," the barkeep said, shrugging. "I didn't see how it happened."

"There's a room full of people who did," Grace said.

"No disrespect," he replied, "but I wouldn't bet on them coming to your defense."

"I didn't realize I needed one. Let's go, Charlie."

Grace and I crossed the road and headed toward the town common.

"The story wasn't this big in Canada."

"It made *The New York Times,*" I said.

"Somehow, I don't think that's where most of the people in there read it."

"Welcome to Massholes where everybody knows your name."

"It's not only there. It's a state of mind around here."

"You understand the bar was named after the state and not the other way around?"

"I've never been so glad to be leaving."

"I'm glad you pulled me away."

She stopped and looked at me. "We're leaving Massachusetts."

"I hate to tell you, but I think they heard about it in Tehran."

"That's where I would have expected this kind of reaction. It's not even the first time it happened."

"The Skydome only opened in June."

"I wish we could claim credit for the idea, but the Toronto Police told us some guy beat us to it."

"Some guy?"

"See, you don't even have to bring a date."

"Thanks."

"Sorry, I wasn't suggesting anything."

We crossed over Main Street to the empty common and took a seat in the gazebo. A carousel, an inflatable castle, and a couple of coin-operated kiddie rides left behind from the holiday cast a pall over the green like a shadow in the squinting sunlight.

"I guess it's just not my thing," I said.

"What is your thing?"

"I don't think I have one."

"Sorry, it's none of my business. I forget I'm not in California."

"Is even California like California? I mean, people take their kids to Dodger Stadium..."

"And seeing us would have scarred them for life?"

"Well, how would you have explained it to Cece?"

"Remember when we went to the park and you asked me about those dogs who were stuck together?"

"I guess this is why you're the parent."

"I'm not, really. Cece is my niece. Mitch and I took her when my sister was hospitalized."

"You're shitting me."

"I shit you not. You're the only person here who knows."

"I'm honored, I guess. But why me? We hardly know each other."

"I received a kind note from your mom. I think the two of you might be the only non-judgmental people in this town—and if I'm wrong, we'll probably never see each other again, anyway."

"So, you lost your baby?"

"No, she's with parents who didn't get cold feet about having a child."

"Oh. I'm sorry."

"Why?"

"I don't know. I couldn't think of what else to say."

"Of all the reasons not to have a baby: to placate parents would be at the top of my list. To save a marriage would be a close second. Still, it takes an immature forty-year-old not to be able to decide until it's too late."

"Are you religious?"

"More spiritual. Why?"

"You couldn't end the pregnancy?"

"It felt even more selfish. Sorry, I didn't mean to make you uncomfortable."

"I just don't have a lot of experience with tears—or emotion of any kind."

"Okay, you're going to want to give me a hug. Rest my head against your shoulder. There. Are you sure you aren't related to Mitchell?"

"So, you didn't want to be parents and now you're raising someone else's kid. How is that selfish?"

"What choice did I have? Carrie is a single parent with schizophrenia. She's in McLean. It was either Mitchell and me, or our mom, who is even less equipped to take care of a kid than we are."

"Cece doesn't know?"

"She thinks Carrie is her aunt. We adopted her and moved here so Cece could visit her. Of course, now that we're moving back to California they'll see each other on the occasional holiday—assuming we don't lose custody after Toronto."

"What about your job?"

"Yesterday was my last day. No surprise there. Tambrands has their image to consider. You did a good job comforting me. You can release me now."

"Sorry, right. This is none of my business, but—"

"You've already heard my big secrets. You might as well ask."

"You lost your job, your house."

"Was it worth it? This is what keeps my marriage going. Or our sex life, anyway. Which pretty much is the marriage. Mitch and I have the same fetish. Probably more than you wanted to know."

"Other ballparks?"

"That was a first, but it's always about an audience. Mitch can't perform without one."

"I guess that explains the Polaroids you left around the house."

"That was more of a tip for housesitting."

"I'm glad I found those Polaroids before my mom did."

"You brought your mother?"

"Sorry, she always wanted to see what Ashton House looked like on the inside."

"No, that's fine. She's obviously open-minded. So, what did she think of the house?"

"She said it was immaculate."

"Hmm..."

"Sorry, I'm not good at ad-libbing. Her tastes run more toward modern."

"So do mine. Mitch was the one who wanted to live in *This Old House*. So, what did you do with the photos?"

"Don't worry. Nobody will ever see them."

"Obviously, I'm not too worried about being seen. It's kind of the point."

"Did you want them back?"

"Not if you're enjoying them."

"Right. Did I say thank you?"

"I figured—single guy, they might come in handy, if you know what I mean. Unless I'm not your type."

"I don't think I have a type."

"Who do you fantasize about, if that's not too personal?"

"I don't know. Dame Edna?"

"Sorry, I don't know who that is."

"I don't fantasize."

"Have you ever seen a therapist?"

"I live with one."

"And she doesn't see any boundary issues with treating her son?"

"I'm guessing you didn't ask to meet about my untraditional family dynamic."

"So you're the one who sets the boundaries. That's fine. I only came here to buy you a drink."

"For what?"

"Services rendered."

"I didn't do anything. The Blue Jay Pie was from my shrink."

"Is that what you called it?"

"That's what she called it, but she thought you might take it the wrong way."

"Actually, it's kind of funny. I didn't mean now. Ever since we moved to Wilbraham, we felt like aliens."

"I know the feeling."

"Well, you made us feel welcome—or at least less unwelcome. I wish there were someone here who could do that for you."

"That's what the years of therapy were for."

"Well, since the Polaroids didn't get much use and the drink is out, is there anything else—maybe a piece of furniture you guys like? Why are you smiling? It's not your style, I know. It's not mine, either."

"I think it would just remind Mel of Mitchell."

"She doesn't like him?"

"I probably shouldn't have said that."

"No, I get it. He's not everyone's cup of tea."

"As long as he's yours."

"It's complicated. Why do you call your mom Mel? I thought her name was Lucy."

"At the high school, they call her Miss Lucy. I use M.L. for short."

"Got it. And which of Mitchell's challenging attributes rubbed her the wrong way?"

"She doesn't even know him. She made a snap judgment. Which is kind of ironic, because she has this reputation for being so non-judgmental with her kids."

"I thought you were an only child."

"Her students at the high school are her kids. I'm her investment."

"Making snap judgments is what good therapists do, right? It's being intuitive."

"Sometimes I wish the intuition came with a filter."

"She didn't tell me, Charlie. You did."

On our way home, Grace managed to segway into the mundane naturally with no awkward pause. Would Derek's one-man barfight make its way into *The Republican*? Could James Garner and Mariette Hartley be pressed back into service to rescue Polaroid from the onslaught of video and 35-millimeter cameras? Would Mitchell and her radioactive status prevent nasty neighbors from attending a yard sale for his inventory? The only curveball she threw was a question about the other half of my parentage. I mentioned something about him "not being in the picture" and tried to pivot to a question about her dad.

"Maybe we should talk about your family for a change."

"That's okay, if you're not comfortable talking about your father."

"Now there's something I don't hear often."

"What?"

"The thing where you turn every personal question back on the person who asked it. You probably inherited it from your mom, right? I mean, she does it for a living."

"I already know my story. It's more interesting to hear someone else's."

"There are a lot of women who would find that quality refreshing in a man. I mean if they didn't die of shock first."

"Thanks, I guess."

"We still haven't settled up here. Maybe I could take you to Hojo's before we move?"

"If you don't mind a drive, the nearest one is in Holyoke."

"For a last chance to try a frappe, I think it's worth a few extra miles."

I reminded Grace that Hojo's only served milkshakes—that we'd have to go to Herrell's in Northampton for a frappe. She said she wasn't game and left me at the curb. I saw Cece careening into her arms at the front door and began walking home, trying to remember what I did with those Polaroids.

CHAPTER ELEVEN

I DON'T SEE THIS ENDING WELL

MEL CAME in waving *The Pilot* like it was *The Chicago Tribune* "Dewey Defeats Truman" cover. The headline read "DEFINE PALACE," and it ran above a photo of Christos King emerging with his fingers pinching his nostrils from a Pee Palace portable toilet. Predictably, the Throne King himself, an advertiser for *The Pilot*, had made the news rather than being the reason rows of porta-potties had been deployed along the perimeter of Sugar Box Farm. King was enraged that an out-of-town competitor was selected over his company.

"I guarantee we underbid them," he told *The Pilot*. "The town administrator was pissed because my other business Mass-holes challenged his brother-in-law's application for a liquor license. All these years, we donated portable toilets to this town for the Fourth of July. Next year, he can ask (expletive) Pee Palace."

"Good news." Mel settled into her Freudian office chair.

"If you own stock in Pee Palace."

"I meant for us. No toxic waste site as our new next-door neighbor."

"Let me guess: a shopping mall."

"Nope."

"An office park?"

"Not even close. The new owners are basically preserving it as open space, just like you wanted."

"Where did you hear this?"

"The assistant vice principal is on the board of the Islamic Society of Western Massachusetts. They bought the land."

"I thought it was owned by Hampden Real Estate Holdings."

"They must have sold it to them."

"So, we're going to have a giant mosque next door?"

"Nope. They bought it for a Muslim cemetery. Isn't that great?"

I knew where this was leading. One of Mel's most oft-told stories was from her days living in a boarding house while attending Katharine Gibbs College, the secretarial school where her parents had sent her. Their hope was to train her as a receptionist for the family business while minoring in "husbandry"—the search for the father of their future grandchildren. The building was strategically located next to the dorm for a business college filled with eligible bachelors. One side faced train tracks and the other a cemetery. Spooked by the prospect of overlooking a graveyard, most girls requested a room with a view of the rails. Mel shrugged off the spirits and opted for the "quieter neighbors." Unable to master touch-typing, switchboard mechanics, or other foundational courses, she lasted at the secretarial school for less than a semester.

Another one of Mel's greatest hits was an admissions essay to Smith which began, "I owe my life to a silver fox jacket." She went on to describe how her dad persuaded his wife to bear a child neither of them particularly wanted with the incentive of the garment she desperately did want. He would get a son and heir to the business. Instead, of course, he got a daughter whose rebellion carried over from preschool to finishing school and straight on past his retirement. Her conclusion—that she, her mother, and even her dad were all victims of the gender roles of the times—won her a place at Smith. Evidently, the strongest impressions from her short stay as a "Gibbs Girl" were her ineptitude at answering the phone and the fearlessness I, unfortunately, did not inherit.

Even my lifelong death wish did not exempt me from holding my breath every time I walked past a graveyard, a superstition that supposedly prevented nightmares. In high school, I was strategically absent the day our art teacher planned a field trip to the cemetery for gravestone rubbings. Knowing my angst, Mel even suggested I bid a fond farewell to her dad at the church and skip the graveside service. So, I assumed the effusively positive spin she put on our potential would-be neighbors was as much about my anxiety as her lack of it.

"Remember when you used to be scared of mirrors?" she asked.

"I wasn't scared of mirrors. I was afraid of looking into them."

"I noticed. Even the one in your crib. When you started shaving without a mirror, I thought you were going to slit your throat."

"I thought *you* were going to slit my throat."

"I responded more therapeutically. I was reading a chapter on exposure therapy in grad school, and they recommended desensitizing gradually. So we started with that little strip of glass that reflected your face from your nose down, remember?"

"Painfully."

"Then you graduated to the rear-view mirror in driver ed."

"And now, I'll be able to watch in the distance. By the time dead bodies are in our backyard, I'll be completely comfortable doing gravestone rubbings."

"Lots of people have picnics in cemeteries. You can't ask for better neighbors. They don't make noise. They don't bring in traffic. They don't overcrowd the schools."

Personally, I would have preferred the Love Canal. If people were going to spend eternity with the dead, cemeteries should be located as far from the living as possible. Mel, on the other hand, reacted as if they would provide much needed diversity. "Hell," she said, "some of my best friends are dead."

The following morning, *The Pilot* revealed the buyers with a headline that read "THEY BOUGHT THE FARM," above a photo of bearded men wearing robes in front of a mosque. Already, they reported, some residents were raising thinly veiled objections not to the cemetery but to its religious affiliation. One urinary palace was painted with graffiti reading "Ayatollah Assahola," and a Halloween decoration, a plastic gravestone, sprung from the ground with a line across a crescent and star and the words "Not in my backyard." Fearing a lawsuit based on religious discrimination, the town had apparently fast-tracked approval.

Pushing the paper away and shaking her head, Mel grabbed her Thermos. "Maybe we can register a few of our new neighbors to vote," she said heading out the door.

As soon as I saw her car backing out of the driveway, I took a walk to Ashton House and scribbled down the name "Skye Mountain Realty" and a phone number from the lawn sign. That afternoon I gave a young agent named Patti the grand tour, starting with Mel's room. We walked under the constantly changing hues of the skies, the azaleas and forsythias, the foliage accented by the occasional fiery crimson of a cardinal—the peaceful, pastoral view Mel never tired of outside her bedroom window.

CHAPTER TWELVE

THIS EXPLAINS A LOT

NEARLY EVERY HOLIDAY held a horror all its own. Thanksgiving and Christmas amplified the absence of family and precariousness of the future. Valentine's Day and New Year's Eve reinforced the solitude of single life. Independence Day and Halloween were for children, parents, and revelers. Choose your metaphor—rock-bottom, sinking into the abyss free-floating dread—no annual ritual approached the dread of the first Monday in September. As a child, I avoided even an inadvertent encounter with the tux-wrapped, sleep-deprived, sweat-drenched, triple-bypass Patron Saint of Labor Day, Jerry Lewis. Watching him chain-smoke his way through the Muscular Dystrophy telethon reminded me what was ahead: the grind of school and the short days and long nights of endless winters. Once I was an adult, Labor Day meant watching everyone else return to routines from the outside looking in.

One year, Mel joined a couple of teachers for a long weekend at the retreat where they held the O-M sessions in the Berkshires. Please, I thought, let her stick with yoga and macrobiotic cooking classes. Whether it was the silence of an empty, television-free house, the photos in *The Pilot* of students moving into the dorms at the five colleges, the blindingly bright day that somehow accentuated the solitude, something pushed me over the edge.

I pulled up to Ashton House in Mel's Valiant with the top-down and the radio presets on WPVR and Pioneer Valley Radio; she'd toggle between classical music and public radio talk shows. The front door was wide open, and I could hear the faint sound of music leading to the backyard where Grace wore a wide straw hat, white polo shirt, pink shorts, and flip-flops revealing bright red toenails. A Fisher Price cassette recorder on the lawn was playing a song about waking up and brushing your teeth just for the fun of it. She snapped it off with a big toe and folded her arms across her chest.

"Am I too late?" I asked.

Moments later, we were barreling down Stony Hill Road as her right foot draped over the passenger door. I'd caught her at a good time. Although the weather suggested mini-golf, Mitchell and Cece were getting in a final string of candlepin bowling, the New England oddity she'd be deprived of after the move to California. Grace stayed home, ostensibly, to pack but more likely to avoid skirmishes, like the one at Massholes, in front of the kid.

Their agent had found a buyer for Ashton House off-market and furnished, so they could bypass movers and memories and make a quick, clean break from Wilbraham. I told Grace we were thinking of using her agent to sell our house. Remarkably, she had missed the news about the sale of Saltbox Farm in *The Republican.* She said she wasn't sure how she'd feel about death on her doorstep, although back home she and Mitchell once squeezed in a quickie between the gravesites of Marilyn Munroe and Hugh Hefner at Westwood Village Memorial Park.

"Did anyone see you?"

"Unfortunately not."

"You're lucky you found someone so compatible," I said.

"A lot of people find it easier to perform in front of an audience. Maybe they wouldn't go to quite the same lengths, but it's not like we have the patent."

"Is it the idea of getting caught?"

"Charlie, don't you ever look in the mirror?"

"I try not to."

"Turn here."

"We have three more exits..."

Grace placed her hands over mine, guiding us into an empty rest stop off I-90. As she reached toward my belt, I thought of the pair of hands guiding mine in O-Ming and intercepted, grasping her shorts, As I lifted my head, she pulled it back into place like her arms were spring-loaded. From there, my tongue switched to autopilot. I'm not sure I honestly felt much, but it seemed to do the trick. She caught her breath and pulled up her shorts.

"Sorry, I should have asked," I said.

"No complaints here. For someone who doesn't see much action, you sure have good instincts."

"I took a crash course at the Monastery."

"That place is amazing. It's like the opposite of the whole uptight East Coast vibe."

"That's Wilbraham. You guys would have fit in much better in Stockbridge or Northampton."

"Too late now. Listen, not that I don't appreciate your generosity, but the original plan was to give you a parting gift. The least I can do is return the favor."

"We're good."

I put the top back down and punched the first pre-set on the radio. Pachelbel's "Canon in D," the only piece of classical music I knew by name, always brought me back to my high school graduation where it was the processional. I shared with Grace the memory of warning Mel about a small afterparty when I watched the kitchen fill with chips and dips, trays of mini-Napoleons and eclairs, and all the ingredients for her zero-proof Red Bull Punch. After the ceremony, the backyard was empty. She tried to distract me with Scrabble; I felt so humiliated that I snuck out of the house and sought refuge in the library. I had made it through school without ever reading a book cover-to-cover, but a short story collection on the summer reading table caught my eye and I somehow made it through two stories— "Elephant" and "Boxes" by Raymond Carver. Although I sensed they were meant to be profoundly sad, I found them vaguely funny. This was how I discovered I was not cut out to be a reader—even before I realized I was not cut out to be a writer.

I returned home to find several cars parked in front of our house and a few kids emerging from the backyard, with some of them carrying gowns and mortar boards. I recognized the back of Brendan Foster's mullet, and I was fairly certain his arm was around Karen Nyman. I waited across the street for the last car to leave and found Mel hauling a garbage bag to the garage.

"Everyone was asking for you," she lied.

I wanted to ask her to name one. I knew they were there for her. Throughout school, I had never been part of the "in" or "out" crowd. I had simply faded into the background.

I looked at Grace. This was the first time I had shared the graduation story with anyone.

Her shoulders lifted and fell. "She must have been mad that you cut out after she planned this party for you."

"She invited friends I didn't have to a party I didn't want."

"Maybe the party wasn't for you."

I took the Holyoke exit off the Pike and pulled into Howard Johnson's. Our waitress Barb looked like a character in a Roz

Chast cartoon, with her cat eyeglasses dangling from a chain, a hairnet, and a white apron.

Grace announced there weren't many guys who would choose butter pecan over a blow job. I placed a hand over my eyes and looked down at the paper menu.

"Relax, Charlie," she continued. "I'm sure it's nothing Barb hasn't heard a thousand times before."

"That one's a first," Barb said as she walked away.

"You think she recognized you?"

"In L.A., we're famous. In Holyoke, we're infamous," Grace shrugged. "I was worried Patti wouldn't find a buyer for Ashton House. She found the only one in town who thought our history was a bigger selling point than the house's."

"Anyone I know?"

"Anyone you don't know? This is the guy who owns Massholes."

"What use would Christos King have for a historic house?"

"I think he's envisioning a sort of Playboy Mansion East."

"With portable toilets on the lawn, no doubt. Now I'm twice as glad we're moving."

"You're leaving, too? Is your mom retiring?"

"She'll never leave her kids unless they force her. I haven't told her I contacted Patti about putting the house on the market."

"You're selling her house without asking her? What if she wants to stay?"

"Would you want your mother living in a house where her only neighbors were six feet under?"

"With my mother, I'd worry for the neighbors."

"I assume she's not your therapist."

"No but she is the main reason I saw a therapist all these years."

"You don't seem irreparably damaged."

"The one-two punch of therapy and Xanax."

"Whatever works."

"At least now the weirdness seems more age appropriate. Every time she calls, she starts the conversation with 'I can't talk now.' Or she'll rattle off a string of F-bombs in the supermarket —little signs the filter is disappearing."

"If that's a sign, I think my mom became a senior citizen seventy years ago."

Barb returned, grabbed a pencil from her ear, and took a notepad from her apron. I ordered a single scoop of Fudge Ripple as Grace scanned the ice cream list.

"You can get that anyplace. I want to try something that gives me the Hojo's experience."

"Grace has never been here," I explained to Barb. "How about butterscotch, butter pecan, butter crunch?"

"They sound a little rich. I don't think I've ever seen fruit salad as an ice cream flavor. What do you think, Barb?"

Her face was unmoving. "Nobody has ever ordered it. Something tells me you're going to be the first."

"This is why Barb gets the big tips. She knows her customers."

"I always used to think so."

"I was going to say you reminded me of my mother, but you probably hear that all the time."

"This is my day for firsts." Barb collected our menus and left.

"Actually, she's warmer than my mother," Grace said.

"Anything you'd like to share?"

"In all fairness part of it is genetic. My family has this warped sense of humor. Friends used to say, 'I can't believe you talk to each other like that.'"

"My mom is kind of like that."

"That's what made me feel right at home with her. I love the fact that she swears like Andrew Dice Clay. But your mom is the opposite of mean. In my family sarcasm was our weapon of choice and sentimentality was the ultimate weakness. When we watched "Love Story" as a family, my mom was like 'For God's sake, would you just die already?'"

"I hear it was pretty sappy."

"You never saw it?"

"I'm not much of a moviegoer. Your whole family was like that?"

"It was the way we communicated. Other families were Hallmark; we were 'The Far Side,' if that makes sense. So, now that we've thoroughly covered my warped childhood." She clasped her hands together on the table. "About the hat."

"You want to know what I'm covering?"

"You always wear it. I'm wondering if it's some kind of security blanket."

"A lawyer who dabbles in therapy."

"I'm surprised you took it off at the rest stop."

"Don't you have a watch, a pair of glasses—I don't know, maybe your wedding ring—"

"Mitch and I don't wear rings. It inhibits our dating lives."

"Bummer. There must be something that has become like a part of your body."

"I have nothing I'm looking to hide."

"You think this cap is some kind of disguise?"

"You tell me."

"Sometimes a hat is just a hat."

"If I can be perfectly honest— back at the rest stop felt, well, mechanical."

"I didn't have any time to rehearse."

"No, you hit all your marks. It just seemed like an out-of-body experience."

"I thought that was the idea."

"Any top-of-the-line Japanese vibrator can provide precision. We like to feel something reciprocal, don't we, Barb?"

The waitress set the bowls of ice cream down. "Fudge ripple, *fruit salad*."

"I've got this, by the way."

Grace slid her bowl over. "Let me at least get the tip."

"No, I've got a tip for you," Barb said, dropping the check onto the counter.

"Mom!" Grace called after her.

"No wonder you're moving back home," I said.

"Good times ahead. So much to catch up on."

"How long has it been since you've seen her?"

"We haven't spoken since we moved here. Now I'll get to hear her weigh in on Carrie and Cece." She took a bite.

"And how her daughter got to be the Blue Jays' most famous fan."

"We still haven't had the 'This is where babies come from' conversation."

"I had that conversation with my mom when I was five, along with how you give a woman an orgasm."

"It's great that Mel's so open."

"Sometimes. There are a few topics I'd prefer to leave off the table."

"If your therapist wasn't family, you could tell them everything."

"I can't imagine anyone I would tell everything."

"If it was a stranger, you wouldn't have to care what they thought."

"It's not that."

"What secret could you possibly be hiding that they haven't heard of before?"

The list of all the things that were off-limits wasn't long, but it was deep. Before Mel began working at the high school, she had a private home practice. I remember she once told me of an older patient—her "crazy client," she called her—who said she'd never had a happy day in her life. "Can you imagine?" Mel asked. I think I rolled my eyes and probably attempted a forced smile. My surprise didn't seem to register. All I remember for sure is she kept talking and, at that point, I had tuned out. That ever-present state of mind, my lack of happiness, was the only topic besides the afterlife (mine, after she was gone) I could never share with my therapist.

Heading home, I tried shifting the conversation back to Grace—her family in California, her career plans, whether she'd found a new home. She either responded perfunctorily or deflected my questions. As we drove by the 'Entering Wilbraham' sign, I confessed that I had no idea why I was burdening a near-stranger with these personal confessions.

"Do you trust me?" Grace asked.

"How could I not trust someone I've shared such a long history with?"

"That's the point. Maybe this is your opportunity to unburden yourself to someone you'll never see again."

"Where do you want to start?"

"Well, how about the biggest taboo." Her eyebrows lifted. "Would you like to talk about orgasms?"

"I was hoping the work would speak for itself."

"I was thinking of yours. If this makes you uncomfortable—"

"I'm not sure I've ever had one," I told her.

"You would know it."

"I've never felt anything close to the way I've heard it described."

"A lot of guys your age find hormone treatments helpful."

"How many fourteen-year-olds do you know who haven't experienced it?"

"Oh my God! Every guy I knew at that age seemed on the verge every time they took a breath."

"This is going to sound warped—" I paused.

"What's that saying—we're only as sick as our secrets."

"In that case, I must be terminal. The only time I experience that level of—I don't know the word, out-of-control euphoria—is from food."

"You're lucky you don't have an eating disorder."

"I don't know—maybe I do."

"Well, you certainly aren't overweight. But you should be able to experience pleasure from both. That's part of being human."

"So many parts elude me."

"This is a bigger conversation than we're going to have in your car. With all due respect to your lovely mother, you've got to find someone with a little distance so you can tell them anything."

As we pulled into the driveway at Ashton House, Mitchell and Cece were playing croquet on the front lawn.

Grace placed a hand on my shoulder. "And in the meantime, I think you should tell your mom you're planning to sell her home before strangers show up in her living room for the open house."

"You want to play?" Mitchell called. "We can have two teams."

"I was thinking you might have chosen a game with fewer pieces to pack when the movers are coming," Grace told him through the window.

"So," I whispered to Grace, "do you and Mitchell tell each other everything?"

"Relax," she said extending a hand with mock formality. "Your secrets are safe."

CHAPTER THIRTEEN

A FIGURE OF SPEECH

I NEVER TOOK it for granted that the anxieties of a non-paying tenant would win out over the house that Lucy Braun built. Never mind that it was technically prefabricated, a word Mel had banished from her vocabulary since the beginning; our house was always her creation. From the reclaimed woods she chose for the floors to the mobiles she hung from the soaring ceilings, and the textiles she chose for the walls or the carefully curated accessories and Japanese-inspired landscaping—it was a personal statement. The idea of trying to talk her out of it left me wracked with guilt. I knew my fears amounted to what she often described as "magical thinking," but I couldn't imagine living in a haunted house or leaving her alone in one.

Mel was financially secure, and finances would never be a factor. Even the most inflated estimate Patti the realtor might present would be meaningless. I postponed her visit indefinitely, hoping I could think of some rational reason to move. If living next door to a sectarian cemetery did not spook Mel, perhaps the prospect of The Playboy Mansion East as a neighbor would. For all her liberal egalitarianism, Mel bristled at the ostentatious, the tasteless, and the nouveau riche. The noise, the parties, the traffic—this was not what she had moved here for.

Yet Mel was convinced that neither of us had anything to worry about. Wilbraham did not take kindly to change, particularly when it came without any financial benefit. A cemetery would do nothing for the tax base, the only incentive for town officials and voters. In a town where Muslims represented 0.2% of the population (one notch above Buddhists at 0.0%), the constituency and the interest in diversifying even the deceased population simply weren't there. She had this on good authority from the assistant vice principal, whose family probably accounted for the 0.2%. After getting an earful from residents, the town's lawyer pushed back. On the record, the mosque was still resolute. Behind the scenes, there were whispers of reselling the property.

As a historic property, Ashton House was protected from demolition, even from significant structural changes. Christos King thought he was buying a trophy property, surely a shortcut to the class he could never earn as the proprietor of a dive bar and a portable toilet empire. In the moment he moved in and realized he'd bought a museum, it would be back on the market —if he moved in at all.

Instead of selling the house, Mel suggested we wait it out. She was so certain we would have new "new neighbors" that if she were wrong on either count, she offered to give Patti a call. I didn't share her confidence, but I trusted her judgment. Months went by with no news and no visible signs of change on either front. Finally, the first shoe dropped. One morning, three trucks pulled up in front of Ashton House. By day's end, a dozen wrought iron pedestals had been placed around the perimeter of the property.

Mel and I took a walk to see if we could find any clues. She took the craftsmanship of each platform as a positive sign the new owner had taste. I suggested they were probably meant as a base for the port-a-johns that had suddenly disappeared from the farm. Perhaps this meant Christos was planning to turn Ashton House into a showroom, and the farm had a new buyer.

More trucks arrived two days later. I watched as crews of six unloaded each shrouded object one at a time and placed it on a platform. The covers shimmied in the wind so that from a distance they appeared like ghosts. Somehow, we must have been left off the list for the unveiling.

The next day, a dozen statues of what appeared to be Greek gods surrounded the property—all naked, each rendered in fine anatomical detail. The color suggested alabaster or marble, with strategic points around the groin and armpits in black. I could hardly wait for Mel to get home from school.

"Brace yourself," I said as she came through the front door.

As we made our way to Ashton House, Mel's descriptions grew more intense from "gauche," "tacky," and "hideous," to a string of expletives that concluded with "fucking grotesque" as we reached an extremely well-endowed, hirsute goddess.

"You were right. He really is planning The Best Little Whorehouse in Wilbraham. I can't believe Grace and Mitchell sold an architectural treasure like Ashton House to someone who wants to turn it into a sex club."

"Maybe you missed it, but they aren't exactly uptight about sex."

"Neither am I. It's his taste in art I find obscene," she said running her fingers through the patch of pubic hair on a statue. "Although I'll admit the craftsmanship is pretty impressive."

"Why don't you start a petition? In this prudish town, you'll get lots of signatures."

"We're the only ones with a direct view. Nobody will even notice."

In the next morning, the headline—in *The Republican*, no

less—was "Big Nudes in Wilbraham." In the story, Christos King insisted he had absolutely no intention of opening an adult resort or any other kind of business. Ashton House was zoned as residential, he noted. And he intended to use it as a private residence. The gods were simply an impulse buy while visiting a statuary on a vacation in Greece. By noontime, crowds had gathered, a mix of locals armed with fig leaves and gawkers with disposable cameras. In a letter to the editor the next day, one resident wondered why Christos couldn't have settled with one of those little boys peeing into a fountain. The story was picked up by the wire services, putting Wilbraham back on the map nationally for the second time in a year. For a moment it seemed like all everyone talked about. Then, the crowds dissipated, the scandal faded, and Ashton House receded into oblivion. Occasionally, workers would appear to do yard work, but there were never cars in the driveway or the garage. A few statues were vandalized, and it didn't even make the newspaper.

Occasional rumors surfaced: King would turn Ashton House into his version of an upscale inn or donate it to the historical society as a tax write-off; the mosque would sell the farm to a developer for affordable housing; the mosque would turn the land into an office park (wrong zoning); the mosque would build an actual mosque, not only a cemetery.

As the months turned into years, the threats to our neighborhood seemingly receded without ever being resolved. We were grateful for the respite which we tried to transform into a feeling of normalcy. I would scan *The Republican* every day. Mel would share what she heard at work or at a town meeting. But we moved on without ever feeling settled. Instead of facing crowds and construction, the neighborhood felt eerily quiet, as if we were its only inhabitants.

Ever since I had been fired from *The Pilot*, I'd taken on the shopping, cooking, cleaning and all the responsibilities of running the house and Mel's finances. She had never needed the income from her job, but now it had been thirteen years since she had reached the district's mandatory retirement age of seventy. I tried to persuade her with the prospect of travel, moving to a warmer climate, or even waking up late, enjoying breakfast in bed, or joining the professional Scrabble circuit. It became a source of friction, a conversation she quickly shut down.

The administration worked out an arrangement for her to job share and mentor a student getting his master's in school counseling at Assumption College in Worcester. But he took a job in Palmer, and the subject of her replacement never came up again. The school wasn't going to find a seasoned counselor for her meager salary, and, so, they colluded to continue.

Physically, Mel showed few signs of aging, but I noticed cracks in her façade: less energy and confidence, more anxiety and doubt. The thought of her driving, even a few miles to the high school, in her ancient convertible or my erratic subcompact during winter, left me counting the minutes whenever she arrived late. Had I offered to drive her a few years earlier, I would have been reminded that she was quite capable of taking care of herself. Much to my surprise, when I asked again, she was clearly relieved and took me up on the offer.

I even noticed a less aggressive, more focused style in her Scrabble game. She would still consistently rout me, but where she once would change letters before considering a word under fifteen points, lately, she'd settle for a mere half dozen. She often slept during the day on weekends and seemed fatigued after a full night's sleep. I wondered if any cracks were starting to show at work, but I was encouraged that she remained razor-sharp and fully engaged in my daily therapy sessions.

None of these changes prepared me for the call. I'm still not convinced there was any connection or any missed signs. I will never know precisely what happened, because on a day that remains a blur, in my one moment of clarity, I was able to make my wishes clear with three words: "Don't tell me." I said it once to Maxine, one of Mel's closest friends and the school librarian, who was waiting in the faculty parking lot with a hug but no winter coat on a twenty-degree day. I repeated it to everyone from the policeman waiting in the office, to the school nurse, to the principal who said how sorry he was to meet me under such circumstances despite the fact he'd played a similar role when I went to school there. Students were gathering in the halls; teachers and administrators looked morose. I was the only one not in tears. People kept asking if there was anyone they could call. To get Mel? To get me? At first, a few words broke through: "shell-shocked" is one I recall. Every voice, every sound blurred into background noise like the pool scene in *The Graduate*.

I got into my car with no idea where I was going. The late-day-September-sun streamed through the windshield like the lights in a police interrogation room. I pulled over into the parking lot of the elementary school and hit play on the 8-track.

If this moment had been in a movie, I would have slammed the director for a soundtrack so on-the-nose. I'd never given Pink Floyd a second thought, but if I hadn't been taught to know better, I would have taken the lyrics about a ribbon so black in the distance as a sign. I strayed onto the empty playground and climbed the tower to the landing of a circular slide. I sat there for moments, and then minutes, maybe longer. The stillness was interrupted by occasional flourishes of wind chimes in the distance. Every time an image made its way into my head, I'd clear it with some practical question: Whom should I call? Where am I going? What do I do next? A stern, gravely, voice pierced the silence.

"Could I ask you to relive your childhood someplace else?"

"Am I holding up a line?" I gestured toward the ladder.

"I have to wonder why a grown man might be in our tot lot."

"I could ask you the same question," I replied coasting to the ground. "But today, I'm going to let it slide."

As I drove on autopilot across the border from Palmer to Wilbraham, the word "despondent" on a billboard pierced the static, and the phone number became my mantra. I hadn't planned on returning home, but the next thing I knew I was standing in Mel's home office, staring at a photo of myself wearing the infamous crimson denim jacket I'd worn to school for years. The same woman, who left a pack of condoms on my pillow when I was in ninth grade simply because they were half-price at CVS, could not resist a 75% automatic markdown from Filene's Basement, even if it was from the women's department. No, I insisted, clothes are not "unisex," and her decision made me an unwitting transvestite and her an accomplice. I glanced over at the Chemex on the counter, which was half-filled with thick brown sludge that congealed for hours because she felt compelled to brew a full carafe every day. Maxine, Wilbraham's one-woman Jewish community, had once suggested it was for Elijah. I suspected it was the same reason Mel would carefully position a wool throw across furniture—to make the place look lived in. I tried to avert my gaze from the kitchen table where the Scrabble board was set.

I picked up the phone to call when I heard the clicks and listened to the first of eighteen voicemails: "Charlie, this is Karen Nyman. We were classmates at MRHS. I just heard the news, and I can't even imagine your loss. You probably have half the school calling but I want to help. Please call me."

That day, I didn't get through the rest of the messages. Some were from school, others from members of Mel's family I had never even met. One was a sales call from a funeral home. I returned a call from someone I barely knew in high school and hadn't seen since. There was something in the tone of her voice.

I don't know if you'd describe it as a sense of urgency or empathy—I couldn't ignore it.

"I'm really glad you called," she said.

"I'm not sure why I did. I mean, I appreciate your offer, but I don't know what you can do."

"I want to take all of the arrangements off your hands."

"The arrangements?"

"For the service, like settling the estate, whatever you need —unless you have everything already planned."

"I don't have plans for what I'm going to do after we hang up the phone."

"I heard you were in shock. Understandably so."

"I thought you lived in Connecticut."

"I used to. How did you know?"

"You sent your engagement notice to *The Pilot*. I used to work there."

"I moved back a couple years ago. I forgot to send in my divorce announcement."

"Didn't you work in advertising?"

"You have an amazing memory."

"For some things."

"We're talking about me. We should be talking about you and your amazing mother."

"You know her? I mean, you knew her?"

"Everybody did."

She took a deep breath, then quickly filled the space with questions. Did I have the power of attorney? Did Mel have other relatives to inform? Did she have a religious affiliation or a clergy member or friend she would want to perform the service?

Up until this point, I'd been able to maintain the façade of a reasonably coherent, mature adult. Then she asked about my mother's posthumous wishes. I told her we had never had that conversation. Karen said she knew I had a lot on my mind but to try and make a list of what I thought she would want.

We agreed to meet the next morning to go over details. Karen suggested Palmiere as a way for me to get away, but I thought she should see the house in case we held the service there.

I had no other place to go and no other plan in mind, but, during that sleepless night, every corner felt alien, and every once-familiar object was a landmine spiked with memories I was determined to avoid. I dragged out my word processor and tethered myself to the dining room table, creating a to-do list and four folders named "Service," "Finances," "Wishes," and "Next." The first provided details for whatever memorial Karen had in mind, including lists of guests and speakers, music, and food.

The second compiled what I knew of our family finances and Mel's will for the probate attorney. The "Wishes" folder was filled with the places I thought she might want certain cherished pieces to go, and "Next" contained all the loose ends I'd need to tie together to put closure on my own life.

Clothes were piled on the floor, a reminder that sometime during the night I'd managed to shower and change into a fresh, striped polar shirt and a pair of painter's pants. I hadn't noticed the sunrise, the draft from the front door left open all night, the muted television tuned to CNN, or the blinking cursor on my word processor still awaiting instructions.

It was close to nine a.m. when I saw a brown Plymouth Voyager Woody pull into the driveway, and it hit me that the Karen Nyman I'd be meeting was *that* Karen Nyman. I raced to the bathroom to brush my teeth. My eyes were so bloodshot that, for a moment, I didn't recognize my reflection in the mirror. I ran a comb through my hair, tucked the greying strands behind my ears, then concealed the whole, matted mop beneath my cap. I had to take a piss wicked bad but didn't want Karen's first impression to be the toilet flushing like on *All in the Family*. I slapped on a few drops of Drakkar Noir from a bottle Mel had left on my bed after a Filene's Basement run when I was in sixth grade, perhaps a hint that Right Guard alone was not sufficient.

"Charlie?"

"Door's open. Be right there."

"Take your time."

During high school, I recalled snippets of hall conversations between some girls who could not understand boys' universal attraction to Karen. I thought of the line "Don't hate me because I'm beautiful" from the Pantene commercials, and a derisive description of golden retrievers as the Farrah Fawcett of dogs. Every teenage male who had her swimsuit poster on their bedroom wall might have responded, "Your point being?"

I'm not sure what I was expecting. I hadn't attended my prom, never mind all the MRHS reunions that followed, so my only markers for aging classmates were the photos they sent to *The Pilot*. The few I had of Karen were in my yearbook, and her wedding picture.

I hadn't yet constructed a composite of how the images frozen in my mind might look decades later. The idea that Karen Nyman was also capable of turning sixty simply hadn't registered. The woman before me had sterling silver hair but few creases in her face, and it was hard to imagine her as someone's mother, let alone old enough to be a grandmother.

"Charlie," she said leaning in for an embrace. "I'm so sorry."

"This was such a surprise."

"For everyone."

"I mean you calling."

"I didn't want to be intrusive. Maybe you want to be around family."

"You're looking at it."

She backed off, swallowed hard and glanced around.

"Whenever I used to drive by this house, I wondered what it looked like inside."

"The outside only seems exotic in Wilbraham. It's a prefab."

"Really? It looks so original."

"The inside is all Mel's quirky taste."

"Mel?"

"My mom—Miss Lucy. That's what her kids at the high school called her."

"Of course. My daughter, Adrienne, was hassled when she went through a goth phase. She said Miss Lucy was the reason she made it through MRHS."

"It's a difficult place to be different."

"I guess high school is difficult everywhere."

"I mean Wilbraham. My mom wasn't popular with a lot of parents."

"I think you'll be surprised how many lives she touched. Have you given any thought to the arrangements?"

I knew I'd never be able to say it aloud. How could I explain to anyone why I could not bring myself to hear how my mother died and decide what and where—or, even, if she would be laid to rest? What possible reason would a decent son and her only family member have for not wanting to be there for her service? I told Karen I had written down a few notes and made a folder for the services. She marveled at my being so organized at such a challenging time. I handed her the page, and she took out a pair of reading glasses.

I excused myself to avoid watching her reaction.

So, Karen Nyman looked sixty, drove a minivan, wore readers, and had a goth daughter. I felt relieved. If time was not the great equalizer, at least it took some of the pressure off. Still, I reached for a few drops of Visine and ran the shower to mask the sound of the toilet flushing. When I returned, she was still reading so I made coffee. Her expression was intense but blank. I placed a mug with a pitcher of 2% in lieu of cream and a bowl of brown sugar on a cocktail table beside her. She looked up from the page and into my eyes.

"I got this."

"You don't understand. I can't arrange a service, I can't decide where she should spend eternity, I can't do any of it, Karen. I don't know why. I just can't."

"Do you know her wishes?"

"She left everything up to me. She should have known I couldn't manage it. When the school called with the news, I told them not to tell me what happened. I still don't know."

"I heard."

"They had to contact some cousin I'd never met to be her next of kin." I watched her face. "I'd never be able to get the picture out of my mind—just like with a final resting place. It's too concrete. It's too real."

"Whatever you need to get yourself through this."

"I know it sounds crazy, but the only way I can get through this is to block it out."

"If that's really what you want, I can figure it out. All I need is your budget and the names of anyone your mother would want to be at the service."

"There are no limits, but I wonder if she would have preferred to skip the ceremony and donate the money to some radical organization to tweak the memory of her dad."

"Tell me more about her, and we'll figure it all out."

I couldn't handle life. I couldn't handle death, and now, I was handing off the responsibilities of my only family member to a stranger. Worse still, I was feeling more relieved than guilty. And I was confused. Was Karen going to these lengths because of her connection to my mother or to me? Most confounding of all, I had no explanation for her timing. Even the devout nonbeliever in me could not write off the way she reappeared in my life exactly at the breaking point—a simple stroke of good luck. It was the kind of coincidence I normally would have dismissed as an implausible, if not impossible, plot-turn in a hackneyed novel. For the better part of an hour, I found myself in curiously unfamiliar territory, on the receiving end of an interview. I shared anecdotes I hoped might provide clues for some kind of proper tribute: our nightly Scrabble games; her collection of pins from political campaigns she volunteered for; the beloved pastoral view from her bedroom window with the constantly changing hues of the skies, the azaleas, the foliage accented by the occasional fiery crimson of a cardinal. Karen took notes, smiling or nodding silently. Slowly, tiny vestiges of her features reemerged: the large, wide-set and green-gray eyes beneath the readers; the cleft chin; the soft, full lips set off against the angular features of her face. I'm quite sure my imagination added the scent of Love's Baby Soft.

"I've got to pick up Nicole in fifteen minutes. They have an early-release day at Mile Tree."

"You have a kid in elementary school?"

"Adrienne's youngest. My granddaughter."

"Karen, how do I thank you?"

"Como se dice: Duerme un poco."

"Que?"

"Get some sleep."

CHAPTER FOURTEEN

A FATE WORSE THAN DEATH

"THERE ARE NO WORDS..."

"She had a good life."

"She will always live in your heart."

"At least she didn't linger."

"I know how you feel."

"She would want you to be happy."

"Everything happens for a reason."

"Time heals all wounds."

"It's okay to cry."

Of all the sage advice I received at the memorial service, the one which resonated for me most strongly was from Mark Rossmore, who had retired about the same time as Mel.

"We all have to go sometime."

"I guess."

"It's a fact, Charlie. Look it up."

"I'll take your word."

"And I say this as someone with affection for your mom."

"Thanks for coming, Mark."

"I wouldn't have missed it for the world. She used to flirt with me, you know?"

"I'm guessing she took a lot of your secrets with her."

"You be strong, Charlie. She is with God now."

"There's a first time for everything."

Karen suggested a memorial service instead of a funeral, after Mel had been dispatched to her final resting place. I told her my mother would have probably instructed us not to do it on her account, and Karen reminded me that these rituals are not for the departed and that they are for their loved ones who need to process their loss and celebrate their life. The advice sounded exactly like what my therapist would have said, which was a thought that had occurred to me countless times in the past week.

I'd been dreading the day, but it was hard not to be moved by the outpouring and especially by the number of students from the high school. The social work student from Assumption, with whom Mel had almost job shared, returned for the full-time position; he'd been handling grief counselling all week. Once it became clear how many people were likely to attend, the service was moved from our backyard to the high school where the auditorium was so small they had to add close-circuit coverage in the gym for overflow.

I hid myself in the back of the auditorium, but I could see Karen near the stage scanning the room. She had asked me for musical selections for the school's chamber orchestra, a mix of students and faculty members. On my list were her two favorites: the "Four Seasons" and "Ave Maria." I recognized Frankie Valli's "December, 1963 (Oh What a Night)," even as an instrumental, and realized I should have specified Vivaldi. Most likely, Ted Weeks would have probably been the last person Mel would choose to be the master of ceremonies at her sendoff. As the former Falcons football coach, he was drafted into administration as assistant principal—the enforcer, Mel called him—before replacing the retiring principal, Grant

Sandoe, who had hired my mom. Ted clashed with Mel frequently, and he once accused her of not behaving in a lady-like manner, a comment that prompted her to wear her mother's wedding dress to school the next day. This fashion choice cemented her legendary status, as word of the story behind it spread. Little did Ted know that Mel later filed a supposedly anonymous complaint about his remark with human resources. Ted's own sartorial evolution ranged from Falcon sweatsuits to an impossibly wide striped tie tucked into poly dress slacks, and a Captain Kangaroo style jacket in MRHS school colors (green with white piping). His spiky Chia Pet coif, a fusion of crew and bowl cuts and impossibly hairy forearms (revealed in short-sleeved white dress shirts at staff meetings) gave Ted the simple elegance of a Moe Howard/Jerry Lewis lovechild. The last thing anyone expected was to see him making his way to the podium wearing a wedding dress with two members of the Falcons football team dressed as angels carrying his train.

"While it is no secret that MRHS's beloved longtime school counselor and I sparred on many occasions," he said when the laughter finally abated, "today, we are all Miss Lucy Braun. So many people asked to share a few words, which tells you how many lives she touched. The way she affected mine was as a worthy adversary who earned my respect in the way she always —always—put our students, her kids, first. I'd like to introduce you to one of them."

A woman stepped onto the stage dressed in a sleeveless top, leather skirt, and heels all in black and offset only by a string of pearls. She looked to be in her early thirties, with an intense, unsettled expression.

"My name is Adrienne Hammond and the last time I stepped on this stage was seven years ago when I graduated. Back then, I swore I'd never set foot in this building again. Here I am wearing black like I never left. For many of you, this might be a happy place. For some of us, it was something else. Now, I realize it wasn't just school, it was the time. My parents were divorced while my mom lived out of state, and my dad was travelling for work so often he didn't see who I was hanging out with and what was going on. Some of you may be wondering why I'm sharing my life story at a memorial service —at least, the ones who don't know the ending. Whatever was waiting for us at home or at school, we knew we could crash in the most cheerful place in the building: that windowless bunker in the basement with the piñata and the mobile and the sign on the door that said, "The doctor is in." And she always was. The only time the door was closed was when she was with another student. We knew that whenever we came back, even if it was after school, Miss Lucy would be waiting for us with a bowl of Kit Kats, or, on less lucky days, orange slices, and the can that held our nickels as payment. What a bargain! She was the one adult I could share all my secrets with, and I had a few big ones. Let's just say if it wasn't for her, I wouldn't be here today. When I think of what a grim time it was for me, I couldn't have imagined working at the Youth Center in Springfield. Then, I thought of Miss Lucy and how many lives she had changed and how many she had saved. How often do you get to make that kind of a difference? Now I'm thinking, damn you, Miss Lucy, you dragged me back here again. I mean, how could I not say goodbye and thanks? You earned every nickel."

A few stray claps broke the awkward silence. Students rose with heartier applause followed by a handful of adults. Others remained seated and were apparently shell-shocked or trying to read the room. I made my way to the front and pulled Karen aside into the hall. She had a forced smile, but her mascara was running.

"Now you know," she said.

"It's always easier to give someone else's parents the credit than our own."

"She was right. Your mom filled the gap I left so I could have this second chance. I owe her everything."

"Consider the debt repaid with interest."

"I just hope the idea for the sculpture didn't get lost in the translation."

All week long, Karen had been careful to use "sculpture" instead of "gravestone" or even "marker," words which might have offered a clue. My therapist would have described it as "therapeutic denial," a valid coping strategy in her book. Karen played along as if it was a completely ordinary request. She did reveal that the members of the school community had pitched in to create some kind of monument and that the results would be unveiled at today's memorial.

Maxine was at the podium, sharing a story I knew well. For weeks, Mel would come home increasingly incensed by the efforts of a small group of parents to remove certain books from the school library. First, it was her beloved *Our Bodies, Ourselves*, then *The Outsiders* and *Forever*, the adult Judy Blume novel. As the list grew longer, she talked about running for the school committee against one of the parents who served on the board. When she found out school employees were ineligible to run, she told me she might quit her job. I knew she was venting, but I could see it making her an even more polarizing figure in the community. So, I suggested she go underground and move the books to her office where she could make them available to students. The book ban never materialized, but Mel's efforts to circumvent it won respect. Maxine confessed she hadn't been brave enough to take on the fight herself.

Ted had returned in his usual business attire and announced that with the help of MRHS alumni Karen Nyman the school community had pitched in to commission a monument to Lucy Braun, which they would like to invite Miss Lucy's son to unveil. A woman standing next to me said she didn't know Lucy had a son and another woman next to her said she didn't even know Lucy was married. I pulled my cap down a little further over my eyes and rushed toward the stage like a contestant on *The Price Is Right*.

Ted placed an arm around my shoulder and asked me to help him lift the cover from the sculpture. In place of a headstone, Karen had commissioned a marker with the letters "L-U-C-Y" resembling Scrabble tiles in a formation based on the Robert Indiana "LOVE" design. I heard more murmuring and laughter than applause. Ted said he was sure there was a good story behind this.

I stayed on stage as long as I had to and then walked off. "Game over," I said beneath my breath, "wherever you are."

CHAPTER FIFTEEN

ALL THE TIME IN THE WORLD

AFTER THEIR FIRST MEETING, Candace began describing Maeve as "Miss G&T," an acronym, I assumed, for gin and tonic but which turned out to be a stand-in for "gifted and talented." And what exactly were her gifts? Maeve, Candace said, was one of those people with a knack for being in the right place at the right time. When I pointed out that was pure luck and not a gift, Candace said, "Wait and see," and smiled. I didn't understand how a New Haven hospice room was anyone's idea of "the right place." The suggestion that Maeve had some ulterior motive seemed to be an overreaction to a simple misunderstanding. Whenever Maeve visited, she walked past Candace and began talking with me as if we were alone. Candace told me that visitors often assumed she was there to empty the trash or a bedpan.

"Something I said?" Maeve asked one day as Candace made a silent exit, shaking her head.

"Something you didn't," I said. "Like: Hello, nice to meet you. My name is Maeve."

"She could have introduced herself. Every time I come in, she gives me a look like I'm here to steal the Waterford."

"She thinks you're here to steal something else."

"Oh yes, my ulterior motive. What did you tell her?"

"I said if you were after the family money, you probably wouldn't have advised me to move to a private hospice that costs more than the Four Seasons."

"Hardly a ringing defense of someone who visits you almost daily on her own time."

"Why is that?"

"If you didn't want me here, Charlie, all you had to do was say so."

"I appreciate your being here. I just don't understand it. I mean, you can't possibly visit every caller."

"I started the helpline after my dad took his life. He was about your age."

"Maybe I should be helping you."

She shrugged. "Maybe you are."

"I can't imagine how."

"For years, I was disappointed he wasn't there for me or my brother. Talking with you opens my mind to what he must have been going through."

"And that makes you more forgiving?"

"More understanding. That's one way you are better off than my dad was. He had the burden of leaving family and friends behind, but you say you have no responsibilities and no attachments.

"So much for getting married and starting a family."

"Or you can do that! You are in a position many would envy —the only feelings you need to consider are your own. That's a rare luxury."

"The world is my fucking oyster."

She put her sneakers up on the edge of the bed frame. "As for marriage, any woman who says yes will make you put that promise of suicide in writing after you add her to your will."

"Thanks for the vote of confidence."

"Nothing personal, but a guy your age who has never been married before raises all kinds of red flags."

"As opposed to a guy who had been married seven times before?"

"If he has been married seven times before, it tells us they are desirable."

"*Were* desirable."

"We think we can fix them. When we see a sixty-year-old man with no dating history, we think of a 75% markdown bin. Even if we don't see the rip or the stain, we're thinking: why is it still here? What's wrong with it?"

"Does 'we' include you?"

"It includes every woman who is being honest. I'm not discouraging you from socializing, but I want to make sure your expectations are realistic."

"I wasn't about to sign up for a dating service. I'm considering options, and having fewer makes the decision easier."

She shook her head, clearly exasperated. "You just suffered the biggest loss of your life. Don't rush into anything. You have all the time in the world."

"Tell that to Gini, my long-suffering caseworker."

"Haven isn't the only hospice. You could also check yourself into McLean."

"I've spent a lifetime in therapy."

"You made this decision a long time ago. Now, reality is catching up with you."

"What do you mean?"

"You can no longer tell yourself you are here for your mom. Maybe one of the reasons you were so afraid to face her mortality was the fear of your own. For the first time in your life, there is nothing standing in the way."

"It's kind of terrifying. So is the alternative."

"It's your decision but remember—you're not alone."

CHAPTER SIXTEEN

STREAM OF UNCONSCIOUSNESS

MANY NEW ENGLANDERS believe March is the cruelest month: the dregs of winter weather; the barren landscape; the brave and foolish crocus emerging like a preemie before toppling under a new blanket of snow. Even navigating the shit-faced crowds outside Massholes on St. Patrick's Day, it had always been my favorite holiday simply by virtue of what lay ahead. By late June when Mel would point out the longest day of the year, I was already counting the days left until September. So, as I watched the hailstorm through the window and the mercury topping out at the nineteen-degree mark on the thermometer, I imagined the same scene a month from now. It seemed I could never relax in whatever season it was.

Vic waved as he steered Mr. Martin's wheelchair in my direction. My next-door neighbor and I had never been introduced because he was always asleep or "practicing"—this is how Vic described Mr. Martin's perpetual supine state. All I knew was that he had been downgraded—or upgraded—from hospice to palliative care so often that he had emerged as a challenger for Haven's longest-surviving resident. Vic placed his money on me in the office pool, a wager he attributed to the fact that Mr.

Martin was thirty years my senior. Also, his children were contemplating having him transferred to a state facility if he defied his prognosis much longer. Vic parked the wheelchair and took a seat by the window near me. His wife, Arlene, had put him on a macrobiotic diet, and he cheerfully lamented the end of food as he knew it. I suggested *The Moosewood Cookbook,* which provided vegetarian recipes fit for human consumption. Vic's skepticism bordered on indignation, but he promised to give it a try.

Mel's copy was back in Wilbraham, and I had a meeting there with our probate attorney the next week. When I told Maeve I was petrified by the thought of returning home, she mentioned that she'd been through the probate process with her dad's estate and offered to attend as my representative. Who was this extraordinarily generous friend willing to volunteer as my proxy? he asked (with the words "extraordinarily," "generous," and "friend" all accentuated). Was Maeve a random good Samaritan, a lifelong friend, or a legal scholar? But he knew exactly who I was talking about. Clearly, he'd been tipped off by Candace (or "The Rev," as he called her).

"Candace has it out for her," I said.

"Maybe she's only concerned about you."

"She doesn't even know Maeve."

"How well do you know her?"

"I know she has dedicated her life to helping desperate people. I know she has come to visit me here nearly every day."

"I'm wondering if that's why The Rev is suspicious."

"Why would you guys assume I'm too naïve to know if I'm being played?"

"Speaking for myself, I would describe you as an admirably trusting soul."

"Nice save."

"You know her better than we do. Let's assume she has the best intentions. Does she really have expertise in probate law?"

I looked away from the window to face him. "All I know is when she offered to do it pro bono it didn't feel right to ask for her diploma."

"At least you know what your mom would have wanted—and what you want."

"If I did, I wouldn't be here."

"Well, choices are limited here. Did someone mention this is a hospice? We don't do spiritual enlightenment."

"I noticed. Even your chaplain doesn't seem interested in recruiting me."

"We must be beyond salvation. Hey, bonjour, Ox."

Vic was interrupted by an orderly who had come to claim Mr. Martin. Densely packed with the frame of a man whose every step was behind a wheelchair, bed, or high-speed floor buffer, he waved at Vic and spun the wheelchair around.

"Ox?" I asked.

"His real name is Emmanuel."

"So, wouldn't that make him Manny?"

Vic shrugged. "The moniker comes from Oxford as in Mississippi."

"That's where he's from?"

"His family is in Haiti. He sends most of his paycheck to them every month. I don't know how he can feed himself with the shit they pay him."

"So how do you take care of your family?"

"They're a little more generous when you have the R.N. after your name. If they screw with us, I can make three times the money as a travel nurse."

"Why don't you?"

"Did I mention it requires travel? I'm tethered here by my damn family."

"You still haven't made the Oxford connection."

"I think it was from the comma, or the university."

"That sounds like something the poet in you would have come up with."

He chuckled. "The literary society here is small. Most of the staff assume it was because he works like an ox."

"He always seems to be on his feet."

"A few of the more lowlifes here call him "Oxymoron" behind his back. It's kind of ironic, since they don't know what the word means. I can tell you for a fact he is smarter than any of them."

"You know, Vic, I kind of wish you were my probate proxy."

"That's very flattering. Of course, I would have said no."

"Of course."

"Hell no."

"That's flattering, too."

"Fuck no!"

"Forget I mentioned it."

"This is a job you need to do yourself. It will bring back all these memories and you'll be miserable for days, but you'll suck it up and a year from now you'll be wondering how you could have considered leaving it to anyone else."

"I'm not planning that far ahead, but thanks."

"Any real friend would tell you that."

CHAPTER SEVENTEEN

CHECK, PLEASE

EVERYONE BELIEVES that alcohol impairs the senses, but I was an exception to that notion. It wasn't merely that I could hold my liquor; I had never gotten close to being truly shitfaced. Without proms, dorm life, bachelor parties, weddings, after-work barhopping, or other social occasions—or the benefit of alcoholic parents as role models—the only real opportunity would have been to drink alone. Sometimes, I wondered if an altered state of reality could take the edge off my real one, but, somehow, I never got beyond a sip or two. I could not distinguish red wine from white, and liquor tasted generically medicinal, while mixed drinks always seemed like they'd be more appealing without alcohol.

Sitting at the Cask' n Flagon near Fenway Park, I glanced nervously at my watch as I waited for Maeve to arrive. We had arranged to meet in Boston, where she was observing volunteers in training at a local suicide prevention hotline. The plan was for her to share details of the meeting with the probate attorney, which she attended in my place after I backed out at the last minute. It was also a chance to repay her kindness. She had refused when I proposed compensating her. Instead, I'd take her to see an Irish band at The Paradise, the legendary rock club that hosted bands from Talking Heads and The Cars to Blondie and U2.

For most Wilbraham residents, driving to the city meant Worcester. Though Boston was only an hour further east, it might as well have been New York. Mel and I had ventured forth one time, a celebration of my graduation from Holyoke Community College. I chose dinner at Another Season, an elegant subterranean restaurant on Beacon Hill, and a performance of *Sister Mary Ignatius Explains It All for You*, a suitably sacrilegious satire at the Charles Playhouse nearby. Mel scored twice, the first time when the waiter assumed we were siblings, and again when Sister Mary asks the audience whether all prayers are answered. The nun replies that the answer may not always be the one we wanted; for example, your toothache might be alleviated right before you're run over by a car. For Mel, this became scripture, a concept she'd share any time religion was discussed.

At dinner, the bartender refilled my glass of Perrier with lime and asked if I was sure I didn't want to order something while I waited. When Maeve finally arrived, she took the barstool next to mine and rattled off a string of Gaelic that required no translation. She had caught pre-rush-hour traffic on the Pike, extending her drive from Wilmington to nearly four hours. Before properly acknowledging me, she managed to catch the bartender's eye and order a draft.

Maeve had none of the classic features associated with Irish beauty. Salted black wiry hair, a slightly hooked nose, close-set, brown eyes, and skin pocked with liver spots, which gave her a slightly witchy look. But in a leather skirt and jacket, spiky heels, and makeup, Maeve had the look of a seductively weathered Lucinda-Williams-style cowgirl. I had suggested she stay overnight in Wilbraham if the idea of a haunted house wasn't going to deter her. Maeve said she could feel my mother's presence there, a remark that reminded me how little I knew her. What if she was into crystals and psychics, astrology or Scientology? Suppose her motivation for helping me was to get a green card? Was it possible that Vic was right, that this stranger had now learned details of my life, making me vulnerable to blackmail?

Maeve handed me an envelope. "The good news is that you are a wealthy man, Mr. Braun. But you probably knew that."

"And the bad news?"

"I didn't say there was any."

"There always is."

Her eyes were steady. "Maybe that money doesn't buy happiness. But you knew that, too. Essentially, your mom left it all to you and your uncle."

"What uncle? My mom was an only child."

"Uncle Sam. He'll get a decent cut. She also set aside money to start a teen center."

"She was planning to serve on the board in her retirement."

"I admire her ambition. That's what I've been trying to do with the helpline."

"How did your observation go?"

"It was interesting. They train volunteers to listen to and befriend callers. But we also need to provide callers with options, don't you think?"

"I'm not an expert."

"If you aren't, I don't know who is. You said you've been thinking about suicide your whole life."

"Here I am nearing sixty, and I still haven't figured it out. If I wait much longer, the decision will be made for me."

"Did you call the helpline to hear a friendly voice on the other end of the line, or were you looking for answers?"

"We're not here to talk about my problems."

"Oh right, your estate."

"You told me what happened at the meeting. I have the papers from Marcus. Let's talk about you for a change."

"I may need another Guinness for that."

"It's easier being the one asking the questions."

Maeve tapped her painted nails on the table. "Where to begin? Feral childhood, angst-filled adolescence—"

"Maybe start with adulthood and work backwards. I don't know anything. Are you married? Divorced?"

"We don't get the luxury of divorce like you do in the States. It would be annulled. Twice."

"Kids?"

"Twenty-year-old son back in Limerick. Lives with my first ex."

"You see him often?"

"Not often enough. I make an annual pilgrimage."

"What keeps you here?"

"Depression is so much a part of our being in Ireland that we have a name for it: "The Black Dog." When we lost my dad, it felt like if I didn't get away, I'd be next."

"And you chose to become a therapist?"

"I hate to tell you this, but many of us pursue the profession to work out our own problems."

"Did it help?"

"It helped me find my calling with the helpline."

We were interrupted by Joe Camel making his rounds to hand out Camel Cash, a currency good for tee shirts, beer cozies, duffel bags, and other Smooth Character gear. Maeve inquired if it was hot inside the giant, plastic, phallic head, and he nodded. I asked if handing out accessories without cigarettes was like offering toys for a Happy Meal without the hamburger. He shrugged.

As we headed to the concert, we walked past the Citgo sign

in Kenmore Square and cut over to Commonwealth Avenue. Maeve asked if I'd ever been to a concert. I figured Pink Floyd and The Boomtown Rats would sound better than The Carpenters. Maeve sounded impressed that I would know Bob Geldof and reminded me of his Irish heritage. The new band we were seeing that night was from her hometown. They were rising stars with radio hits like "Dreams." Trying to hold my own, I told her I preferred the original version by Fleetwood Mac. She laughed and told me only the titles were the same.

Attempting to change the subject, I told her that the dream I'd had the previous night was a keeper.

We looked up to see the tour bus for The Cranberries. The bus was parked outside The Paradise. The place was packed, and I asked if we could wait outside to escape the noise and smoke. But she wanted to stake out a place close to the stage. When the band came on, I was relieved by their mellow vibe. Even a song they introduced from their next unreleased album with wailing vocals and crunching guitars was melodic beneath the din. For an encore, the lead singer covered Close to You in such a hushed tone that she made Karen Carpenter seem like Ann Wilson. Filing out, I noticed that even Maeve was among the oldest members of the audience. Many of the accents in the crowd sounded like fellow expats, and I asked Maeve for a few translations of words like "banjaxed," "gobdaw," and "craic."

At the next exit, the Brasco & Sons Funeral Home sign implored customers, "Slow down—we can wait." The crowds from a night game at Fenway were just breaking, and, on the walk back to her car, Maeve asked about my dream. In the dream, I walked into Brasco's baroque parlor and announced I had two months to live. A receptionist took my hand and led me to an anteroom where a Brasco son waited. I asked if he had a recommendation for the ultimate existential decision—burial or cremation. It was a matter of personal preference, he said, one often influenced by the three F's: faith, family traditions, and finances. When it came to a home for eternity, I said, money was no object, but I was anxious to make the right decision. He said he completely understood, but when I asked if it would be possible to sample both options, he looked at me quizzically. For comparison, I proposed a two-night trial. First, I would spend a night in a coffin to get a feel for the environment and decide if it would be a good fit. The Brasco son eyes me quizzically and said he would check with his older brother. He had a question: would the simulation need to take place underground or would a night in a demonstrator on the showroom floor suffice? And, if the floor model was okay, could it be open casket or would they need to find a way to shut the lid so I could still breathe? Above ground would be fine, I said, but the only way to tell if it would feel claustrophobic would be if the coffin was lid-down.

At this point, the Brasco son was writing notes, some of which I could decipher upside-down: "Showroom/burial?" "Casket O or C?" I asked if the linings provided reasonably good support, and he said if money really were no object we could go as plush or firm as I would like. As far as cremation, he asked, how exactly would that work? I confessed I knew little about the process and wondered if it basically would be like being placed into a pizza oven. He thought for a moment and said he was working front of the house and would have to check with the furnace master, adding "pizza" to his notepad. I asked if it would be possible to spend a second night in the oven without firing it up. He said he couldn't promise anything, but he would find out my options and get back to me.

"No wonder you have trouble sleeping," Maeve said as we neared the parking lot. "If I had nightmares like that, I don't think I'd ever close my eyes."

"You'd describe it as a nightmare?"

"You think of it as aspirational?"

"Sorry, I have very little for comparison. I rarely dream."

"You rarely *remember* your dreams. Your subconscious probably blocks them out."

"An act of self-preservation, I guess."

"Except it doesn't work that way. We think we're blocking out our thoughts, but we're really pushing them down further where they grow stronger. It's like buried nuclear waste. We assume it's dormant, but it's always simmering beneath the surface."

"I used to lose sleep over my insomnia. Now, I can worry about falling asleep, too."

"If I were your therapist, I'd want to know how you became so obsessed with death."

"I'm not sure I'd use the word 'obsessed'".

"I'm not sure how else to describe it. It feels like when something takes up every waking moment, holding your mind captive in sleep."

I looked at her. "Maybe I've always had a kind of love/hate relationship with death."

"Don't you think that might be worth exploring?"

"I doubt there are support groups for people like me. I'm not even sure there's a name for it."

"A diagnosis might be a good place to start."

"So I can confirm I'm even more fucked up than I think I am?"

"Maybe we need to get out of your head for a moment."

"Gladly."

"Your mom wasn't only generous with you. A sizeable portion of her estate is designated to charity."

"I know. She was talking about that teen center when I was still in high school."

"That's how she wanted to make a difference. Do you ever think of how you will?"

CHAPTER EIGHTEEN

A CERTAIN TIME, A CERTAIN PLACE

AS THE ONLY resident of Haven House who received mail and deliveries, I was able to keep up the gift subscription to *The New Yorker* Mel had sent since my fourteenth birthday. I read the magazine like most teenage boys read Playboy, skipping over the text for the visuals; in their case, it was for the centerfolds, but in mine, it was the cartoons. Charles Addams, Gahan Wilson, occasional cameos from Edward Gorey—the work of artists with a macabre style evoked both a fascination and anxiety that felt acutely familiar.

I received two sympathy cards, both forwarded from Wilbraham. One showed a gull flying across a lavender sky with the caption, "Heaven has welcomed a bright and beautiful spirit." Mel would have gotten a laugh out of that one, which reminded me of "Deep Thoughts" on *Saturday Night Live*. It was signed "Love, Michelle" and included a surprising note about Mel. Michelle recalled how the "Bus A14" students from Springfield saw Mel as the one staff member in Wilbraham on their side. When an A14 point guard got into a fight with a townie member of his own team—who used the "n" word and told him to "go back home"—both students were suspended.

Mel intervened to have the Springfield student reinstated. Other A14 students visited her to confide how unwelcome they often felt. Some spoke of teachers who didn't call on them in class or acted surprised when they had the right answer or aced an exam. One girl said she would never have made it through MRHS, if not for her daily visits to Mel's office. Michelle, a straight-A student, never experienced these sleights personally (perhaps because she could pass for white,) but she was bullied for her academic success and excluded by A14 students and Wilbraham locals, neither of whom saw her as one of them. Michelle would visit Mel during a free block to teach her knitting or to play a game of Scrabble. I was surprised Mel had never mentioned Michelle and wondered if they had ever spoken of me. Mel would often come home, railing about what a racist town we lived in and how MRHS reflected it and why she thought the administration was to blame. But she was also frustrated with local students, who told her the reason the A14 students didn't feel accepted is because they kept to themselves. "Why can't you sit at their lunch table instead of waiting for them to come to you?" she often asked.

The second card I received pictured Colonel Sanders at the pearly gates. Atop each is a chicken deity, and the caption read "Uh-oh." It was a Far Side card from Grace, who had heard about Mel from Christos King, who called to ask how to reach me about the bill for the mirror at Massholes. She wrote: "There are apparently no official Far Side sympathy cards, but the Hallmarks all seemed too sappy, and this had an irreverent spirit I think your mom would have appreciated. Although I didn't know her well, I would bet her greatest wish would be that you begin the life you say you've never had. It's not too late. Thinking of you. Yours truly, Grace."

I also kept up on events in Pioneer Valley through my subscription to *The Springfield Republican*. One morning, I was surprised to see a photo of Mel on the cover with a story about the teen center. Trustees had been named, with Maxine appointed as chair, per Mel's directions. Most of the other names were unfamiliar but one stood out: Liam Thompson, son of Derek at *The Pilot*. This was not a choice Mel would have made. It reeked of retribution, yet it also fit with The Thompson family's interest in being seen as pillars of the community. Apparently, the location for the center had already become a point of contention, with one camp advocating for the high school and a second pressing for a standalone site.

I was surprised Mel had not spelled out her wishes, but I was certain I knew her preference. Placing the Center at MRHS would keep it under the control of Ted Weeks, who would ensure it served the interests of the administration and not the students. There would be no shelf of banned books, no candy dish filled with condoms, and, certainly, no rogue counselors.

I was reading the anniversary issue of *The New Yorker* with Eustace Tilley on the cover when Vic burst into my room, triumphantly waving a bag of coffee beans and announcing he had won the lottery. Not only had I never bought a ticket in my life, but the thought hadn't occurred to me. Like everyone, I'd seen stories about players winning windfalls to an early retirement. I asked if perhaps we should celebrate the occasion with something a little more festive like champagne. No, he explained, coffee would be the most appropriate. He would receive a pound a month for a year, his haul from a Dunkin' Donuts scratch card, the only time in his life, he noted, he'd ever won anything. I congratulated him as if he had won Megabucks.

"You know Dunkin' is my middle name?"

"Yes, it's on all your paperwork. Your mom must have been quite the coffee drinker." Vic perched himself at the foot of my bed. "So, how was the concert?"

"I had no idea we'd have to stand for two hours."

"Where was the show?"

"The Paradise. I assume the name was meant to be ironic."

"Some great bands have come through that place: Tom Petty, Lou Reed, U2..."

"I'm surprised they survived the smell."

"Come on, man. That's called atmosphere. That place rocks."

"That place reeks."

"As any real rock club should."

"Then this one is the genuine article."

"Now, if you're looking for pure urine-soaked authenticity, you will do no better than The Rat."

"Because what goes better with piss than vermin?"

"It's short for The Rathskellar. Their restrooms would make the ones at The Paradise seem like The Ritz."

"The floors of The Paradise were so sticky that I didn't even attempt the bathrooms."

"Then you may want to skip The Rat. In the battle of authentic club restrooms, it's only rival is CBGB's in the East Village."

"How did you get to be such an expert on the Boston music and restroom scene?"

"I did a short tour of duty at Boston University's School of Nursing before I transferred to UConn. It was right on Comm Avenue, with The Paradise on one end of the campus and The Rat on the other. A real mecca for live music. Who did you see there?"

"Some new Irish band called The Cranberries. They're from Limerick where Maeve is from."

"I'll have to ask Carter if he's heard of them. When he was a kid, I took him to see all these great bands. Now, I get to see him perform."

"He's in a band?"

"I guess you'd call him a solo artist. It's only him and his gear. He plays techno shit, like, Kraftwerk, New Order, you know."

"I don't know, but it sounds like you're not a fan."

"I'm a fan of Carter, but I'm not sure I'd describe it as music. Damn, I sound like my dad when I played Tom Petty."

"Isn't the whole point of music to annoy your parents?"

"Mission accomplished. He follows a British band, if you can call it that, The Black Dog..."

"Funny, Maeve said that's the name the Irish have for depression."

"I can see why. Did our pal join you for the probate meeting?"

"Um." I looked away from his incredulous expression.

"You sent her alone!"

"I wasn't ready to face that yet."

"Dunkin,' my man."

"I asked her, Vic. She was helping me out."

"And I suppose she wanted nothing in return."

"I offered to pay her, and she said no."

"Sooner or later, I'm guessing you'll be getting the bill."

"The only thing she accepted was my offer to take her to this concert."

"I have some televangelist friends I'd like to introduce you to."

"And, by the way, that hospital she recommended? They advertise here in *The New Yorker*."

I opened the copy to a dog-eared page with an ad for McLean Hospital roughly the half the size of a business card. Vic pulled a pair of readers from a utility pocket to examine it.

"Ah yes, McLean Hospital, asylum to the rich and famous."

"Asylum as in insane?"

"As far as I know, the only admissions requirements are an 800 SAT score on reading and writing and an Amex Platinum card. They specialize in substance abuse."

"I knew I should have bought that weed from Ray in high school."

"You'd have been up against some heavyweights: James Taylor, Marianne Faithfull, Ray Charles."

"Maeve mentioned a couple famous poets who were alum, like Sylvia Plath and Anne Sexton."

"Fame is relative whenever you're talking about poets. But I find it curious she chose two people who took their own lives."

Candace popped her head into the room. "Sorry, gentlemen, I didn't mean to interrupt a heart-to-heart."

"No, Rev, come in. I was just emptying Charlie's bedpan."

"Don't think I wouldn't do it," Candace said.

"Charlie's pal Maeve Mullen recommended McLean Hospital for his next stop."

"Ah yes, celebrity rehab."

"I kind of think of myself as—what's the opposite of celebrity—nonentity?"

"It's a strange recommendation."

"You think it's a crazy idea?"

"For someone dealing with depression? No more than a hospice, I guess. I'd consider the source."

"I've been trying to tell him that ever since Maeve blew her cover and paid him a visit here."

"What cover? I knew she was from the helpline."

"Isn't the whole point that the volunteers are supposed to be anonymous?"

"I thought the point was that the *callers* were anonymous."

"The whole conversation is supposed to be anonymous."

"That's what I told him."

"Charlie is a big boy. He'll figure it out. I stopped by with the information you requested about donating your body to science."

Vic threw his hands out. "Is everyone trying to kill this man?"

"I asked Candace hypothetically," I said, "because she mentioned her cousin was in med school in Maine."

"According to Luis," she said, "you may want to rethink the idea."

"What did you hear?"

She shook her head and shuddered. "I've visited a slaughter-house. I have worked at a sewage treatment plant, and I've seen Cannibal Holocaust. His description was too gory even for me."

"What did he say?"

"The first-year med students in his class collected gold fillings, played Hacky Sack with organs, and trash-talked donors' bodies."

"I wondered if they might notice certain imperfections."

"Oh, they notice everything."

"On second thought, I think I'll be an organ donor. Or maybe I can list the whole package in the classified ads as 'barely used.'"

"This seems like a decision you could probably defer for a decade or two. Candace gave a Vulcan salute before she exited. "Live long and prosper."

CHAPTER NINETEEN

DON'T ASK

IF I DIDN'T KNOW her last name, I never would have guessed that Erma Tomassini shared DNA with her son. The lack of physical resemblance was striking. Even at her relatively advanced age, you could imagine that hers was an Arthur Miller/Marilyn Munroe marriage where, in a cruel twist of fate, the kids inherited his looks and her skills as a theoretical physicist. Which was not to say that Erma wasn't amply endowed with intellect. I learned from Vic that she had attended Choate Rosemary Hall, then an elite girl's school, and UConn on full scholarships. However, the career she envisioned as a nutritionist was derailed by motherhood, first caring for young children, then mourning the loss of her oldest son, Eamon, a firefighter who was killed on duty. For years, she was paralyzed by despair, withdrawing from family and friends into near isolation. When Erma finally emerged as a semblance of her old self, she channeled her despondence into her work as a dietician at Haven.

Although Vic was an open book about the most minute and sometimes seemingly personal details of his life, I learned this chapter of his family story entirely from Erma, who paid a visit to my room after the memorial for Mel at the high school. Though less gregarious than Vic, I could sense a baseline exuberance that had been subsumed by layer upon layer of anguish. By the end of our conversation, I knew as much about her as she knew about me. But unlike Vic, who relished center stage, Erma parceled out personal information judiciously to establish a bond over mutual bereavement. I wasn't sure how much most of the other staff knew about the real reason I was there, but, with Erma, I assumed Vic had clued her in. So, one day, when she asked what I would miss about life, I knew it was an exercise and not an existential question. My reply, the New Haven Original Clam Pie at Sally's Pizza, was met with "Yes, I heard about you." We developed a rapport; I'd routinely trash the hospice cuisine, and she would bemoan the eating habits of her sons whose four basic food groups were fat, sodium, sugar, and liquid hops.

When I told Maeve about Erma's question, she transformed it into a more open-ended assignment: make a list of pros and cons for living or write a letter to the departed.

I opted for the latter.

"You told me so," I wrote to Mel. *"You always tried to warn me to plan for a future without you, and I refused to acknowledge the possibility. Now, here I am, exactly as you feared, with no next move, wondering why I'm still here. You will not take comfort in this, but there is a sense of relief in knowing that if I was gone tomorrow, nobody would notice. The one advantage to truly being alone is that you have no sense of responsibility toward anyone else. If you have trouble understanding, think how you would feel if the tables were turned, and I had made it out first.*

Or maybe I am overestimating my place in your world. Thankfully, you had a life apart from me. You had your kids at school and friends at work, and you made a difference to a lot of people. If you had any doubt about that, you should have seen the outpouring of love at your memorial service. (Yes, I know you said you didn't want one. This wasn't my initiative, and I couldn't have stopped it if I tried).

I used to believe that for the first half of my life you were completely devoted to me, and, in the second half, I was completely devoted to you. As an adult, I told myself no matter how bad life got for me, it was my job to stick around and take care of you. Now, I'm not so sure I was being honest with myself. Without you, I am forced to consider the possibility that I stood in the way of you having a more fulfilling life. I wonder now if my fear of your mortality was really masking a fear of my own.

The best I can do now is to try to live out your wishes for the teen center. When it opens, my first contribution will be our Scrabble board, which I retired, followed by your beloved copy of Our Bodies, Ourselves and the rest of your infamous library of banned books.

In the meantime, the location of the center has already become a point of contention—the first of what I'm sure will be many controversies you have stirred up here in 01095 with your generosity. Well played. I am proud to have inherited your talent for making all the right enemies.

Speaking of inheritances, Christos King is after compensation for an irreplaceable piece of artwork which he claims I destroyed at Massholes (don't ask); Mark Rossmore sent me a sympathy card with an invoice for the outstanding balance; and, speaking of Massholes, Ted Weeks wants me to kick in for your memorial at MRHS. (I shit you not.)

I take some solace in the idea that you won our unspoken battle. Ours was clearly never the conventional mother/son relationship, blurring all kinds of lines between therapist and patient, parent and friend, caretaker and caregiver. A cynic might say we used each other. A more objective therapist might have described us as co-dependents. You, who bristled at absolutes by questioning every convention and always looking for practical solutions, might have said "We used each other well."

Somehow, I was never bothered by the fact that you called me Charlie and your students "my kids." In the same way parents of adopted children often tell them they are special because they were chosen, we were connected by something less random than blood. Whatever you were to me, I always knew you had my back. Do you remember the call you got from Mrs. Volk when I was in third grade? She had asked us what we wanted to be when we grew up. The other kids probably named all the usual occupations. I have no idea why I responded "black." It was just the first thing that came out of my mouth. I remember it made everyone laugh, but she was surprised that such a polite, quiet kid would respond so flippantly. She knew I was "making do" without a father and wondered if there was something going on at home. I remember you asking me what I meant—something she never did. When I didn't have an answer, you asked if I meant I wanted to be like Martin Luther King, Jr. or Sam Cooke, whose songs were in heavy rotation on our turntable. I'm guessing you were disappointed to hear it was merely "my favorite color," but I was proud that you told Mrs. Volk you weren't worried, and she shouldn't be, either.

Despite all the years we spent together, for all the talks we had and ways we were on the same page, I'm not sure we knew each other well. There are so many things I still don't know. Did you really become a single mother because you feared you would miss the opportunity before you found a partner, as you always told me, or was I the excuse you were seeking to give up the burden of dating and marriage? Did you sacrifice opportunities to avoid leaving me alone?

We avoided asking each other the hard questions and pressing for honest answers. It worked until it didn't. Here, at the end, I'm left to wonder how much you knew about what was circling in my head but was left unsaid. Did you realize how detached I was from everyone and everything? When you told me about your "crazy" client—the one you said never had a happy day in her life—did you not realize you were describing me as well? Or were you too close to see? What would you want for me now if you knew there was no happy ending?

Wish you were here.

Yours still,

Charlie

CHAPTER TWENTY

AFTERLIFE

WALT: LISTENERS OF "VALLEY SPEAK," our daily dialogue on WPVR/Pioneer Valley Radio, know that the name Francis Carr has come up often when we open up the lines, something which we will not do today. *The Times* correspondent was raised in Northampton, and on a visit home, he learned about the strange-but-true saga of a Wilbraham man whose suicide was chronicled in a series of articles in *The Daily Hampden Gazette* over a decade ago. Carr's new book, *Posthumously Yours*, has been making headlines of its own for several reasons. Let's begin there, Francis—welcome home and thanks for joining us on "Valley Speak."

Francis: Thanks, Walt. Not to begin with a correction, but I should note that my homecoming is virtual. For the record, I am back in New York.

Walt: Noted. So then I'm assuming you have not been following the local coverage of your book, which includes an oped in *The Gazette* cheekily titled "Well, Exhummmme Me."

Francis: My publicist forwarded that one, and I must admit that while the claim has no merit, the headline was amusing.

Walt: Then you know that the reporter for *The Gazette*,

Odette Curry, claims you dug up your protagonist's story from her series without proper attribution to her or the paper.

Francis: She's quoted saying as much in every interview I've done on this book tour. So, yes, I was aware. It's quite the opposite. As a reporter for the hometown newspaper, she wrote about it first and covered it comprehensively, but the story was picked up nationally so I could have read about it in any number of newspapers, right? I chose to voluntarily disclose where I read it.

Walt: She seemed to find your description of her as a reporter particularly dismissive.

Francis: First, let me note that in my business the title of "reporter" is considered a sign of respect, not a pejorative. That said, Odette's series was not the basis for my book. I did my own research and the results you see in *Posthumously Yours* are entirely my own. Personally, I think it's presumptuous of any reporter or writer to claim ownership of any non-fiction story. Let's not exaggerate our importance. We are the conduits. This was a real life, and it wasn't mine, Odette's, or any other reporter's or writer's. The story belonged to Charles Braun.

Walt: Of course, he's gone. Both of you are trying to lay claim to it, along with any ancillary benefits.

Francis: You mean like the benefit of having strangers attack you for sympathizing with someone they perceive as having encouraged a man to take his life?

Walt: We're certainly going to get into that, but I was thinking of financial benefits like advances, royalties, movie rights.

Francis: It's certainly not my area of expertise. Frankly, I can't imagine a book less suited for translation into a movie.

Walt: Because?

Francis: My understanding about movies—again, purely from the perspective of someone who has bought tickets to them

—is that they are essentially a visual medium. This story is basically all on the page. As far as the book is concerned, it is the first one written about this case, but I doubt it will be the last. In fact, I suspect we'll eventually see one from the woman at the center of this case.

Walt: And here—we need to say for listeners who may be coming into this cold—we're talking about Maeve Mullen, the founder of the Hampden County Helpline, who befriended a sixty-year-old man who had long contemplated suicide, and who was charged with manslaughter for encouraging him.

Francis: Maeve initially sat down with me for a series of interviews which I used in the book to describe conversations she had with Charles Braun, her son Jack, and others in this drama. I found some of those conversations so illuminating I thought about abandoning the book and offered to help her write an account from her perspective. She declined, but I could see the lightbulb go off. The next thing I knew our interviews were over.

Walt: Did she say why?

Francis: She didn't, but I'm guessing she'd decided to tell her own story. Like I said, these aren't our lives—they belong to the participants like her and Charles Braun. Obviously, he can't tell his side, so I relied on accounts from people in his orbit. Maeve clearly has strong feelings about how she was represented in the trial, and I can understand why she might want to speak for herself.

Walt: You said you don't see this story as a movie. What made you think it would be a worthwhile book?

Francis: It starts as a mystery—what was this woman's motivation? There are some people who believe she manipulated Charles into making the helpline she founded as a beneficiary of his estate and then tacitly encouraged him to kill himself to collect.

Walt: Which I think would fairly describe the view of most of our callers.

Francis: It certainly calls her motivation into question. There are examples of instances when her advice to him, if you can call it that, seems more ambiguous. Perhaps she wasn't *advocating* suicide, as I've seen some more hyperbolic commentors suggest. Maybe she was just trying to be supportive and build trust as he sorted things out and came to his own conclusions.

Walt: The question is whether the job of a suicide prevention counselor is to prevent callers from killing themselves or to help them consider the pros and cons.

Francis: Perhaps she wasn't quote unquote "aggressive" enough in dissuading him.

Walt: For example, instead of telling him she would support whatever he chose and then staying on the line with him as he overdosed, she could have called 911, no?

Francis: See, this is a perfect example of the kind of misinformation I've been hearing on this book tour. She did not say she would *support* whatever he chose. She said she would stay with him on the line either way.

Walt: Some reviewers have described that point as a distinction without a difference. They see the book as making the case for Maeve Mullen's position.

Francis: She turned down my offer to work together. In retrospect, I'm glad she did because it enabled me to present an account representing all different points of view. If anything, I would've had an incentive to be critical of her. Instead, I presented a balanced portrait.

Walt: So why do you think the book has not been received that way?

Francis: If readers see bias here, it's not because I'm expressing an opinion—it's because I'm not expressing *their* opinion. Remaining objective is not enough. They want me to demonize this woman. That's not my job. I believe the reader is intelligent and can draw their own conclusions.

Walt: I don't know about demonize but, yeah, they were troubled that you seemed morally ambiguous about someone who clearly had a conflict of interest and whose behavior as a therapist violates every conventional set of ethics in treating people who are suicidal.

Francis: Are these people mental health ethicists?

Wait: We spoke with a number of therapists and hoped to present a range of views. So far, we have not been able to find one who was willing to defend Maeve Mullen's conduct as a therapist if you want to call her that. And a number of book critics noted a parallel in the way your neutrality about her professional conduct mirrored hers—the way she presented and weighed options Charles Braun about whether he should take his own life.

Francis: Some of those critics seem to be basing that view not on anything in the book but on excerpts from interviews like this one, often quoting me out of context. I've even had callers on talk shows suggest I'm somehow aiding and abetting a homicidal maniac, with some vitriolic, vaguely threatening message attached.

Walt: Which is why—although I'm sure none of our civil Valley Speak listeners are responsible for these threatening messages—we're not taking their calls today. So, let me ask you a question I suspect many may have: Let's say that instead of having written this book, you just finished reading this objective portrait you painted. What opinion would you come away with as to Maeve Mullen's innocence or guilt?

Francis: Of course, that's another way of asking me to show bias here, but I'll play along. And this is going to sound like avoiding your question instead of answering it, but my honest response is I don't know. There is compelling evidence on both sides. For example, I think Maeve Mullen's efforts to get Charlie Braun to add her charitable organization to his will certainly bears explanation, and I'm not sure that her lawyer, Bordie Hammond, satisfactorily addressed it. Perhaps most troubling, I don't think Maeve herself ever satisfactorily explained why she withheld a letter Lucy Braun had written to her son and given to the family's probate attorney, Marcus Miles.

Walt: And here, we need to explain that Charles Braun asked Maeve to attend a meeting with the attorney on his behalf, at which she was given a copy of his mother's will and the letter. She gave him the will but withheld the letter, so he never saw it before he took his life.

Francis: In court, Maeve claimed she was trying to protect Charlie, who was grief stricken and vulnerable. I would say this wasn't her call to make. When the probate attorney read that his client never received the letter, he brought it to the court's attention. On the other hand, the money Maeve persuaded Charlie to contribute went to the suicide prevention hotline she founded, so there is nothing she gained personally. You also must wonder, if this case were really black and white and Maeve purely sinister, wouldn't the juries have picked up on that and convicted her? Instead, this has dragged out for years, which tells me that when confronted with the facts, impartial observers see some ambiguity.

Walt: The delays may just reflect how slowly the wheels turn in our justice system. But let's step back here and give listeners a sense of how this story wound up on your radar in the first place. You were doing some research about your own family history on a visit to Northampton—

Francis: Shout out to Northampton's own Forbes Library. I brought along my daughter to visit her grandparents, and while she was watching a dance recital, I decided to go through some back issues of *The Gazette*. I came across Odette's series about this story I had somehow missed.

Walt: You hadn't written a book before. Is there something about Charlie Braun's story that resonated for you personally?

Francis: God, I hope not. I'm an upbeat person, and I have a good support system around me. I don't think most people would describe me as troubled, which is not to say I didn't empathize with him. This was someone who had somehow made it to nearly sixty without fully experiencing life.

Walt: Which also might explain why he placed so much trust in a significantly younger relative stranger.

Francis: She certainly had more life experience.

Walt: What was it he said, that he never had a happy day in his life?

Francis: That was a comment one of his mother's clients made, and Charlie said he could relate. Imagine feeling so emotionally detached and joyless. What made me want to dig deeper and ultimately find the story so compelling were the ambiguities, not just with Charlie but with Maeve. I don't think anyone would suggest she put the idea of ending his life into his head.

Walt: In the book, you wrote that he half-seriously believed he came out of the womb suicidal.

Francis: "Half-seriously" is your description. After reading about him, I'd say he was completely serious.

Walt: So, the question becomes, did Maeve Mullen encourage him? Persuade him? Or was she simply negligent for not having tried more vigorously to stop him?

Francis: You left out one. You're framing it as though it's murder two versus manslaughter.

Walt: What did I miss?

Francis: The possibility that she is not guilty.

Walt: I wasn't speaking about legal responsibility. I was thinking morally responsible.

Francis: So was I. People can disagree with her judgment without questioning her motivation.

Walt: You interviewed many of the people who figured into this story. Some relayed conversations they had personally, others described exchanges between those who wouldn't or couldn't cooperate, like Charles and his mom. One I found particularly revealing was a meeting Maeve had with her lawyer, Bordie Hammond. Can you share it?

Francis: My guess was he would have dissuaded her from talking. If he did, he was unsuccessful.

Walt: Bordie Hammond constructed a defense based on the premise that maybe she went too far—or not far enough, depending on how you look at it—in explicitly discouraging Charlie Braun from killing himself, but she wasn't the one who actually pulled the trigger, so to speak?

Francis: Basically, he had to create what I'd describe as a sort dual-defense strategy: first, she unequivocally did not encourage Mr. Braun to take his life, and second, he was not an impressionable teenager but an adult who'd been contemplating suicide all his life. Even if she had said the wrong thing, it was his decision and his alone.

Walt: Among the more controversial things Maeve reportedly told Charlie—and I'm paraphrasing here—was that if she had led his life and was his age, she would not continue her life. Now, she also qualified this by acknowledging she wasn't suggesting what he should do. But can you see how some might construe this more as a legal disclaimer than a genuine reservation?

Francis: I understand how people could see it that way, but I also think there's something missing here: the intonations that could only have been gleaned from hearing their actual conversation. She could have been showing sarcasm, for example.

Walt: If there weren't recordings and with Charlie not around to corroborate Maeve's version, how did their conversations come to light?

Francis: Sean Byrne, a priest in New Haven, had heard Maeve's confessions. When he read about the case, he went to the police to share what he knew.

Walt: Risking excommunication for violating a fundamental duty of priests to maintain absolute secrecy in the seal of confession.

Francis: He left the priesthood to testify.

Walt: Why was he willing to disregard one of his most sacred vows and step away from the church?

Francis: The Catholic Church holds that suicide is a grave offense, one of the three requirements of a mortal sin. Father Sean told me he believed aiding and abetting a suicide to be tantamount in aiding and abetting a murder.

Walt: He saw Maeve's conduct as a crime.

Francis: Morally, yes. He also met Charlie briefly a couple of times when he was the priest at a parish in Palmer, Massachusetts, near Charlie's hometown of Wilbraham. Sean wasn't very forthcoming with the details, but even though Charlie wasn't Catholic, he apparently visited the church and reached out for help.

Walt: The plot thickens. What else did he tell you about the conversations between Maeve and Charlie?

Francis: He described the final one.

Charlie: Every time I get here, I can't decide which option is scarier, living or dying, so I do nothing.

Maeve: Doing nothing is doing something.

Charlie: Okay, well, I always made the same choice.

Maeve: And how has that worked out?

Charlie: You think I should go with Plan B.

Maeve: We've been down this road so many times. You're asking for permission. I can't give it to you, and you don't need it. I'm only here to support you—whatever decision you make.

Charlie: Let's say I go ahead with this. Do you think five hundred dollars is enough for housekeeping?

Maeve: What are they cleaning, the White House?

Charlie: I'm talking about a tip for the maid at the hotel.

Maeve: I believe the going rate is around two bucks a day. How long have you been staying there?

Charlie: I checked in today, but by the time they find me—

Maeve: Oh, right, that might require a few extra bucks. Five hundred should cover it. How about your estate? Is everything in order?

Charlie: I think so.

Maeve: Marcus made all the amendments?

Charlie: All you need to do is make sure he gets paid, since, obviously, I won't be able to. Sorry, I've had all the time in the world, but I still have a hard time saying it out loud.

Maeve: You're sure you want to go through with it?

Charlie: I've never been sure, but you've gotten me this far.

Maeve: Let's be clear, Charlie. You asked what I would do if I were you. I'm not. If I thought I could give my life meaning by ending it to help others, would that be enough to get over the fear? I think so, but that's me. This is a decision only you can make.

Charlie: I think I already made it. I'm a little more movie literate, and I sampled some nightlife. I still don't get the fascination with football, but at least I finally understand how it's played—sort of. At this point, I can't imagine anything that would turn my life around. Now, I have to find the courage to go through with it.

Maeve: Whatever you decide, do it because you've made a conscious decision, not out of fear.

Walt: That was the last thing they said to each other.

Francis: She promised to stay on the line as long as it took and told him he was not alone. After a minute or two, she thought he was gone. Suddenly, she heard laughter. He'd been holding his breath as a sort of preview, but he kept hearing "Late Lament," the spoken-word interlude on "Nights in White Satin." He said it always reminded him of a Hallmark sympathy card.

Walt: A moment of unintended levity there.

Francis: I guess. He took a deep breath, said, "Okay, here goes nothing," and he was gone.

Walt: You know, what occurred to me when you were reading that was the mixed messages Maeve was sending. It's like she was leading him to the proverbial ledge, then pulling him back.

Francis: I can see how it could be read that way.

Walt: Although I think it's clear what she thought he should do. So how do you interpret those conflicting statements? Was she ambivalent herself or allowing him the space to make a choice? Or is it possible she was thinking ahead and insulating herself and her organization from liability?

Francis: Remember, she had no way of knowing their conversations would end up public.

Walt: Okay, then how do you explain her motivation?

Francis: The only way we can ever know someone else's motivation would be to read their mind. I have yet to master that ability. Based on my conversations with Maeve, I can only speculate that she was trying to balance being honest about her personal views and being an honest broker, if you will.

Walt: What does that mean?

Francis: Trying to act responsibly in her capacity as the leader of a suicide prevention program.

Walt: That's where I think it's unclear. Does Hampden County Helpline actively promote suicide prevention, or provide the message, "We're here to listen and support you whatever you do?"

Francis: Their mission is in their name. It's about helping callers, not mandating their behaviors. Maeve told me that "prevention" is the goal, but the word is misleading because ultimately—at least with adults—the decision is up to the individual. That philosophy differs somewhat from other hotlines.

Walt: I can imagine why.

Francis: Charlie was also something of an outlier. I mean, typically, the process is all over the phone. Here, it evolved into something more like a personal relationship, a friendship of sorts, although I'm not sure Maeve would have described it that way. Let's say she took a personal interest.

Walt: Was that crossing a line?

Francis: No question. In fact, I think that may be the biggest mistake she made.

Walt: Getting involved in the first place.

Francis: Visiting a caller in person. Even if he welcomed it, the whole premise of a hotline is based on anonymity.

Walt: So why did she do it?

Francis: She saw parallels between her father, who took his own life, and this caller, at least in terms of their age and what seemed to be a lifelong pursuit to end their lives. Maeve looked at Charlie's life objectively and said if she were in his shoes, she would not continue her life. Now, that may have been a mistake tactically, even ethically, but it was based on her personal experience, not any ulterior motive. Remember, when Maeve decided to visit Charlie, she didn't know his financial status—all she knew was there was a man she wanted to help. So, if we're looking for motivation to confirm her status as a villain, it becomes a little more complicated.

Walt: In the book, you wrote that Maeve's lawyer was worried that she might be seen as playing God.

Francis: Bordie Hammond wanted to be sure the prosecution wouldn't frame it in those simplistic terms.

Walt: This defendant made a value judgment about the worthiness of a man's life, someone who was not terminally ill, someone who, arguably, was simply depressed. Is that not the definition of playing God?

Francis: It's a good thing for the defense you weren't on the jury.

Walt: I'm only voicing the way many see it. She played God by deeming the life he had lived as unworthy, then she played clairvoyant about the path it would take if left to evolve on its own.

Francis: Again, I don't want to come off as defending the defense here, but when I heard what Maeve told Charlie, I thought she seemed to go to great lengths to clarify she wasn't speaking in a professional capacity.

Walt: Still, who was she to make a diagnosis?

Francis: She'd say she was only telling him what she would've done in his position. He told her he'd contemplated suicide nearly his whole life. You don't have to be clairvoyant to assume that if things hadn't changed in Charlie's first sixty years, they were unlikely to change in his future.

Walt: Tell that to all the late bloomers.

Francis: Every time I hear that, I try to find one who was

Charlie's age. The only example I came up with was Grandma Moses.

Walt: So, life is over after sixty and people should just hang it up?

Francis: By sixty, most people already have lived at least one life. They've had jobs, relationships, marriages, children, divorces. Charlie Braun would've been starting from scratch. I'm not aware of anyone else who has pulled that off.

Walt: Before we take a break, I want to ask about legal strategy. This case raises some questions I'm not sure have been directly addressed before. So, in the thirty seconds remaining, can you summarize the basis for the defense?

Francis: Bordie Hammond saw this as a First Amendment issue. Since Maeve had not broken any laws, he argued that finding her guilty would mean curtailing her free speech. He also cited the Fifth Amendment in violating due process. Had she been convicted, it would have taken society places we're probably not prepared to go.

Walt: You're listening to Valley Speak. My guest is Francis Carr, reporter for the *Times* and author of the book *Posthumously Yours*. The book chronicles the life of Charles Braun who ended his own life. Some believe he did so under the encouragement of a suicide prevention counselor. I'm Walt Kennedy, this is WPVR, public radio for the Pioneer Valley. Back after this...

Dear, dear Charlie,

There is a part of me—or whatever came after—that is happily surprised you are reading this. My greatest worry was always what would happen to you when I was gone. You never allowed me to talk about it, but I feared you wouldn't give yourself a chance to find out what was next. I'm glad you proved me wrong. Here you are, on your own, hopefully trying all the things you should have been doing had I not held you back.

I suppose it's ironic that I was able to be a mother naturally to so many other people's kids but not my own. I preached honesty and candor to them, while the two of us colluded to avoid certain topics and keep secrets from each other. Even living under the same roof as you, I knew there was so much I didn't know about you: why you stayed all these years, why you never pursued friendships or relationships, what gave you happiness (or whether you experienced it at all). And there was so much you didn't know about me. The secret I regret keeping most is the lie I always told you about how you came into the world.

You are not the result of an anonymous donor. I knew the man well. We had been together for more than a year, and all that time he had been completely honest about not wanting children. When I told him I had become pregnant accidentally, he knew it wasn't true and ended our relationship, not because of you but because of me. He realized I was not to be trusted, and he was right. I got what I wanted, but it cost me the (first) love of my life. I don't regret it, and I am the only one to blame, which is why I never told you this before.

You'll notice I have not used the word "father." That's because I don't see him that way. He could not have been clearer —this was not something he ever wanted to be. So, I tried to protect his privacy and your feelings from the response I felt sure you would have received if you attempted to contact him. Truth be told, I probably also wanted to protect myself from your reaction. I'm sharing this now because although you will never meet him, I want you to know there is still someone else in the world you are connected to.

A few years ago, Maxine told me I was smart to create the perfect companion for myself. I'm sure she meant it as a compliment, but I was so mad that I didn't speak to her for days. I couldn't handle the thought that I was so diabolical, manipulative, and selfish, but the reason it stung so badly was because it was true. I never gave you the real mother you deserved. When I think about what Maxine said, I'm not even sure I was a good friend, because of the way I put my need for companionship above your need for a life of your own.

One thing I know for certain—as a therapist, I sold you short. From the beginning, I knew it was a mistake. I could never give you the objectivity that makes therapy valuable. Grace Cullen told me in her profession they have a saying, "A person who represents himself has a fool for a client." She was gently suggesting a parallel with being professionally treated by a family member. There isn't the distance a therapist needs to be effective.

So many topics were off-limits between us. You couldn't share your honest feelings about me. Whenever I tried to ask about relationships and sex, you changed the subject. I never recall you mentioning any friends. As a parent, I didn't want to be intrusive, but if I was going to be of any help to you as a therapist, I knew it was my job to ask uncomfortable questions. I tried to steer you toward someone else, but you always rejected the idea out of hand, and I figured it was better for you to have me as a sounding board than no one at all. I wondered how candid you would have been if you had agreed to see another therapist. In my master's program, one of the professors reminded us that a therapist can only work with the information they are given. She said that even Freud (Anna, not her father Sigmund; this was Smith, after all) could not help a client who withheld details or presented a skewed picture. Was I wrong to believe some thoughts would always stay in your head, no matter who was asking the questions? If I'm completely honest, maybe I also kept tabs on you in case you ever left. Whatever my reasons, you deserved someone who was an advocate for you and you alone and not someone with a conflict of interest.

I know I fell short as a parent, too, which is ironic because I swore I could do a better job than my parents did with me. You often heard me say their greatest gift was being absent in my life. I like to think their neglect insulated me from any damage they could have done. Perhaps I went in the opposite direction with you because I was unable to let you go. I tell myself it was the better of two extremes even as I wonder whether it left you paralyzed and unable to feel the confidence to become independent as a child who is tethered to me by responsibility as an adult.

Now you are free, Charlie. I honestly believe it's never too late. You can start by finding a new therapist, someone you can tell everything, who can help you sort it all out and is bound to keep your secrets. One thing you will discover: whatever you have been keeping inside, thinking nobody else in the world could possibly be feeling, you are not alone.

Then, as the wordsmith in our family, I hope you'll consider these. The first is from the book you gave me for my "final" retirement by our former family doctor and Springfield neighbor: "You have brains in your head. You have feet in your shoes. You can steer yourself any direction you choose. You're on your own. And you know what you know. And YOU are the guy who'll decide where to go."

The second is from that time when I took you to Paul and Elizabeth's for risotto cakes and tofu kebabs, and you took me to the Iron Horse to see that unknown singer who became so well known. A line from one of her songs stuck with me. It was something about having nothing to lose when you start from zero.

Maybe you'll decide to pursue your master's in journalism and the career you always wanted. Wouldn't it feel fun to send an announcement of your new job as a reporter at the Times to The Pilot and stick it to that fucker? Or maybe you'll decide to move somewhere warm and start your own newspaper. Or travel the world. Whatever you decide, you'll start out with one advan-

tage few others have: financial security. While money can't buy happiness, it can help you make up for lost time, open doors, and pay for a lot of slices. And Charlie, even though neither of us are believers, wherever you decided to put me, I promise I'll always be with you.

Forever,

Mel

Walt: Walt Kennedy, back with our guest on Valley Speak, *Times* reporter Francis Carr. Mr. Carr's book, *Posthumously Yours,* offers a more expansive, intimate account of a story first reported by Odette Curry in *The Daily Hampden Gazette*. The suicide of a Wilbraham man raised questions about whether he was encouraged to take his life and, more broadly, if such encouragement should have legal consequences. Francis, hearing that letter from Lucy Braun to her son, Charles, I had several thoughts, the first being that he deserved to read it.

Francis: Without a doubt. I believe withholding it was Maeve Mullen's greatest mistake. She said as much herself. Again, she claimed her intention was to protect Charlie from these revelations, particularly about the identity of his biological father, but I don't think it was her decision to make.

Walt: You could make the case that if Charlie had read the letter, he might have been persuaded not to end his life.

Francis: How he might have been impacted is speculative. What is certain is that Lucy Braun wrote the letter to her son, and it should have been delivered to him without anyone interfering.

Walt: The other thought that crossed my mind was how it contrasted with his letter to her.

Francis: The easy read was that their relationship was too close and conflicted, but, in some ways, they seemed to have reached almost opposite conclusions. Here you have two people who spent all these years together, who also had a client/patient dynamic yet didn't truly know each other. And when they finally put it out there on the table in these letters, both end up in the dead letter office. Sorry, no bad pun intended.

Walt: I'd like to ask you to read the third chapter in which you describe an arbitration hearing to settle the claim by the hotline Maeve Mullen founded and directed. They argued that Charles Braun re-wrote his will to include the organization, and his wishes should be respected. A group—I don't know if you'd call them friends or acquaintances—stepped forward to suggest the provision was essentially coerced and therefore, should be invalid.

Francis: Several staff members at the hospice where Charles Braun spent the final year of his life—again, not because of any terminal illness—and a few friends of his mother's formed a kind of ad hoc group opposed to the organization's claim. They had no standing and decided to pursue it through arbitration.

Walt: And again, we should remind listeners that your description of events is based on interviews with people who attended.

Francis: Right, and I should note that the dialogue from the arbitration came directly from transcripts of that meeting, as well as the final conversation between Charles Braun and Maeve Mullen, which she described to Sean Byrne, and he shared with reporters. Hopefully, it will all make sense when you hear it.

Walt: You might want to top off your waterglass here, Francis. This is chapter three of *Posthumously Yours* by the *Times* reporter, Francis Carr, our guest today on Valley Speak:

. . .

Traveler's Tower in downtown Hartford is roughly equidistant between New Haven and Wilbraham, Connecticut's third-largest city and the small Massachusetts town most notable as the home of the Friendly's Ice Cream chain. So, it was the place where interested parties from both locations agreed to meet for hearing in the arbitration process over the estate of Lucy Braun, transferred to and amended by her son, Charles, upon her passing. He added the Hampden County Helpline, a suicide prevention hotline founded by Maeve Mullen, as a beneficiary before taking his own life.

Marcus Miles, the Braun family's probate attorney and Borden Hammond, the Helpline's lawyer, were at the hearing—one of several unusual aspects of this case. Miles—tall, slender, bald, sporting a goatee, bowtie and suspenders—was representing the estate in attempting to remove the Hampden County Helpline as a beneficiary. As an executor, he was approached by a group whose members knew Lucy, Charles, or both, and believed the helpline's founder, Maeve Mullen, coerced Charles into making the bequest before encouraging him to take his life. The Wilbraham members of the group included one of his high school classmates, Karen Nyman; a friend and colleague of his mother's, Maxine Folkman, and a retired priest, Sean Bryne, who had served at parishes in Palmer, Massachusetts, near Wilbraham, and in New Haven. The Connecticut contingent was Victor Palmino, a nurse, and Candace Delgado, chaplain at Haven House, the hospice facility where Charles Braun spent his final months. The atmosphere was surprisingly relaxed. Marcus introduced the Wilbraham and New Haven groups, neither of whom had met in person before. Folkman brought apple cider donuts, and Nyman poured coffee from a Dunkin' Donuts Box 'o Joe. Bryne sat apart reading The Catholic Free Press while puffing on Captain Black Cherry from a briarwood pipe. Even Hammond and Nyman, both of whom had seen each other in person only twice since their divorce was finalized a year earlier, waived to each other cordially.

The plan was for the Hampden County Helpline to be represented solely by Hammond, who proposed emphasizing the gift was not for Mullen personally but a bequest to an organization with a critical, lifesaving mission. However unfairly, she had become a polarizing figure. For Mullen to appear as the face of the Help Line would only be a reminder of the connection they sought to downplay. Hammond asked if a board member might represent the organization but as academic and civic leaders. They were wary of publicly risking their own reputations—at least until the media storm had blown over.

"Right now, your reputation has made you radioactive," he told Mullen. "If you really want to protect your baby, the best thing you can do is abandon it."

Mullen felt hurt but realized it was a sound strategy. They agreed he would go it alone.

This was before Mullen had been charged criminally, but stories were swirling that an announcement from the district attorney's office was imminent. Hammond believed that litigating such a case would offer opportunities to enhance his career, and representing the helpline would demonstrate his legal prowess. He reached out to offer his services pro bono to the organization she founded, an investment of time he believed would be rewarded by the exposure he'd receive in a criminal case.

So, when Mullen arrived at the conference room, soaking wet from a downpour, and took a seat next to her lawyer, the relative calm quickly dissipated. Hammond thought he smelled alcohol on her breath and admonished her for showing up. Bryne appeared shellshocked. He'd been assured Mullen would not be at the hearing. He looked over at Miles, who raised his arms and shook his head to suggest he was equally surprised.

Mullen told Hammond she'd made a stop at Kenney's, a local pub with Gaelic roots, only to warm up. She maintained she had a single Irish Coffee and was not compromised in the least; nevertheless, she agreed to let him do the talking. Hammond was not satisfied. He lit into her for giving Miles the opportunity to disparage the helpline through guilt by association and for reneging on their arrangement to allow him to fly solo at the hearing. She shot back that everyone already knew she'd founded the helpline, and distancing herself would only make it appear they had something to hide. The altercation became so intense that the other side of the room grew silent.

When she first walked into the conference room, Lawana Robinson looked as if she might have wandered into the wrong place. As the arbitrator for the case, Robinson wore a tailored navy pantsuit and cream-colored blouse with a string of pearls, the uniform of defense attorneys. She whispered something to Miles, then made her way to the other end of the conference table where Hammond and Mullen were having their heated exchange.

She introduced herself and said, "My understanding was that the Hampden County Helpline would be represented by council," she said.

"Correct," Hammond replied extending a hand. "Borden Hammond. I'm here on behalf of the Helpline."

Mullen introduced herself as the founder of the helpline and said she was there to observe. Robinson asked if they were on the same page. They nodded and took their seats.

"Congratulations," Hammond muttered to his client. "You just connected the dots for the estate."

Bryne gathered his coat and newspaper like he was prepared to bolt, but Robinson introduced herself and began the hearing before he could escape. Noting the number of people who had come to speak on behalf of the estate, she began with an explanation of how the arbitration process differed from court proceedings, emphasizing that often there are no witnesses or even lawyers. "So," she said in a vain attempt to ease the tension, "I'd like to thank all of you for making me feel like a real judge."

Addressing the elephant in the room, she emphasized that the parties in the arbitration process were the Braun estate and the Hampden County Helpline and not any individuals. The scope was limited to whether the estate was compelled to honor the bequest to the Helpline. The message was clear: her decision would not be impacted by an individual's innocence or guilt in any potential criminal cases. It was an ethical, professional, fitting disclaimer. It was also completely untethered to reality. There was no way to separate The Hampden County Helpline from its founder, leader and, until now, its public face. Any line drawn between the two was artificial. Presumably, the conduct of the founder was reflected in the philosophy of the helpline. If suicide were presented as a viable option for one physically sound caller, presumably it would be valid for others.

The five individuals who were there to speak on behalf of the estate's position were not motivated to take time off from work and make the drive out of an interest in protecting its assets. They saw no distinction between the organization and its founder, and they wanted to make sure she was not the beneficiary of a death they held her responsible for. It was inevitable they would blur the lines Robinson had drawn, but this was an arbitration, not a trial, and the rules were more flexible. She swore them in simultaneously and gave each a chance to have their say.

Maxine Folkman, a librarian at the high school where Lucy Braun was the guidance counselor, and her closest friend at work, was the most dramatic speaker. With wild gray curls, a gypsy dress and dangling earrings that brushed her shoulders, she had the earth mother look of an Ed Koren character, perhaps one of his affable anthropomorphic monsters. Her rapid-fire, pressure-of- speech delivery was punctuated by quieter, more reflective, tearful moments.

As chair of the teen center that was Lucy Braun's dream and philanthropic priority, Folkman had attended a meeting with Miles, where she first heard about the bequest for the Help Line which Charles had added.

"I received the news as if I was channeling Lucy," she said. "Her estate was supporting the organization that took her son's life. The whole thing felt like cruel irony, and there was nothing she could do to stop it. I felt like it was my job to speak on her behalf."

Hammond asked if Folkman believed the teen center stood to receive additional funds redirected from the Help Line. She said the thought never occurred to her, and the suggestion that she was profiting off her opposition to the help line was insulting. "All the people planning the teen center are volunteers," she snapped. "The reason we are donating our time on the project and are here today is because we want to honor Lucy Braun." Hammond said he wasn't suggesting anyone was profiting personally, only that if the helpline's claim on the estate was rejected, the funds might be redirected to the other charitable organization in the will, the teen center.

"Seriously, Bordie," Nyman said. "That's where you want to take this?"

"We're at a hearing, Karen," Hammond replied.

"It sounds like I'm missing something good here," Robinson interjected. "Does someone want to enlighten me?"

"My ex-wife is another member of the teen center's advisory board, Madam Arbitrator," Hammond said.

"I'm sure she is capable of sharing her own credentials, Mr. Hammond," Robinson replied. "As much as a good personal drama would probably be more entertaining, we're going to stick with the dry details of this estate matter. Ms. Nyman, can you do that, please?"

With shoulder-length silver hair, chiseled, still taut features, and striking blue eyes, Karen Nyman had that unnaturally natural youthful appearance like actors who seem to suspiciously age in reverse. Soft-spoken and succinct, she made listeners lean in. Nyman said that she and Charles Braun were high school classmates, but it was through her daughter that she came to understand the community's attachment to Miss Lucy. Planning for the teen center, she realized why it was her dream. Without a word about the helpline, Nyman seemed to suggest that this was Lucy Braun's real vision.

Next up were Vic Tomassini and Candace Delgado from Haven House. Delgado, the hospice chaplain, kept her anorak zipped to the top all morning, checking her watch frequently and leaning back in her chair with her arms folded. With straight black hair and coffee toned, makeup-free skin, she exhibited no angst, sense of mourning, nor personal connection.

Despite having nearly daily conversations with Charles Braun since his arrival at Haven House, she described him as a "hard nut to crack," then caught herself and added that she was describing his demeanor rather than intending any clinical diagnosis. As he was not religious, she said most of their conversations hovered on the surface. "I'll be honest, when I first met Charlie, I was thinking, 'What are you doing here using a hospice as a hotel?' It felt a little, I don't know—"

"Entitled?" Tomassini interjected.

"I was going to say bougie, but yeah," Delgado continued. "That was the first time it really hit me what a slog life had been for him. In a way, he was right, you know? Living all those years that way took a kind of resilience, so when this stranger suggested his life wasn't worth anything, I thought—what is she doing here?"

Mullen rose to speak, but Hammond tugged on her arm to sit down.

"You'll get your chance," Robinson said. "First, we'll hear from all the witnesses."

"I mean, Vic and I were, like, since when do counselors at anonymous hotlines make house calls? We asked our case manager flat out if we could bar this chick from the building, but she said Charles was a grown man and we couldn't decide on his visitors. I mean he was old enough to be my father. How did he not see through this?"

"I really need to interject here," Hammond said.

"That's okay" Delgado said. "That's all I got."

Tomassini winked at his colleague and took a swig from his cup. Bald and blue-eyed with an early five o'clock shadow, he wore blue scrubs which he began by apologizing for, explaining that he had a shift immediately after the hearing and would not have time to change.

"I'm here because my mother instructed me to be," he began. "She got to know Charlie as a volunteer at Haven House. I told her that Candace here had it covered, but mom insisted I represent her because she was afraid she'd get too emotional. And she said I knew him even better, which I guess is true, to the extent that we spent more time together. I'm not sure anyone could say they really knew him. Charlie kept his cards close to his chest. What I can tell you is that he described Maeve Mullen as a friend, but some of the things she told him that he shared with me didn't seem like anything a friend would say, never mind someone who works to prevent suicide. I remember many examples, but the one that probably sticks with me most is when she told him his estate could do so much good for others."

Mullen shot up from her seat and demanded to be heard and this time without constraint from her counsel. Robinson coaxed her back into her seat with a reminder that she'd get her chance to respond. It was clear that she, too, found Tomassini's comment problematic. Had there been a jury, she would have likely instructed them to disregard the remark, but as she reminded the attorneys, both parties had agreed to binding arbitration and it was up to them to keep their witnesses on point, even if it meant omitting the most powerful soundbites. Tomassini said he had watched enough episodes of "L.A. Law" to know his comment might be ruled speculative or prejudicial and apologized, before looking Mullen in the eye and adding "I guess I don't understand why his donations wouldn't have been just as valuable to you while he was alive."

Before Robinson could speak, Miles stood, shot her an assuring look and escorted Tomassini into the hall. When they returned, Tomassini asked for a moment to apologize. "Madam Arbitrator," he said, "I had a "Come to Jesus" conversation with the counsel for the estate. Mr. Marcus explained why you were upset, and I understand my outburst was out of line. Forgive me."

Fortunately, they were not in court, Robinson said, turning to Sean Byrne. It was likely that the story of the Brauns, their estate, and Maeve Mullen and the helpline she founded would not have come to light were it not for the retired priest. The confessions he heard and subsequently revealed to a reporter for *The Daily Hampden Gazette* in Northampton, Massachusetts, not far from Wilbraham, led to the dispute between the estate and the helpline. Now, the disclosures he made appeared to be heading from arbitration to criminal court. Bryne was the parish priest at St. Anne's Church in Palmer, Massachusetts, when Charles Braun wandered into a confessional. Though Braun said he didn't have any religious affiliation, Byrne said he could see this man needed help, so he slipped him a card with the phone number of the Hampden County Helpline. Years later, when Bryne had been transferred to a church in New Haven, he heard the confession of Mullen, who had founded the helpline.

What she described troubled him enough that he considered reaching out to leadership in the archdiocese. Priests were bound by the Seal of the Confessional, a solemn commitment to confidentiality. He had no doubt there would be no exemption from the oath to protect a parishioner's privacy in confession, an infraction punishable by excommunication. At seventy-one, Bryne was pondering retirement anyway, but he knew he would need to resolve the dilemma on his own. In the end, he chose to contact Odette Curry at *The Daily Hampden Gazette*. Knowing the consequences, she offered him anonymity, but he declined. Once the story broke, Mullen would surely name him anyway (which he said she had every right to do). Besides, he thought, making the hard choice meant living with the consequences. Bryne read most of his statement from cards, stammering occasionally and seeming rattled throughout.

"The oath we take as priests to keep every confession private is no different than the promise therapists make to their patients and hotline workers offer their callers," Bryne said, looking Maeve straight in the eye. "If we make exceptions, we risk the trust we need to establish for people to come to us. The Church is right to go after priests who violate the agreement like me, which is one of the reasons why I retired rather than requested an exemption.

Yet another doctrine I hold equally sacred is the culture of life from the womb to the prison cell. In the Catholic church, we view the taking of life, whether by suicide or murder, as an attack on God. It is not our life—it is his. So, if we are encouraging or even condoning a suicide, we are aiding and abetting a murder. I'm not going to compound my sin of violating the Sacramental Seal by disclosing more of what I heard in confession but there were many comments I found troubling. One I will repeat here, because it has already been widely reported. It penetrated my mind deeply when I first heard it and has been lodged there ever since. He looked down to read from the cards. 'In some ways, I envy you. Most of us linger and decline, but you're able to bypass the infirmities and indignities and make a clean break from this world. You will be able to simply vanish. And I know you aren't a believer but in helping others, you will go to a better place.' *A better place.*"

Here, Bryne looked directly at Mullen, whose eyes were tightly shut; her hands were clasped atop the conference table, and her lips moved as if in prayer.

"It hardly mattered that he wasn't a member of our faith. You were telling a man that he would be rewarded for committing a grave sin. When I put the pieces together, I realized I had inadvertently referred a man to his death. It was my obligation to understand the philosophy of an organization when I make a referral. It was my parishioner's job to recognize the power her words have and the responsibility her organization must unambiguously, unconditionally support life. Both of us fell short. I hope you'll forgive me, Maeve. This was something I had to do."

Robinson thanked Bryne and the other witnesses, asking if any wanted to escape before the "endless minutia of arbitration." Bryne was the only one to take her up on the offer, making his way out wordlessly and avoiding eye contact. He had looked uneasy from the start, but the moment Mullen made her surprise entrance, he seemed ready to bolt. Hammond later revealed he was worried Bryne's quick exit might give Robinson the impression he couldn't face Mullen. He was also concerned that, in her inebriated state, she might go off script and reveal some incendiary comment she made to Braun, or Robinson might interpret his trying to prevent his client from speaking as an admission she had something to hide. "Brevity is the soul of wit," he whispered into her ear.

"Haste makes waste," she replied before launching into a rambling monologue.

***Walt: That's the third chapter of *Posthumously Yours* as read by its author, t*he Times* Reporter Francis Carr, our guest today on Valley Speak. Francis, you earned a sip of water. Here, a chance to catch your breath.

Francis: This is why they had a professional read for the audiobook. I'm obviously a writer, not a reader.

Walt: You acquitted yourself nicely. When you wrote "rambling," you weren't kidding. Maeve Mullen's speech went on longer than her attorney's statement.

Francis: Longer than either attorney's statement.

Walt: I won't ask you to read it in its entirety, but can you extract the essence of her remarks?

Francis: Maeve Mullen later acknowledged that she'd had four too many. I can't repeat the actual two-word description on the radio except to say the second word was "faced."

Walt: We'll use our imaginations.

Francis: As you might expect, the word "betrayal" was a recurring theme. She began by saying that she was praying for Sean—that was all anyone could do for someone who betrayed their church, their own vows, and the parishioners who trusted them. She recalled her first confession—she used the word reconciliation—in Ireland when she was eight years old. The whole sin part hadn't really registered yet; she thought it was a place where you told secrets. So, she told this poor priest in great detail about what she found her thirteen-year-old brother was doing in the bathroom—a sin once removed. But even when she was older and figured out what confession was for, she looked forward to it. Therapy was not really an option then, and she felt the priest was her confidante. She also spoke of losing her own father to suicide and how it inspired her to pursue a career in counseling and start the helpline.

Walt: It may have played differently, but it sounded coherent to me, especially for someone in her state.

Francis: I am making it more linear than it was. By all accounts, there were moments that were genuinely moving, but the word "rambling" is the one I kept hearing. And she never denied Bryne's version of what she said in the confessional. She didn't address it at all, in fact, which was surprising. I mean, she could easily have denied every word, and it would have been her word against his.

Walt: Why do you think she didn't?

Francis: Maybe because she was too inebriated to remember it, but I never heard her dispute Bryne's memory of that confession in any news story or interview. Was that because she didn't think anyone would take her word over a priest's? Was it practical to avoid lying under oath? Or did she own the comments and assume others would as well? I have no idea.

Walt: Did her attorney, Bordie Hammond, address the veracity of the confessions Bryne claims Mullen made?

Francis: Did you want me to read his remarks from the arbitration?

Walt: And the statement from Marcus Miles, the attorney for the estate, if you would.

Francis: I'll begin with Miles, then.

Miles: Madame Arbitrator, as the attorney for the Braun family estate, I initially had no intention of seeking to omit The Hampden County Helpline as a beneficiary. Charles Braun, the last surviving member of the family, added it in a completely lucid state of mind, and I always see my role as following the instructions of my clients to a T. On a personal note, however, I should add that suicide prevention struck me as a worthwhile cause that was particularly relevant here.

I received the request to remove The Hampden County Helpline as a recipient from the individuals here today, most of whom knew Lucy or Charles Braun. They come from two separate entities in two different states, neither of whom knew the other, and yet they reached the same conclusion: that rewarding an organization and its leader for their role in the death of the benefactor would be the ultimate miscarriage of justice. What was their agenda in approaching me, taking time off, and traveling here to speak to you? They have no skin in the game. They were simply troubled by the outcome. Mr. Bryne was not affiliated with this ad hoc group and was not here on behalf of the estate, but you could see how troubled he was by that outcome and by his decision to retire early from the priesthood.

Now, Mr. Hammond will undoubtedly suggest that even if you believe the founder of the Helpline handled Charles Braun's situation poorly, that is no reason to punish the organization itself. However he would like to spin it, the two are inexorably linked. Maeve Mullen is not only the founder of the Helpline, but she is also its executive director and its guiding force. Her personal involvement is the reason you see her here today. Just as her philosophy about suicide prevention was reflected in the way she advised Charles Braun, we must assume it extends to the helpline's other callers. That should concern us all. To borrow from the Hippocratic Oath, "first do no harm."

As I have said, I view the requirements of my job to be following the wishes of my clients. Once they are gone, I must consider their intentions as well. I've served as Lucy Braun's attorney for years. I can't imagine that she would possibly want her estate to benefit an individual or an organization—in this case, one in the same—that might have had a role in the suicide of her only child. As a dedicated and beloved school counselor, she would certainly feel the same about other people's children. I am confident it would be the exact opposite of her wishes. And, if her son had been able to recognize how he was being manipulated, I feel sure he would never have added the helpline as a beneficiary to the family's estate."

And here is Borden Hammond's summation: "Madame Arbitrator, as the attorney for the Hampden County Helpline, I am representing an organization, not an individual. Its founder is on leave from her role as executive director and is not involved in day-to-day operations. To be clear, even if you completely disagree with what she told Charles Braun based on everything you've read, this case is not about her. If you find in favor of the estate's position here, it will not be Maeve Mullen who is deprived; it will be countless anguished, often desperate individuals who reach out to the Hampden County Helpline each month when they feel nobody else is there for them. For many, they are literally the last line of support.

Now, their methods have been misrepresented here and, in the press, so let me summarize them in a single word: listening. These volunteers—and I should emphasize that the people who answer the calls are not paid a penny—are carefully trained to offer support and referrals to mental health professionals and other resources whenever possible but above all to listen attentively and compassionately. For a caller who believes there is no one in their life who cares, their presence alone is often the initial deterrent to a desperate, irreversible decision.

Charles Braun sought to support the Hampden County Helpline because it played that role for him. He did not so much amend the resources handed down to him by his mother but amplified them. I have yet to see this reported but Lucy Braun, whom Mr. Marcus accurately described as "a dedicated, beloved school counselor," routinely handed out cards with the

Helpline's phone number to her students. Now, I don't know if her son knew that, but clearly, she had enough confidence in the helpline to refer her "kids," as she described them. Do we really want to substitute our own judgment for hers?

This case is not about Maeve Mullen, but our opinions can't help but be shaped by what we've observed. We've all read the most provocative quotes from Sean Byrne about what he heard in the confessional. Some of us have focused on other statements that presented a more nuanced portrait. On that final call, time and time again, she asked, 'Are you sure you want to do this?' and reminded him he was not compelled to. Most of us never heard that Maeve told Sean Byrne, 'Every word I told him, I would want someone to tell me if I was in his position, so help me, Jesus."

We can have an argument about whether it was her role to simply forbid a sixty-year-old man from acting on his plan, but that is a conversation for letters to the editor, for call-in shows and bar conversations. What we are here today to decide is completely different. It is much narrower, much more technical, and far less interesting. It is simply whether you should intervene in the Braun family's intentions to support a suicide prevention hotline.

I was interested to hear Mr. Miles mention that his witnesses who came here today have no agenda. The same could be said for Maeve Mullen. You can believe she is a compassionate person who didn't want to see a man suffer. You can agree with those who vilify her as the angel of death. But there is no disputing she had nothing to gain financially or otherwise.

I will tell you candidly: I advised her to stay away today to avoid guilt by association. But like all the other witnesses here today, Maeve felt she had to be here not to defend herself but to support a mission she firmly believes in."

. . .

Walt: I found it interesting that the attorney for the helpline, Borden Hammond, acknowledged that Maeve Mullen's presence was a detriment to his client. Was that theatrics or do you think he genuinely believed it?

Francis: Oh no, he clearly felt his case was hampered by her appearance. He felt ambushed. There is no question he was angry she failed to honor their agreement.

Walt: Without putting words in your mouth, I get the impression you also felt her showing up did nothing to help the helpline.

Francis: First, she was lucky it was an arbitration rather than a court trial, where her testimony would have opened her up to all sorts of cross-examination she would have been in no state to handle. And yeah, I mean, I'm not a lawyer, but it seems to me if you are trying to make the argument that this case was about an organization and not an individual, it doesn't help for that individual to show up with all their baggage. On the other hand, you look at the results, and her appearance didn't seem to have a negative impact—or at least not a fatal one.

Walt: Before we get to that ruling, I realize you weren't in the room, but based on your interviews with the folks who were, what were their expectations?

Francis: Well, this was not a black and white case. Both sides made compelling arguments. Certainly, some of Maeve Mullen's confessions to Sean Byrne sounded troubling and since they were fundamentally undisputed, it's fair to assume they were accurate. At the same time, this particular case wasn't supposed to be about the phone manner of an individual or even the philosophy of an organization. That would all be decided later by the courts. This process was simply to determine whether a family's wishes should be nullified. Which is why I was surprised not by the arbitrator's decision but by how quickly it was issued and how she saw the case.

Walt: Spoiler alert here for those listeners who may not have followed the arbitration process.

Francis: Yes, go out and buy the book.

Walt: No cliffhangers here on "Valley Speak."

Francis: In this process, the arbitrator issued what is known as a "reasoned" award which provides not only the ruling but an explanation. Her decision was in favor of the helpline but what stood out to me in her explanation was that she seemed to view this as an open-and-shut case. Lawana Robinson commended the witnesses, who approached the attorney for the Braun family's estate, for trying to right what they saw as an egregious wrong. She credited Sean Byrne for resolving his crisis of conscience so conscientiously and with such a high degree of personal sacrifice. She acknowledged that it was possible to see the founder of the helpline in a positive or negative light. However, she said none of these factors were relevant to this specific case, which was not about the founder, not even about the philosophy of the organization, but simply about carrying out the wishes and explicit directions of Charles Braun. The rest, she wrote, was for a court or perhaps an ethical conduct board that governs mental health hotlines to determine.

Walt: So, she basically threw up her hands and said the larger questions weren't for her to decide.

Francis: She viewed the scope of the arbitration as extremely limited. She made the point that estates are filled with recipients many could view as unworthy, like pets who receive bequests for millions of dollars. A suicide prevention hotline hardly seemed frivolous. No one was suggesting this one was fraudulent or corrupt. If there were concerns about its approach, there were other venues to raise them.

Walt: How much did the helpline receive?

Francis: The award was $1.7 million plus attorney costs. Fortunately for the estate, Bordie Hammond agreed to take the case pro bono. He said his family had been touched, and this was his way of supporting suicide prevention. A cynic might say he also wanted to seal the deal to represent Maeve Mullen in the criminal trial which seemed imminent.

Walt: I would have thought losing in arbitration might have slowed the momentum for charging her.

Francis: If anything, it brought the whole matter back into the public eye. It would have been difficult for the D.A. to ignore it.

Walt: Now, that case received even more media attention and you cover it extensively in your book. It's been a few years now. For those who may not have followed that trial, can you provide a summary?

Francis: About three weeks after the award was announced, the Hampden County D.A.'s office charged Maeve Mullen with involuntary manslaughter. Bordie Hammond represented her but, this time, full fare. Mullen agreed to step aside from the helpline, but she asked that some of the arbitration award cover her legal expenses. The board granted her request. That raised a lot of eyebrows, including some who questioned how resolute this divorce between Mullen and the helpline really was. Marcus Miles, the estate's attorney, and the witnesses from the arbitration were incensed that funds meant to support a suicide prevention hotline were being diverted to pay the legal expenses of an individual they held responsible for Charles Braun's suicide. All the witnesses from the arbitration testified for the prosecution in the jury trial. After two weeks of deliberations, the jury was unable to reach a unanimous verdict, resulting in a mistrial.

Walt: I think a lot of observers were surprised that the D.A. declined to re-try the case.

Francis: He said that while he believed in the merits of the case, it was such unchartered territory it would not have been a good investment of his office's resources. He would not comment beyond that statement, so make of it what you will of it. Today, Maeve is back in Ireland.

Walt: We should emphasize that while your book covers both the arbitration and the trial in detail, it is also about the lives of the Braun family, Maeve Mullen, and the people around them before and after these events. So, I would not describe it as a courtroom drama. That was just one small slice.

Francis: I'm glad you mentioned that because I'm not a legal reporter. I certainly didn't approach this thinking these cases were the most compelling part of the story. The lives of the two protagonists, if you will, are what initially intrigued me. Having said that, their personal narratives raise some complicated ethical and legal issues. Suppose I said to you—not in any professional capacity but simply as someone who has known you since we met an hour ago, "Walt, I don't think your life is worth a plugged nickel." You've been wondering yourself, teetering back and forth, and now, here's this guy Francis—he's smart, he writes for the *Times*, he's known me for more than an hour. Maybe you're thinking, he knows something I don't. And the next thing we know, you're on a ledge.

Walt: We obviously don't want to make light of this.

Francis: But you see where I'm going here. Was Maeve Mullen being held accountable because she initially met Charles Braun in the capacity of a helpline worker and therefore should have known better, or could the ruling apply to anyone who said something similar to a friend? Now, suppose Braun was in hospice with stage four cancer and wanted to end his life quickly and painlessly. As his social worker, you don't physically facilitate his death, but you communicate that you are supportive of his wishes.

Walt: Now we're getting into euthanasia, which I think is a whole different issue.

Francis: I certainly could imagine some overlap. If we're going to hold people accountable not for physically enabling someone to take their life but simply for concurring with their decision, we'd better decide which people: mental health professionals? Friends? Everyone? You can see how it becomes a slippery slope.

Walt: I'm unaware of any situation known to mankind that is not a slippery slope, but I take your point. In the time we have left, I'd like to circle back to the reaction to this book. We mentioned it has been strong, to say the least. That's usually a good thing for a writer. Here, it sounds like a mixed bag.

Francis: I'm not sure why simply presenting a—let's say *alternative view*—is somehow seen as endorsing it. I played it straight down the middle because that's how I saw it. I didn't see anyone I would characterize as purely a sinner or a saint. Well, I think Sean Bryne might qualify for the latter, but the book's critics haven't zeroed in on the portrayal of him.

Walt: And if you had to take a guess where the vitriol is coming from, you would say?

Francis: As I mentioned, there are a lot of displaced feelings in the criticism. The people who are most vociferous seem to be those who see Maeve Mullen as a murderer, pure and simple, and who would only accept a portrayal of her in this light. And, of course, they are perfectly justified in threatening the life of anyone who writes about someone they see as a murderer without condemning them. Irony is not big with that crowd.

Walt: An eye for an eye, I suppose.

Francis: It's come to that.

Walt: So, Maeve Mullen returns to Ireland. The Hampden County Helpline gets new leadership and an infusion of funding, perhaps part of her legacy. Tie up the other loose ends for us.

Francis: We should point out that prior to her departure the helpline was put into receivership by the A.G.'s office.

Walt: The Massachusetts attorney general.

Francis: They emerged with a new board, a new executive director, and a more explicit policy governing what volunteers can and cannot tell callers. So, the mission is no longer this kind of neutral values clarification. Now, it's "We are here to prevent you from killing yourself, regardless of who you are and what you may be struggling with. No matter how we may feel privately, we are not permitted to go off-script."

Walt: This seems to be a tacit admission that their founder's approach was the wrong one.

Francis: There seems to be this perception that the way Maeve Mullen interacted with Charles Braun was based on some type of grand philosophy. Having interviewed her, one thing I can say is their interaction was situational. So, it's not like 'as an organization, we used to be pro-suicide, now we're opposed.' That kind of analysis doesn't do justice to the volunteers—past and present—who were always there to save lives, not to end them.

Walt: Unfortunately, we'll have to leave it there. For the rest of the story, you'll have to read the book. It is called *Posthumously Yours*, and the author is *Times* reporter Francis Carr, and I appreciate your joining us today on Valley Speak.

Francis: Thanks, Walt and Hampden Valley. It's been nice to be back home.

CHAPTER TWENTY-ONE

IN THE FINAL ANALYSIS

TENTS ARE PITCHED across the front lawn where a local artisan is putting the finishing touches on an etched wood sign. An events crew unloads audio equipment and staging from a truck idling at the mouth of the gravel driveway. Landscapers are adding cherry blossoms to the azaleas and forsythias outside the former bedroom window. Days from now, Wilbraham residents will get their first look inside the new teen center that will be dedicated after years of controversy, but the ghosts inhabiting the house Lucy Braun built are everywhere, from the midcentury furniture that remains in the living (now rec) room, to the Italian espresso machine and "house" brand drip coffeemaker in the new bakery/café.

Anyone who knew its patrons would be shocked that the new Braun Teen Center bears their name, a decision even its planners acknowledge would never have received their approval. "On this one, we overruled them," shrugged Adrienne Hammond, who worked with disadvantaged kids in Springfield before returning to her more affluent hometown to help plan the Braun Center, surely one of the most deluxe youth centers in small town America.

Adrienne, who retains a dancer's physique from her college days at Hampshire and a French crop with a high fade that recalls a touch of her rebellious high school years, seems ambivalent, if not downright remorseful, about her move. She traded a job working with disadvantaged inner-city teens for one where —she says half-kiddingly— "most of the kids are spoiled brats like I was." The opportunity to help build a new program from the ground up with the resources the Springfield center never had proved irresistible, but she swears she will eventually return and apply what she learns to the population that needs help the most. She is quick to add that it wasn't a beautiful building or other amenities that saved her—it was one counselor who made this new facility possible.

As the former home of Lucy Braun and her son Charles, the center includes two amenities that offer vocational training and after-school jobs to local teens. The estate purchased adjacent acreage once known as Saltbox Farm and returned it to its original use as a working vegetable farm to be tended by high school students. Adrienne fought to open opportunities to Springfield teens, but her proposal was shot down by residents who feared the town would become "one of those places with high tops hanging from telephone lines." As a compromise, they agreed to include the A14 students bused in from Springfield to attend Wilbraham schools. The center also won over local skeptics by promising farmer's markets and a community supported agriculture program. An onsite bakery providing additional training and jobs will buy produce from the farm which, at one point, was slated to become a Muslim cemetery. The conversion of the land from death to life is only the first metaphor that would seem too on the nose in fiction.

A drawing of the cartoon character Lucy Van Pelt at her psychiatry booth greets visitors at the entrance to the Center. The artwork was donated by Grace Cullen, a former neighbor of the Brauns who lived in the historic Ashton House mansion down the road before returning to Santa Rosa, California, home of the Charles M. Schulz Museum and Research Center. On a table next to the sketch is a can and sign that reads "Psychiatric Help 5 Cents." Adrienne claims that they'll use the proceeds to buy marijuana plants for the farm.

The original, mid-century furniture is now supplemented with rough and tumble bean bag chairs and comfy couches. A game room with air hockey, ping pong, and billiards is well-stocked with an assortment of board games that could double as another heavy-handed metaphor for the Brauns' complicated narratives: Risk, Life, Trouble, Sorry, and Aggravation. In deference to the patrons' daily ritual, there are also a dozen copies of one particular game for tournaments. Adrienne wryly notes that the center seems to have converted Wilbraham from Candyland to Scrabble.

Café Au Lait, a bakery and café, is an extension of the Brauns' original home donated by Acorn Deckhouse, its builder. The pastry chef, Michelle Ellis, shows off her new kitchen which is still receiving the final touches from a contractor's crew before the grand opening. The original footprint was tiny, but, when Adrienne met Michelle, she persuaded the board to make it large enough to accommodate baking classes. The one and only visit Michelle made to Paris—indeed, her only overseas travel—was for a French Club trip in high school. She is determined to make a return visit someday to perfect her craft. Decked out in a Laura Ashley-style apron, a string of pearls and floral-patterned Merrell clogs, Michelle looks exuberant. Her culinary training was from a local community college, she says, not a "real" cooking school. She imagined being a lifelong apprentice in the kitchen, not a pastry chef and never a culinary instructor. But she worked at a short-lived local patisserie, alternating between the kitchen, waiting on customers and bussing tables. Michelle paid a visit to

Autre Chose, a traditional French Bistro in Cambridge, where the owner, Maurice LeDuc, sent out baskets of otherworldly croissants to every table. Flaky yet thicker and heftier than most, each was bronzed to a near crackling texture. Butter or jam, really any spread would have been superfluous, which is why these were served naked. This was the model Michelle said she wanted to emulate. She confessed to being more of a tea drinker but reached out to a local roaster and dairy farm and decided to sell only the namesake drink. You could get Café Au Lait with light, medium, or dark roast, with milk from a cow, a nut or a plant, but no cappuccinos, mochas, lattes, or even black coffee.

Michelle welcomes her visitor by placing a croissant on a high-top table between them before retrieving their coffee order. "When I was a kid, my mom never gave me coffee, even half-and-half," she recalled. "That was for the kids who called their parents by their first names. So, I wasn't surprised when I heard that Miss Lucy made it for Charlie ever since he was little. It's kind of cute, don't you think?"

How did she feel when she first read a short obituary of Charles in *The Republican*? "Mad," she says, her lips pursing and eyes closing. She holds up a finger to indicate she needs a moment and disappears into the kitchen. A few moments later, she returns, dry-eyed, carrying a copy of MRHS Falcon, her high school yearbook. She opened to a page flagged with a paperclip. Under Charles Dunkin' Braun, there are no photos, superlatives, or honors, only a name above a signature that read: 'Michelle, Good luck in college. Cordially, Charlie.' The patron asked if she thought they were close. She laughed. "I mean if you can be close with a boy who signs your yearbook 'Cordially.'"

Though they came from very different backgrounds, Michelle said she always believed she and Charlie were kindred souls bound by that feeling of not belonging. She said if you look closely at any class photo from kindergarten on, you can usually pick them out: one, sometimes two children whose eyes tell the story: angst, disconnect, maybe resignation. You sense no matter how much they try to engage others they will remain apart. Some are singled out, branded and bullied. The lucky ones simply vanish.

Charlie and Michelle both stayed local as their life trajectories would suggest. When they occasionally ran into each other, Michelle thought it might be worth another try. "I mean, I knew we were both the type who would always be alone, but I thought maybe we could be alone together."

When she read the obit for Lucy Braun, Michelle realized his mother was his only living relative. "When my parents passed, the rest of the family disappeared. I should have figured. I mean, my parents adopted me, but their families didn't. Charlie wasn't adopted, but we both lost our family. I thought it might be something else we had in common."

She sent him a card that offered not merely sympathy but comfort, thinking it might open the door to some kind of response. It turned out to be her final outreach. "I guess it was all in my head," she said as her gaze locked far across the room. In an instant, she shakes her head as if awakening from a dream, having her default sunny temperament restored. She explains that any anger and disappointment disappeared once he was gone and she realized what he'd been dealing with. Now, she sees her good fortune with this new job as his way of finally being recognized.

Often told that her croissant rivals any from the Left Bank to Quebec. Michelle calls it a "work-in-progress" and says she hopes she can perfect it in time for the dedication ceremony. And how does it feel to finally be a local? "My goodness," she laughs, "that's one thing I could never be. They live here. I work here."

Besides the farm and the café, the Braun Center will house Bibliothèque Interdite, a surreptitiously named room filled with books that have been banned in schools and town libraries nationwide. This was the idea of Maxine Folkman, the librarian at MRHS where Lucy Braun worked and one of her closest friends. Each week, she plans to monitor the American Library Association's banned book database. Every time a title is removed anywhere in the country, Maxine says she will order a copy. She believes the idea pays tribute to Lucy Braun's subversive side and the knowledge-is-power mantra she shared with "her kids."

The Braun Center is a fitting legacy to its beloved patron. It also doesn't tell the whole story. Lucy Braun was more complicated than her reputation. Did she empower kids or circumvent the wishes of their parents? Was she a responsible parent herself or did she, as her friend Maxine once half-jokingly suggested, create a playmate and caretaker for herself at the expense of her child? Perhaps what was most puzzling was that Lucy withheld information from him that might have allowed him a connection to one other person in the world—his father. Was she right in believing that opening the door to this man who apparently was so averse to children that he left her would inevitably end up in disappointment? Probably, but what if all those years later, her ex had changed as people occasionally do over the course of a lifetime? What if, like Candace Delgado, the hospice chaplain, Charles had discovered a stepfamily he never knew he had—and it made a difference? Those are a lot of what-ifs, but it's difficult not to wonder who Lucy was really protecting.

There are other seemingly benevolent individuals in this real-life drama whose choices were controversial. Sean Byrne, the unwitting catalyst for the court cases that brought the story to the public's attention, made the decision at the risk of excommunication to violate the Seal of the Confessional, an absolute prohibition against revealing the confessions of a penitent. He was clearly motivated by a crisis of conscience but acknowledges a sense of ambivalence. Rather than challenging the outcome, he retired. Instead of moving to a residence for fellow retired clergy as he had planned, Sean (he no longer cares to be addressed as "Father") resides in a subsidized studio apartment for the elderly.

Sean Byrne grew up in a large Irish Catholic family near New Haven. His older siblings did more parenting than his hard-working, blue-collar father, who was a widower. He describes his upbringing as fundamentally close-knit but without a lot of communicating about feelings. Basically, he recalls it as "every boy and girl for themselves." He found himself drawn to the church in part by the comfort of the rules he was missing at home. Near the top of the list was a reverence for life. From the most innocent infant to the least innocent death row inmate, the message was always that every life had worth.

It's difficult to imagine the gregarious personality his former parishioners described. He seems subdued, perennially preoccupied, as if he was replaying the details of a fatal car accident over and over in his head. Initially, it seems surprising that he has granted a number of interviews, but upon meeting him, it becomes clear he is not as much engaged in a conversation as simply reliving the details yet again.

The only performative note is when Sean mentions that the origin of the phrase "Hobson's Choice," a British stable owner offering customers the option of the stall near the door or none at all. "Some decision," he begins. "They had it easy."

Throughout Maeve's confession, Sean told himself she knew what she'd told Charles Braun was wrong. As the story unfolded, he kept hoping it would take a detour, and she'd proclaim her unambiguous support for life. Instead, she seemed to lead Charles in the opposite direction, at times practically encouraging him to get over his fear and get on with it. How could Sean possibly reconcile this with the church's reverence for life and his own? He worried about her taking other calls and talking to others in dire straits.

Sean wanted to work within the church system but knew he'd never receive permission to reveal a parishioner's confession. Praying for guidance, he said he found none, leaving him wondering if there was a rule about when it was okay to break the rules. Finally, he reasoned that without life, there could be nothing to confess. Although it was an agonizing decision, there was no question about what to do. Yet, as soon as he disclosed the confession, Sean said he felt such a profound feeling of having betrayed a sacred trust that he momentarily considered retracting his account.

Even with the benefit of time and distance, Sean says he feels no more clarity about whether he made the right decision. He knows he has ruined one woman's life and really has no idea if he helped to save others. Sometimes, he is certain Maeve Mullen was consciously encouraging Charlie Braun to end his life and holds her responsible. Other times, he wonders if he and others might have taken some of her words out of context and are holding her responsible unfairly. On one point, he feels certain: "She may have given him mixed messages, even bad advice, but she wanted to help him. What motivation would the founder of a suicide prevention hotline have for purposely leading a caller in the other direction? She did not stand to benefit personally from his estate. This cost her everything."

He wrote to ask forgiveness for his betrayal and received no reply. "I don't blame her," he says. "Maybe she sees me as the person who took *her* life."

This is the one brief point where Sean slips out of the endless internal conversations and rhetorical questions to consider his own culpability. Freed from the boundaries of the clergy, he acknowledges that his initial reaction to Maeve's confession might have been personal. "I realized this man whose life she was describing was only a little younger than me. What would she have said if I were the caller?" The poster priest for Catholic guilt, Sean clearly will be revisiting his decisions for the rest of his life, another example of collateral damage from this strange story.

Although she was not convicted, Maeve Mullen says she felt like a pariah. Returning to Limerick where she was born and raised, Maeve hoped to get a fresh start. But the story had received wide enough attention, and she found the notoriety more difficult to escape than she anticipated. At home in Ireland, she sensed the public was more sympathetic—or at least, more diplomatic—yet every time she met someone, she wondered what they had heard and whether they had an opinion. For a time paranoia set in, and she became mostly housebound in the one-bedroom basement apartment of her son Jack, a customer service agent at Ryanair in Shannon. Jack had been raised by her ex while she completed her education and began a career in the States. After living with his dad throughout college, Jack had finally moved into his own place. He wasn't looking forward to sharing it but didn't know how to turn away his mother, even if he could not bring himself to give her the title she never earned. Jack introduced visitors to "my roommate, Maeve," hoping they wouldn't notice the obvious family resemblance.

Maeve had seen many job openings in her field, from school counselors to case workers, but she knew applying would lead to background checks, questions, and rejections. Instead, she sought something virtually anonymous, replying to a help wanted ad seeking switchboard operators for an answering service. The wages were poor and the work dull, but she could do it without leaving home, the ideal arrangement for a budding agoraphobic. With her son away at work during the day, it was also a good opportunity for an aspiring alcoholic. For most of her life she had fortified her resistance to her father's example with self-awareness, choosing a profession that would insulate her with daily reminders of its consequences. Even all her social work classes at UConn could not fully prepare her for the number of calls to the helpline about alcohol problems—their own or a family member's. It was the callers who mentioned it in passing that surprised her the most. Their lack of self-awareness seemed alarming. She never drank at home and could have a pint with friends without the slightest interest in a second. It was only after Charles Braun ended his life that some of her callers' descriptions of alcohol use began to seem eerily familiar. After Jack left for work one morning, Maeve poured a nip of Jameson's from her son's stash of airline beverages into a juice glass and placed a call to the Health Service Drugs and Alcohol Helpline.

Stateside in Wilbraham, a week later, students in the field were delivering the modest early harvest Adrienne hopefully described to Michelle as a trial run. Her kitchen staff pivoted from croissants to make use of the bread-and-butter corn for muffins, and local wildflowers filled the vases on every table. Already, she was pitching a hydroponic greenhouse for berries in winter and even an onsite apiary for honey. Linda English, the MRHS nurse, wrote "Get out your epi-pens," but nobody said no.

Adrienne knew the opening and dedication ceremony would be dominated by town officials and local businesses sponsoring the event, but she desperately wanted the focus to be on the teenagers. She kept in touch with the kids from Springfield, and she'd heard from a student who had just won a contest—first prize was a visit from a nationally famous artist to play at her prom. In her senior year, Ella was uprooted from her high school in New Zealand while her father, a linguistics professor at The University of Auckland, took his sabbatical year at the headquarters of Merriam-Webster in Springfield. Ella skipped the prom, and Adrienne got her to donate the concert for the dedication. To generate excitement, they decided to keep the identity of the artist a secret. Word had spread so that besides the A14 kids and locals, many of the forbidden Springfield students had shown up. Before the start of the show, some were camped out on the lawn in front of the stages while others milled about. The contingent from Haven House drove up from New Haven. Erma investigated the farm and the kitchen, while her son Vic and Candace hung out with Adrienne and the kids.

The opening of "Raspberry Beret" blasted from the speakers, and everyone sprang to their feet. A few falsetto squeals rose above the track. Adrienne turned to Ella and said she hoped they didn't think Prince was in the house. A line dance broke out with overhead handclaps on the beat.

"Drums, please," a familiar voice announced as the track segued into "Summertime," and the crowd roared with excitement. "Now they're going to think it's the Fresh Prince," Ella laughed as the dance moves morphed into the laid-back vibe of that classic. As the track faded out, a DJ behind the turntables and an offstage voice instructed everyone to put their hands up in the air for P.M. Dawn. Another cheer went up as Prince Be stepped onto the stage in a tie-dye robe, beads, bracelets and headband. DJ Minutemix nodded to his brother and launched into "Set Adrift on Memory Bliss," prompting Vic to exclaim excitedly, "It's Spandau Ballet!" The lawn looked like a mashup of American Bandstand and Soul Train, a psychedelic, utopian mix of wealthy white townies and multi-ethnic urban kids.

"As princes go, I guess C is as good as A and B," Ella said.

"Why don't you join them?" Adrienne replied. "You're still young enough for another month."

"I don't know," Ella replied. "I'm kind of over getting told to throw my hands up in the air."

Michelle and her apprentices greeted parents, town officials, and other adult guests with corn muffins and café au lait dusted with cocoa and cinnamon. Maxine had replaced some of the more controversial titles in the library with *Little Women*, *The Yearling*, and *Anne of Green Gables*, and the condoms in the candy dish with Reese's Pieces. Noting the French sign on the door, the staff writer for *The Daily Hampden Gazette* asked her for the English translation—she said, "The Enchanted Library." *The Republican*, the public radio and television stations in Springfield—WPVR and WGBY—spoke with Adrienne and some of the A14 students. The sales manager for *The Palmer Pilot*, the hometown weekly, bypassed the kids for interviews with the elected officials and local sponsors. Erma returned with a bag of produce and a couple of scones, handing one to Candace and shoving the other into her son's mouth. She pronounced the farm worth the drive from New Haven, the muffins worth the calories, and the center "amazing."

The principal of the local high school where Lucy Braun worked was the first speaker. For most of the years he worked at Minnechaug Regional High School, Ted Weeks thought of his guidance counselor as an adversary, someone who circumvented authority and did as she pleased. Theirs was a battle of polar opposites, politically, professionally, and personally. He believed in order and discipline, while she gleefully championed permissiveness and rebellion. Their antipathy was so apparent that many faculty and staff assumed he would find some way to get rid of her, but he knew better than to try, at least overtly. The military strategist in him knew she had a powerful power base of students, and many parents would come to her rescue. He played the long game, knowing he would likely outlast her, but their clashes were well-known, and he suspected her of rallying students against him. He was not wrong but could never prove it. All of which made his conciliatory remarks at the school's memorial service for her surprising if not suspect. The superintendent and several allies on the school committee advised him to leave it to his deputy, the assistant principal, to represent the administration. The prevailing opinion was two-sided; if he even hinted at his true feelings, he would come across as insensitive and unsympathetic; and that if he were generous and diplomatic, he would seem hypocritical and disingenuous. Everyone offered variations on the advice of Thumper in Bambi: "If you can't say nothing nice, don't say nothing at all." He trashed the grammar and ignored the counsel, delivering a speech that acknowledged their differences but praised her dedication.

For those who had attended the school event, where he was surprisingly generous and conciliatory, hearing the acid tone that seeped into his cursory praise now was jarring.

Those outside the school community were flat-out mystified. Candace, the chaplain at Haven House, noted "It's not often you hear the person who delivers the eulogy trash talking the deceased." The mood was so discordant that Karen Nyman, Adrienne Hammond's mother and one of the center's board members, felt compelled to follow him with an impromptu anecdote about how Lucy Braun saved her daughter's life.

When asked about his talk later, the source of his pique became clearer. Weeks had always wanted the teen center to be part of the high school and located on site, claiming it would be easier for students to access. The board opposed that plan, arguing that the Braun property allowed for the acquisition of the farm; the center should be available to all Wilbraham teenagers, not only high school students. Their most pressing concern, though, was to keep control of the Center out of the hands of school administrators and make its mission true to Lucy Braun's beliefs, and they had the estate and its funding on their side. Seeing how the center had turned out and how positively the community was receiving it, Weeks was so enraged that he even suggested its name was an exercise in hubris. Never mind that she was gone before its name or location were discussed; the outcome felt like her thumbing her nose at him from hell. Not only were his wishes ignored and the school he led deprived of positive attention, but also the center itself was a monument to a bitter adversary.

Perhaps the one omission of all the speakers was the other Braun who'd made the Center possible. The name Charles did not come up once, even though the estate that provided funding had passed through his hands. Then again, maybe it was by design. This was, after all, a man who spoke of the ability to vanish as his greatest aptitude and strongest desire, who, by his own account, had been struggling to find a way out practically since birth. By all accounts, the center was his mother's passion, not his. Sadly, he claimed not to have one. Following through on her vision would likely have been his tribute to her, not to the teenagers the center would serve.

Trying to piece together an accurate portrait of an enigmatic individual like Charles Braun is complicated by the fact that he is no longer with us to tell his side of his story. Certainly, there are people without the advantages he had who were able to overcome similar challenges and not only claim personal accomplishments but make a difference in the lives of others. Instead, he was so stuck in his own head that he was inert. Though it sounded callous in the courtroom, perhaps Maeve Mullen's notion that his greatest value to society was through the good for others his family's estate could do was factually honest.

On the other hand, it was hard to know another person's mind. In this case, the best we can do is create a cut-and-paste portrait based on accounts by people who knew him best—which is to say, hardly at all. The composite which emerges is of a guileless, distant, somewhat amorphous observer. What becomes remarkable is not that he cut his life short but that he endured it as long as he did.

One document that might have provided some clues about Charles Braun's state of mind was a card he mailed to Maeve Mullen right before he checked into the hotel and took his life. She confirmed its existence but declined to release it. It was easy to understand why Maeve did not share this note before her trial. Like nearly everything else about this story, Charles' words could have been interpreted in different ways. On the one hand, he describes her as a caring stranger who became his one true friend, someone willing to tell him the hard truths, even, he hints at her own peril. On the other, she could be seen as an enabler, someone who took his hand and guided him toward the light instead of encouraging him to take a step back. Given the public reaction, especially in the U.S., where her conduct was rarely seen in a favorable light, it's not surprising she ultimately decided to make her case in her own words.

The Easy Way Out by Maeve Mullen

"May you be at the gates of heaven an hour before the devil knows you're dead...May the saddest day of your future be no worse than the happiest day of your past...A good laugh and a long sleep are the two best cures."

We Irish have a proverb for everything, but the first time I saw that last one was in a newspaper story describing my philosophy of life. I couldn't help but wonder who they were talking about. Since you are reading this, you probably already know me (or at least you think you do).

If you came here expecting my confession, you'll have to read Father Sean Byrne's account in the newspapers. Everything I told him in confession and everything he shared was true, but he left out important details. Also, I didn't tell him everything. A reporter called asking to help me tell my story. I'll tell you what I told him: what feckin' story? I was never famous, or I guess you'd say infamous, before this court trial, and there's nothing especially interesting about my life before it. Now that the case is over, I shouldn't care what you think. But then, I'll get a look from someone on the bus or in the market and I know that even back here in Ireland there's no escaping it. For the rest of my life, I will be "Charlie's Angel of Death," "Doctor Death's Daughter," or my personal favorite, "Killer Queen." (You Americans do know the Royal Family live one country to the right?) Every time I meet someone, I wonder what they've read, what they know or think they know. It shouldn't matter but it does. Even though I know I will never really get past it, I felt like I should tell you who I am and why I did what I did. That way, you will judge a person you know, not the one you thought you knew.

I didn't want to write a book, because people would say I shouldn't profit from the tragedy (something I have no desire to do). So, I settled on this magazine because they offered to let me set the record straight, in my own words, without any changes. I began to write about the case, and I realized there were parts that wouldn't make sense if you didn't know where they came from. Before I knew it, I had written my life story which, like I said, was fairly ordinary until I got caught up in the whole—let's call 'em "The Troubles."

So, let me get that business out of the way, and we'll get to the part you came for. I grew up in Limerick, Ireland, yes, the one you read about in *Angela's Ashes*, but my childhood was a little different. Okay, maybe a lot. I'm not saying that alcoholism was absent in the Limerick I grew up in, but in my family, we struggled with different problems. Some experienced poverty, but by the time we were in school, our home was more of an upscale, urban squalor with electricity, plumbing, and, in our case, even toilet seats elegantly covered in the fuchsia shag carpeting on the floors.

The four of us—my dad, Connor, my mom, Fiona, my brother, Ian, and I—lived in a flat on Gerald Griffin Street, not Adare Manor, to be sure, but maybe the higher end of lower middle class. Our dad repaired jewelry and watches in his shop downstairs. Our mum worked in a beauty salon down the block until she was diagnosed with cervical cancer. I was ten and Ian was nine when she basically disappeared, shuttling back and forth between her bedroom and St. John's Hospital.

Truth be told, even before she was ill, the four of us were more like roommates than family. I assume that Ian and I potty trained ourselves because I can't imagine either of our parents having been involved. By the time I was in first class and Ian in second, we walked to primary school together. There was nobody with the ability or the inclination to cook. On Fridays, Ian and I received our allowance and biked down to the Milk Market on Mungret Street to shop for ourselves. We survived on bananas, peanut butter, porridge or McCann's steel cut oatmeal, brown bread, apples, soup and potatoes—the last two being the only reason the stove went on in our kitchen. Dad gathered food for himself and mum when she felt well enough to eat and took their meals in bed. Ian and I sat at the kitchen table watching *The Den*, a show for kids, and *Fair City*, a soap that was definitely not. The exception was Sundays when dad would drive us to his mum for proper meals: boxty or Colcannon Mash and Champ, sometimes Spiced Apple Cake or Bread and Butter Pudding for dessert. We always left with a care package meant to last the week that made it about a day and a half. Our visits to Nan were like going from Oliver to Eloise.

I'm making our childhood seem a lot more feral than it was. We had a place to sleep, an allowance for food, all the basics. In hindsight, I'd say our parents were less neglectful than absent. Ian described it as a sort of "self-service" childhood. Mum's illness had a lot to do with it, but he and I always relied on each other more than our parents. She was always something of a mysterious figure to me, but I had the feeling I was a disappointment to her from the start. Before she began treatment, mum was a classic Irish beauty with fine strawberry blonde hair, dewy skin, and striking blue eyes. I got my looks from dad whose rough, craggy features live well with a man, not so much with a woman: wiry, wild black hair, bulbous nose, ears a little too prominent. Add bad skin with the occasional unsightly mole, and the way it translates is a little witchy.

Even as a girl, the word that comes to mind is "hag." Now, before you assume I heard it from bullies on the playground, I need to tell you it is a name I gave to myself. And in case you think it was something that caused shame, I should say I claimed it with pride. I know it may be hard to believe, but my looks have given me confidence, resilience, and maybe some of the independence I developed from being my own parent. Growing up, girls were never threatened by me, and boys treated me as one of the bunch. I hung out with three of Ian's football teammates who were his closest friends and had—I don't want to say relationships, more like training sessions--with each of them. None had much experience and to be able to practice on someone who wasn't intimidating improved their technique and boosted their confidence. Which is not to say I was much more experienced myself, but I could tell them what worked and what didn't—which was more than they could say for Resusci Annie, the CPR training mannequin which Ian compared me to the first time he realized his friends were using his sister as a sex doll. Except they weren't using me; I was volunteering for service. What did I get out of it? I'd be the first to admit that early on, the rewards were rarely physical. Instead, it made me feel powerful and drew me closer to them as friends. If I had been someone they were attracted to or had feelings for, I doubt they would have felt as comfortable.

It wasn't only as a teenager that I found advantages in not having looks to get in the way of friendships and other relationships. Time and again, I saw the way men and other women are more relaxed with people who appear ordinary (at best). When I paged through photos of my mum at my age and her mum at Nan's age, I saw the "before" and "after" and realized how much more difficult it would be to lose my looks than never to have had them in the first place. The older we get, the more it seemed to work to our advantage. Those who always looked older than their years get compensation when they age and people say they haven't changed, whilst the decline is so much more visible with the people who relied on their looks.

As for my days of shag the hag, I also must admit I had a little fun describing every detail of my shenanigans to poor old Father Driscoll at confession. He sounded uncomfortable, but I suspect appendages he thought had long grown dormant came back to life. Fortunately, he seldom saw my parents—what they might have said was a different matter. From what I can recall of her better days, mum hardly seemed like the type who was chaste at my age, but I think she might have worried about her reputation as a parent. Dad and I had the kind of unspoken bond that would have probably made him concerned, but we never had the kind of conversation that would have provided opportunity to lecture me about my indiscretions. The closest he could get was to wear the concern on his face with a plea to "take care." Ian, who inherited mum's looks and earned something closer to her approval, excused her absence but not his. She was ill, after all. What was his excuse? Back then, I never could have explained it, but today, I would have said: the same one as *his* father, his sister, his cousin. All you had to do was look through the family photos and see the resemblance in their expressions, that look of anguish and desperation before they made their exits.

Suicide was in our DNA. My brother and I fought back in different ways. For Ian, it was humor. After the football season, he and his lads organized a summer basketball league. The name he chose for their team, "Six Feet Under," was supposed to represent their wee stature. I got it. When the others chose Pumas, Panthers, Broncos, Bengals and other animals for names, Ian changed it to the Limerick Lemmings, an inside joke I'm sure nobody else understood. I understood deflecting death by making light of it, but I also saw it as a problem to solve. I found books like *The Butcher Boy* and *Paddy Clarke Ha Ha Ha* that made me think about psychology. I remember reading about high school students in the U.S., who were trained to help others, and asking our school psychologist if we could start a program. I learned about the suicide prevention hotline of The Samaritans and wanted to be a volunteer, but I wasn't old enough.

As I had lived through my mum's final days, I saw the toll it took on my dad and how fragile he became. By my final year of the senior cycle in secondary school, I was hoping to study psychology or social work abroad but decided I needed to keep an eye on things at home. Thinking that spending time with him might draw us closer, I offered to help at his shop during the day and take night classes in psychology at the University of Limerick. He set me up to take care of the customers, but it was so slow, I used the time to read textbooks and write papers. I had never expressed an interest in his work before, so when I asked if I could assist him at his workbench, he smiled, clasped my hands between his, and said he would be fine. Reeling from the loss of mum and tired of a distant, sullen dad, Ian moved in with Nan for his final year of secondary school. I didn't want to desert him, too, but he seemed more remote than ever.

At the library, I found two titles—*Of Soda Bread and Guinness,* which had recipes from every county and *Quick Cooking: Fast Fixin' Recipes with Velveeta Process Cheese Spread*— and tried making dinner for two. I decided to split the difference: macaroni with Velveeta and a bottle of Guinness Stout that had likely been on the mantel above the fireplace when we moved into the flat. Dad said the lovely color brought to mind Yellow Man, the honeycomb candy from Belfast. He tore off a hunk of soda break, stuck a fork in it, and dipped it in the pan like fondue. I asked how he was holding up. "We do what we have to do," he replied turning on the television. That was when I decided there was nothing more I could do there.

That was also the night I decided to mail my application to the School of Social Work at University of Connecticut. I had never travelled to the States, but one of my cousins who was studying at Yale mentioned their divinity school had a program with UConn which was focused on research. Somehow, I got it into my head that I needed to work on a "cure" for suicide. I realize now I was really looking to get as far from home as possible. I applied to universities in Melbourne and Toronto, but UConn offered a full scholarship. My cousin agreed to let me stay in her apartment while I completed my degree. If my dad had so much as said "stay," I would have never left him so soon, but it was difficult to tell grief from his normal state of mind. Instead, he mumbled something about making my way in the world— which was probably what he thought he was supposed to say. Ian told me I should take advantage of the opportunity but didn't say what I wanted to hear—that he would take care of our dad. I left home with an ominous feeling and was ashamed for not feeling more guilty.

The first thing I noticed about the U.S. is the first thing they noticed about me: At home, I was defined by my appearance, but here, it was my accent. Often, people would simply remark what a charming brogue I had. Sometimes, it led to their memory of trips to Ireland, a reference to their family's own heritage, a fondness for Guinness, a U2 concert, step dancing, or St. Paddy's Day. Occasionally, they were just slagging about not understanding me, like when they would ask me to say something again in English or request subtitles. The closest it ever came to criticism—a remark about busing in Southie—went completely over my head until I read *Common Ground* for a class about race nearly a year later. The rest were good-natured and welcoming, promoting me to the status of ambassador of a nation with about the same sized population as my new home of Connecticut.

University was a revelation. I had always made my way through school with neither distinction nor shame, attentive but rarely inspired. My graduate program felt less like preparation for a career than a continuing therapy session unravelling every mystery about my family, culture, and life. Substance abuse, depression, family dynamics, aging, trauma, and suicide—my education had answers to all the questions I never knew to ask. I threw myself into assignments, revealing personal history as if it was confession. I admired Professor Bradshaw, a veteran social worker who shared her experience while encouraging our participation. I became quick friends with my classmates, nearly all of them older and already established in their profession. They shared something of themselves, but I left nothing on the table, even my history as a sex coach for Ian's mates. The other students—all but one woman—weren't buying my explanation that I was the one in control. Never mind that I willingly volunteered my services or that I considered the boys as friends. As the girl, they felt I must have felt exploited, a casualty of poor self-image, or parents who failed to set limits, or males who were only too willing to take advantage of my vulnerabilities. By definition, the teenage girl was the victim, incapable of offering consent. That I claimed not to be damaged or exploited only demonstrated how deeply I had repressed my feelings and how likely it was that the experience would come back to haunt me. But I knew what I was doing, I took precautions, I was nobody's victim, and I was sorry if it contradicted the textbooks. I had no regrets.

The same was true when I told them the nickname I'd given myself. I tried to explain that I never felt diminished by my appearance, that, if anything, it made women less competitive with me, men less intimidated, and everyone more relaxed. They nodded, but I could tell they were thinking I was in denial. One woman said what was on the inside counted and gave me one of those "Isn't she brave?" hugs. I became the class case study, a chance to see if they could rehabilitate this poor, broken soul from a messed-up family. When we broke up into groups for projects, everybody wanted to be my study buddy. Even Professor Bradshaw took me aside and said to remember she was a therapist as well as an instructor and would always be there if I needed her.

It all sounds a little humiliating, but it didn't feel that way. We often went out for a few pops after class, learned more about each other's lives, and supported one another. The compassion, not only for me but every student, was genuine. I thought I would have chosen any of those women—even the lad—as a therapist. Besides serving as a surrogate client, there was one other way I felt good about the contribution I'd made.

We did a variety of role plays in front of the class. Professor Bradshaw would give us a case, and one of the students would be the therapist and another the client; after, we'd share honest feedback about the session. One week, Renee, a human resources director who was making a mid-career change to social work, was assigned to be Frances, a teenager who was being abused by her stepfather and considering harming herself. Her therapist, Roger, the one lad in class, was young enough to be the son of most of the women and the grandson of a few. The rest of us were pursuing clinical work, but Roger had enrolled in the master's program straight out of college to become a community organizer. Earnest to a fault, he took the course to learn more about therapy. So naturally, he seemed slightly awkward in a one-on-one session. The class was critical of how quick he was to offer advice instead of simply affirming the client's feelings; he needed to "talk less and listen more," to "ask questions instead of offering answers," to let Frances "reach her own conclusions instead of trying to solve her problems for her," that last one being a quite "male" way of approaching every situation.

Roger, who typically spoke up less than anyone in the room, apologized for talking too much. Professor Bradshaw, who had been taking notes without showing her hand, suggested he was new to this and the whole point of the exercise was to learn. She referred to a chapter we had read about being comfortable with the silences and, I don't know, something just sat poorly, and I slipped into my Gaelic self: "The textbook is not feckin' scripture, is it?" I asked.

There was a moment of silence before I continued. "I mean, excuse my French, but a fifteen-year-old girl is telling us her fifty-year-old stepfather is climbing into bed and fondling her, and we're supposed to nod and ask how it made her feel? Maybe

I'm an eejit, but I'm afraid I'm going to have something more to say."

Professor Bradshaw clarified that we were not to stay silent. Especially when dealing with a minor, we had a responsibility to make sure they clearly saw this behavior as a crime. We were to help them find a safe adult to confide in and report it. Was that the totality of our job, wordlessly listening to clients spill their guts and occasionally calling the cops? But I wanted to offer what had been missing all my life. In return for sharing my private thoughts and fears, I would get the same prayer of absolution and be called upon for the same act of contrition as the next penitent. I desperately wanted someone to hear *me* but also help me see things more clearly. I was looking for options but also guidance. I didn't need someone to say magic words and make my problems disappear. I was merely seeking an open-minded, objective collaborator. I wanted to be part of a conversation, not perform a monologue for a silent partner. I knew I had found my calling as a social worker, but I wasn't going to learn it from a textbook or a rehearsal or even a wise professor.

My real education was a placement at the Hartford Multi-Service Center. Here was Destiny, looking for a maternity dress for the junior prom; Jenna, planning an escape from her boyfriend who branded her with a tattoo of his name across her backside and monitored her so closely she kept looking out the window for his car; Jermaine, who was trying to decline membership in the Park Street Posse without getting stabbed; Henry, a codger who'd made his way from the nursing home a few blocks away with the aid of a walker anchored by two tennis balls; and Loretta, a fifty-eight-year-old woman on disability who claimed she'd slept sixteen hours a day since she was twenty.

Whenever I did an intake at the Multi, there was one question every client—regardless of age, gender, and income—

answered affirmatively: "Are you having suicidal thoughts right now, or have you had suicidal thoughts in the past?" For some, it might have been a fleeting thought, but for others it was intermittent or persistent. Whether they came in to talk about an eating disorder, an abusive relationship, sexual dysfunction, or financial problems, suicide was always on the table. With my family history, this was obviously a topic I knew something about. During my final semester, as part of my master's thesis, I applied for a grant to launch the Hampden County Helpline. My plan was always to return to Ireland, but, to my great surprise, the funding was approved. I decided to stay on to see it through.

All throughout the trial, I told myself it was worth it for the lives we saved. But when I read what people said about me, I wished I had never tried to help Charlie. Whatever else you may think, that is what I was trying to do. Of all the absurd things I heard, the most ridiculous one was that I pursued him for the money. I never knew he had any until I visited him at the hospice and learned why he was there. I don't ordinarily make house calls, and it was risky. It went against everything we're told, and I understood why. Like the seal of the confessional, the confidentiality of callers is sacred. They need to be confident that the power is in their hands; they can call us anytime they want, but they can hang up on us, too. I didn't ambush this guy. I never forced him to reveal his identity. I saw someone in desperate need. I could tell that nothing I could do on the phone was going to make a difference. His was a lifelong death wish. So, after I had earned his trust, I asked if he would like me to pay him a visit. It was unorthodox, unwise, and unprofessional, but each time we hung up, I thought of him all alone in the world—no family, no friends, no one but the voice of a stranger on the phone. I'll admit, it got to me. But when I made the offer and heard the surprise in his voice, I felt certain I had done the right thing—at least for him.

When we met and I learned he had money, my first thought was that the people caring for him might be taking advantage of him. I mean, what reputable hospice takes in a completely healthy person for months? If they really thought he needed help, why didn't they refer him to a place where he could get it like a psych hospital? I became his advocate and protector—that's why he asked me to meet with the lawyer for his estate on his behalf. When he decided on his own to add the helpline to his will, the beneficiary was not me but a charity instead. I never stood to gain anything personally from his decision. Ask Professor Bradshaw or any of my classmates at UConn who were prepared to testify as character witnesses on my behalf, if getting rich is your motivation, social work is probably the wrong profession.

I struggle with my lapse in judgment, sometimes allowing myself to cross the line. There is a difference between befriending and becoming friends. I still ask, did I allow myself to become too close? Yes, but I put myself in jeopardy, never Charlie. I got to know him as well as any human ever could, except his mom, and I believe having a connection after she died extended his life but did not cut it short. Laughter alone added a few months, I am sure. Usually, Charlie's humor came from the darkest places with an expression so deadpan, I wondered if he might have been serious. As we spent more time together, I started to know when he was joking and realized how therapeutic it was for him.

So many of the words attributed to me by Father Sean or the staff at Haven House were just examples of having someone on but they were presented in the press as if I was serious. Charlie used to say there were so many reasons to kill himself and only fear was keeping him alive. I wanted him to realize all the good things he might have been taking for granted. So, I suggested he make a list of the pros and cons. Whenever I asked how he was doing, he always replied "tired." All his life, he could never recall waking up feeling rested. Most nights, he claimed he would doze off, then wake up after a few hours and remain awake the rest of the night. I asked if catching up on his sleep was at the top of his list of reasons to kill himself. Does that sound like a serious question? Yet, that's how they spun it. I *jokingly* suggested Charlie could add "no more colonoscopies" to his list of pros after he said how much he hated it. Another time, we were talking about his upcoming birthday, and he wondered aloud about whether he could go back and do all the things he missed the first sixty years—prom, dating, marriage, kids, career—when his peers were on their third marriages, grandkids, and retirements. So, I said he might be the first person in hospice asking for a raincheck on his life. Suddenly, it became a headline where this guy was asking for a second chance in life and I'm pulling the plug on him.

Sometimes, I was slagging Charlie, and they twisted my words into something serious. I did want to build credibility with him. This was, after all, a grown man who, ultimately, was going to make the decision on his own. Or I'd acknowledge the obvious: it wasn't a choice between suicide and immortality. We talked like the two adults we were—about watching people like his mom and mine grapple with the challenges of their later years, about how often they'd told us, at a certain point, it might not be worth it. We wondered if maybe old age was God's way of making life so unbearable that it was easier to let go.

Every headline became more absurd. In each article, the person they were writing about became less recognizable. From the words of staff at the hospice to Father Sean's account of my confessions, I might have assumed this deranged therapist was behind the suicide of this confused, impressionable senior myself. It certainly was an easier explanation than this unique, complicated situation required. So, let me tell you how I really saw Charlie Braun:

When I hear about a sixty-year-old man who says he's never had a happy day in his life—something I will confess I had never heard before —my first thought is obviously depression. While there may not be a cure, there are many treatments. The difference was Charlie said he'd never had a sad day, either. What he really felt was *nothing*. Now, any therapist worth their degree will tell you that is a classic description of some type of disorder, and there is a chemical or therapeutic solution to every disorder. The trouble is, Charlie Braun didn't neatly fit into any of the boxes.

Professor Bradshaw, someone I truly respect, once told us that every individual is unique, but she had yet to find anyone with an undiagnosable problem. I would have liked to have introduced her to Charlie. I don't think she or any other mental health professional would have considered him to be crazy. He was rational, sober, and resolute in his belief that, at this stage, his life was not going to fundamentally change. Could he have been wrong? Absolutely. I firmly believe it's possible at any age, and sixty can be the beginning of Act Four, with plenty of unexpected plot turns and twists possible. Some people, I said, might envy someone with the freedom and means to experiment. But I don't think it was unreasonable for him to believe the most likely scenario would be remaining in "purgatory," as he put it, so those of us with a soul might understand it.

I understood it completely. I kept asking myself how I would feel if I were in his position. And what would I do? The truth is, I'm not certain I would have made a different decision. Despite my family history, I am anything but suicidal. Even in the darkest times in my life, I always had something to live for: my work, friendships, even my fraught relationship with my son.

I feel like therapy is a godsend, not only as a vocation but as an alternative to the stony silence of my childhood and the stiff-upper-lip ethos of my culture. Where it falls short for me is our failure to try to see things through our client's eyes while remaining respectful in our response. I could not honestly tell Charlie I wouldn't have the same wish *if I were in his shoes*.

A lot was said (and written) about our final conversation. The most troubling words I can recall compared me to the parent who keeps urging her child to the end of the diving board when he clearly isn't ready. Never mind what it suggested about Charlie, a grown-up who was anything but impulsive in a decision he had spent a lifetime pondering. To be clear: I never said "jump." I never told him to "get on with it." In fact, I said the opposite: there is no pressure to decide. Only one decision would be irrevocable. You have all the time in the world. What I didn't say was "Here's what you must never do." What I didn't do was override his decision by calling the cops. I was there to be with him whatever his choice, so he wouldn't be alone.

For many people, our lives provided entertainment, satisfying a morbid curiosity about a taboo topic. Without sounding self-pitying, I get it. Every good story needs a villain, and I stepped up to fill the role. Nobody forced me to visit him at the hospice, and if I hadn't, you wouldn't be reading this now. I have only myself to blame. Friends ask me if I had to do it over again if I'd handle it differently. Completely. What I have learned about my profession is that boundaries protect the therapist as well as the client. What I have discovered about myself is that I'm too concerned with my own survival to push boundaries and approach a client on a purely human level again.

Why does it matter now after the fact? I suppose I was hoping that even those who are certain I did the wrong thing—me included—would realize it was with the right motivation. So, I'll give Charlie the last word:

Maeve,

Greetings from the far, Far Side.

If you are reading this and I am still around, it is not because you didn't do your job but because I didn't do mine. I mailed it to you before I checked into the hotel because if I didn't ever check out, there were a few loose ends I needed to tie up:

When you suggested I take this time to see if my life might turn around, I never expected miracles, but I did experience something I wasn't expecting—new people in my life that made these past few months interesting. When you spoke of Vic, Candace, and the other people at Haven, I knew you were often "giving out," to draw an expression from your Irish language tutorial. But we had some lively conversations with a few laughs, something probably uncommon in hospice, so I'm going to cast aside modesty and say I'll bet my room there feels a little empty. Hopefully, it will stay that way for a while, and Gini will finally realize how much she misses me. I heard from a former neighbor in Wilbraham who moved back to California and even a couple of classmates from high school who resurfaced to challenge my assumption that I didn't have friends.

The real revelation, of course, was you—partly because your appearance in my life was so unexpected. I'll never know what really made you reach out beyond the anonymity of the Help Line and become a real person in my life. The explanation you offered—that I was close to your dad's age—might have been a small part of the answer but I can't imagine I reminded you of him. He had a family, his work, and a life. You are the first person who realized that I was going through the motions and who understood why that wasn't enough. You helped me put my life into perspective and encouraged me to be courageous rather than paralyzed by fear. It took courage on your part to go off script. Instead of trying to save me, you listened, you heard me, and you responded candidly without ever putting your thumb on the scale. My gift to the helpline is a way of expressing my gratitude and my hope that the volunteers can provide support to others as you have done for me.

I spent years trying to decide where my mom would spend eternity and when the time came, I still couldn't do it. I appreciate your making the arrangements on my behalf. To answer that same question: surprise me.

Posthumously yours,

Charlie

ABOUT THE AUTHOR

Charles D. Braun is the pseudonym of the author who, in six decades of life, never read a word of Shakespeare, watched *Casablanca*, *Star Wars,* or porn, bought a lottery ticket, pulled an all-nighter or experienced a hangover, owned a pet (or even a plant), or wrote a love letter...and whose final act was to leave his novel in trusted hands for publication.

www.ingramcontent.com/pod-product-compliance
Lightning Source LLC
LaVergne TN
LVHW090812050925
819954LV00001B/24

* 9 7 9 8 9 9 8 9 4 7 7 6 6 *